HEAVY METAL FAKK2

KEVIN B. EASTMAN

KEVIN B. EASTMAN's meteoric rise to fame began in the mid-1980s, when he and partner Peter Laird co-created the Teenage Mutant Ninja Turtles, who quickly became pop culture icons and launched a merchandising empire. In 1990, he founded The Words and Pictures Museum of Fine Sequential Art, located in Northampton, Massachusetts, and in 1992, he became publisher and president of *Heavy Metal* magazine. Among Eastman's other comic book accomplishments are *The Melting Pot* (elements of which have been included in *Heavy Metal: F.A.K.K.²*) and *Zombie Wars*. This is his first novel.

STAN TIMMONS

STAN TIMMONS is best known for his comic book work, scripting such titles as *Alien Nation* and *The Man From U.N.C.L.E.* His short fiction work has appeared in the anthologies *The Ultimate X-Men* and *The Ultimate Hulk*. This is his first movie novelization, and if he'd known how hard it would be to make a book out of a movie, he probably still would've done it.

HEAVY METAL

FAKK2

KEVIN B. EASTMAN

AND

STAN TIMMONS

BASED ON A SCREENPLAY BY ROBERT P. CABEEN

ibooks
new york
www.ibooksinc.com

DISTRIBUTED BY SIMON & SCHUSTER, INC

An Original Publication of ibooks, inc.

Pocket Books, a division of Simon & Schuster, Inc.
1230 Avenue of the Americas, New York, NY 10020

Text and artwork copyright © 1999 by Heavy Metal Entertainment.

Heavy Metal is ® and © 1999 Metal Mammoth, Inc.
Heavy Metal: F.A.K.K.² ™ and copyright © 1999 Kevin B. Eastman.
ALL RIGHTS RESERVED.

An ibooks, Inc. Book

ibooks, Inc.
24 West 25th Street
New York, NY 10010

The ibooks World Wide Web Site Address is:
http://www.ibooksinc.com

You can visit the ibooks website for a free read and
download of the first chapter of each of the ibooks titles:
www.ibooksinc.com

ISBN 978-0-671-03896-0 (pb.) | ISBN 978-1-876-96902-8 (hc.)
First ibooks, inc. printing September 1999
10 9 8 7 6 5 4 3 2 1

Edited by Steven Roman

Cover art by Luis Royo
Cover design by Dean Motter
Interior design by Michael Mendelsohn at MM Design 2000, Inc.

This one's for Rose Lowery.
Not only is she the last of her kind,
she's the only one of her kind.
Better days are just ahead . . .
right behind that iceberg.

—Stan Timmons

Share your thoughts about these and other ibooks titles
in the new ibooks virtual reading group at
www.ibooksinc.com

HEAVY METAL

FAKK2

Prologue

Once upon a time . . .

Not so long ago, and not that far away, if you believe in legends . . .

In the beginning, time and space came together in one magnificent fusion, creating a cycle of life and death, with the wheels of the universe spinning in perfect balance, working in sensible harmony.

But nothing, it seems, is ever truly perfect, for there was a flaw. At the very heart of this fusion, a rift was spawned where all the known rules ceased to exist. Had the rift remained unchecked, it would have continued to grow and spread, allowing the otherwise-unalterable nature of time to fully refashion the stuff and dreams of our material universe.

Paralysis, oblivion, and entropy would have been the end result.

The Arakacians—The Dark Forces at play in the universe—wanted this. They encouraged it.

But despite the unraveling of the natural weave of the universe, a sense of balance and harmony yet prevailed, and so the Enlightened Ones recognized the impending catastrophe, and went to great lengths to contain the rift.

But from this rift flowed a liquid capable of bestowing immortality upon any who drank of it. Legend says these waters spilled forth, splashing their secrets of life eternal across several worlds. The Enlightened Ones constructed a monumental device to hold back this negative force, but the Arakacians did not want this. They wanted the chaos and immortality the waters would bring them. But they were greedy, as all evil things are, and they soon drank all the forever fluid that fell upon their planet. Without these rejuvenating waters, the Arakacians would once again become mortal, and fall, and die.

The Arakacians were led by a soulless creature named Rutger, and his bloodthirsty troops rolled across world after world, destroying civilization after civilization, searching for the liquified immortality which they knew had fallen upon other worlds. They were a foolishly prideful race, and could not imagine a universe that no longer contained them. Their desperation escalated, as did their cruelty. They spread only death and devastation.

And at last, they found the planet Uroboris, where the last of the liquid was said to have dropped.

By then, of course, the Enlightened Ones had finished constructing the Chamber with the aid of slave labor pressed into service—a race of reptiles that lived, if not peacefully, at least blissfully ignorant, on the same hellish planet. It could only be opened by a key—one which, if ever lost, would guide its bearer back to the fountainhead of immortality. But to protect its secret, the key was designed to drive all who touched it insane.

The Arakacians by that time were dwindling, their numbers halved, and halved again. Still, they were sufficiently powerful to enslave a peaceful colony and force them into battle with the Enlightened Ones.

It was slaughter, of course. What else could anyone expect? The colonists were easily defeated and routed, but their attack had weakened the Enlightened Ones enough to pave the way for the Arakacians to move. They were desperate; they had not come to fail, but neither would the Enlightened Ones allow them to succeed.

During the uprising, the door to the Chamber of Immortality was locked, and the key cast out . . . deep into space. Without the waters to heal their grievous wounds—suffered in their relentless search for immortality and this last, all-out assault—the Arakacians again became mortal, and were finally defeated.

Rutger's body, however, was never found.

Ironically, the Arakacians, in their mad bid for immortality, were destroyed, and none survives. The universe moved on, and the Arakacians, despite their galaxies-spanning reign of destruction, were soon forgotten.

If you believe in legends. . . .

One

The Earth and her planetary neighbors had long, long ago given up the last of their natural resources, as reluctantly as misers parting with hoarded wealth, who, in the end, all wound up broke, and poor, and all but ignored by their greedy children.

Not that the demand for resources—oil, metal, even water—diminished with the dwindling supply: the palm of desire is always open, always looking for more. Perhaps, if man were not such a rapacious creature, he would never have first looked across the vast plains, over the rise of the tall, tall mountains, or into the star-freckled face of space, wanting more.

Someone, somewhere, always had more. And someone, somewhere, always wanted it.

Of course, certain purists will tell you it's all been pretty much downhill since man decided to come down from the trees and establish an economic system, while still others argue it was an even bigger mistake to climb out of the ocean and evolve legs and grow a brain-stem.

So man kept looking ever outward, farther and farther from home, and soon spread across the galaxies in starships like thistledown in a strong wind, plundering new worlds of their natural wealth, leaving behind ugly, empty husks, like a trail of seduced and spent lovers.

A more philosophical person might begin to see a parallel with the Arakacians and their insatiable hunger that propelled them across the universe.

As one might expect, the private sector didn't take long to step into the breach, and soon giant corporations were sending their own mining ships out. The work was dangerous, and so were the men who did the work. They were often the dregs of society—outcasts, ex-convicts, court-martialed soldiers who had their sentences commuted, men who couldn't find work at home. These were not the type to be trusted, but then, neither were they the type to be missed if anything went wrong with the operation. No one said that, but everyone knew it.

On one such expedition, the crew of the *Cortez*—one of a fleet of such ships owned by Metal Mammoth Mining—came upon an asteroid bearing a rich vein of Lairdium, and the process began again:

First, the mother ship locked onto the asteroid, while the advance crew descended and set up its geodesic structure—a base of operations complete with heat, lights, and artificial gravity. Next, the heavy-duty mining equipment was shuttled down to the surface to begin plowing the craggy, frost-covered terrain. Then came the men, who would descend into the ragged trenches gouged into the cold stone and begin the long, tiresome work of shoring up the walls and bringing up their prize.

From the start, this project seemed cursed. Not that these men were the sort to place any faith in omens—or in anything other than the strength of their own limbs—but it was difficult to ignore the facts.

The men were quarrelsome. Maybe not so big a surprise, but it *usually* didn't end with one of the protagonists getting spiked on a rock pick. Afterwards, the man's killer claimed he was compelled by voices to do the gruesome deed. Not a very original defense, but there was no such thing any- more as original sin; it had all been done by this point. Perhaps the best one could hope for was *unique* sin.

And the machinery was moody. For no apparent reason, the great trenching engines would simply cough to a halt, only to start again, seemingly of their own accord. Certain areas of the asteroid seemed as cursed as ancient burial grounds—the mining equipment would stop, dead cold. But when it was moved to another sector, it would start up smoothly, without a hitch. In retrospect, those unlucky enough to survive the events that spread forth from this operation like ripples in a pool, would later say they felt as if they were being *told* where to dig ... *guided* ... by some- thing that wanted to escape its icy prison.

A flash of light, like a beacon showing ancient sailing ships the way to safe harbor, stabbed upward from a tear in the rocky surface. The light glowed green, and beat in time like a living heart. Several of the men turned from it. They had never seen anything like it before, and doubted it could be anything good.

But not Tyler. He was on a collision course with his des- tiny, and he sensed it, somehow.

Tyler moved forward to the lip of the crevice, drawn by the beating light of Fate as a moth is drawn to a flame. He paused at the edge, peering down, still undecided, still un- committed as to what to do next.

"Sir?" said one of the miners—Callaghan. But even over the comm-link resting in Tyler's ear, Callaghan's voice seemed far, far away. "Should you really touch that? I mean . . ." The nervousness in Callaghan's voice was obvious to everyone else. But not Tyler. Only that light was obvious to him. "It may be a Class-4 biohazard, sir."

"Are you telling me my job?" Tyler replied, never taking his eyes from the odd, pulsing glow. The sound of his own voice, amplified by the comm-link in his helmet, surprised him, almost shocking him out of his thrall. Perhaps, for just a moment, there had been a chance he could turn away, and things could have ended quite differently, if not altogether happily.

But then he felt the voices in his head, tickling his brain like insects skittering over a piece of rotted fruit, and whatever choice Tyler might have had up to this point was gone. He knew somehow that the light had also probed the minds of the others, but they had not been chosen.

The light only wanted him.

"No, sir," Callaghan replied. "It's just—"

Callaghan's mouth worked, but all he could manage was air and vowel sounds, because the light from the object suddenly intensified, doubled, then trebled, as Tyler's gloved hand reached into the crevice and touched it. Even though his bezel was polarized to withstand the light of suns and stars, Callaghan had to throw a protective hand up over his own face to shield his eyes from the glow. Tyler's faceplate was rendered momentarily transparent by the wash of light, and if anyone had been able to look at him, they would have seen a predatory smile smeared across his face. And maybe, just maybe, a look of doomed resignation.

And then the light simply winked out. One moment it

was there, and the next, gone, leaving only its afterburn imprinted on everyone's retinas.

The men blinked, their eyes unable to adjust to what seemed like sudden darkness in the wake of that unearthly glow. Tyler was already moving toward the geodesic dome and its makeshift lab, established for analyzing mineral samples in the geodesic dome. In his hands he carried a shaft of ice. In the center of that ice, now as black as a collapsed star, was a shape only Callaghan had been near enough to glimpse. It looked like a key . . .

Tyler entered the dome and moved directly to the lab, sealing the airlock behind him. He placed the ice-encrusted key on a flat, tabletop scanning bed, and thumbed the scanner's ON button. As the scanning laser probed the imprisoned obelisk, Tyler began stripping out of his mining suit and into the tight, one-piece flight suit he preferred. Over the left breast of the flight suit was emblazoned the Metal Mammoth Mining insignia and, below that, a metal tag bearing his name.

Outside the dome, other members of the mining party began to rap on the metal hatch.

"Tyler? Are you all right in there?" Coleman, by the sound of his voice.

But Tyler did not answer. He continued to dress with the slow, deliberate movements of a dark and brooding man who hurries for no one.

On the scanner, the pencil-thin red light ran the length of the obelisk and, having recorded its longitude, began to read its latitude. Although it was not a heat-emitting laser, the ice surrounding the key began to melt, sloughing off the obelisk and puddling on the scanning bed in pools of liquid that looked like rusty mercury.

Freed of its ancient prison, the obelisk once more began to pulse and throb with a living light.

Now, Tyler could see strange carvings and symbols on the key's surface, and a prominent pictograph depicting twin pillars, between which a sun was setting.

"What are you trying to tell me, hmm?" Tyler mused absently, and removed his heavy lab gloves. "What is it, boy? Did Grampa fall down the well? You want me to follow you? Is that it?"

In a way, that was exactly what it wanted.

"Who's he talking to?" Callaghan asked. Although Tyler had removed his helmet, his comm-link was still open, and the miners on the other side of the door could hear his mutterings.

Coleman shook his head. "Don't know. I didn't even know Tyler had a grandfather."

"This is gettin' creepy," Hazelwood ventured. "Somebody'd better get in touch with the *Cortez*, tell 'em what's goin' on down here."

"What *is* going on down here?" Callaghan asked. The others could only stare back in mute reply.

Tyler moved closer to the obelisk. The ice had completely melted now, and the object itself was as dry as a rock. He ran one rough-callused finger along the pictographs on the key's surface, and felt again that tickling at his thoughts. But this time the insects weren't just skittering over his brain; no, they were stinging and biting and burrowing into the soft, membranous tissue, like miners digging for gold.

Tyler could smell green grass and flowers and fresh well water. He could taste old, burnt copper, but that was just where he'd bitten his tongue hard enough to draw blood.

He could hear chanting, a chorus of a thousand ancient, inhuman voices, and he thought they were calling his name:

Tyler . . . Tyler . . .

"Tyler?" Callaghan called through the bolted door. "Tyler!"

Tyler gripped the glowing obelisk with both hands, fighting to control it, to cast its stinging probes from his mind and its demons back down into hell, but, once activated, the device could not be held in check. Blood began to drip, then gush, from his nose, and ruby tears flowed from the corners of his eyes.

He was making wild, glottal sounds from somewhere deep in the back of his throat: "Tk! Ngk!" The other miners could hear this, but could hardly guess what was causing them.

"Go get a drill," Callaghan ordered. "We're going to force that door open!" The lock wheel was on Tyler's side of the door, but the knuckle and pintel were on the outside. They would remove the door from its massive hinges.

Coleman ran off to the supply dump to do as he had been told. If any of them could have guessed what was on the other side of the door, they wouldn't have been in such a frenzy to open it.

Simultaneously, far away, a guard who has spent the last forty years of his life, as his people reckon time, standing vigil—as did his father and his father before him, and back and back and back through the long chain of years and family—is startled out of his complacent near-doze as an orifice in the ancient altar opens like a sleepy eye. This is not a day he has ever imagined coming, and the light that washes out of the opening in the altar makes the guard take an involuntary step or two backwards.

This can't be, he thinks, but it is, and he knows it. Down deep in the pit of his heart, where the wild beasts of fear live in restless anticipation, he knows it.

As the light from the ancient altar—whose ornate carvings and pictographs mirror exactly those on the newly-discovered obelisk—glows brighter, the guard turns and runs from the great hall. It is as much fear as duty that moves his legs in long, scissoring strides.

The light from the obelisk filled Tyler's wide, unblinking eyes—or perhaps the place behind his eyes—with strange ideograms and subliminal flashes of distant lands yet to come. It was over in a pico-second, but the skull-cinema seemed to go on forever. Tyler had no idea of what forever was, and no concept of what it meant . . . yet.

The blaze from the key went out, but it left a matching glow in Tyler's eyes. It was the whirling, dancing light of insanity. Maybe that fire was always there, just a little, waiting for the right flint and proper kindling to stoke it into a conflagration. Madness is nothing more than saying yes to the wrong impulse at the wrong time, and Tyler had seldom been a man who could say no.

Tyler became aware of his surroundings all at once, and he heard the wasp-whine of the drill-bit as it tried to chew its way through the locked lab door. Already, he could see wisps of smoke pluming around the lock on his side of the hatchway. It wouldn't take long now. He tucked the obelisk into the belt of his flight suit, and turned to the doorway.

"Almost through," Coleman announced. The other two men stood back, letting him man the drill. They held their handguns pointed vaguely down at the floor but ready to bring them up to fire in a moment. They just hoped that moment didn't come.

The door was jerked violently inward, startling the three men into inaction. The sight of Tyler—and the madness painted on his face like some hideous clown makeup—caused their synapses to trip over their own feet, leaving the men rooted to the spot.

It wouldn't have mattered. Tyler moved with a speed no one had ever suspected, and tore the heavy, still-whining drill from Coleman's hands. He flipped the drill around, business-end away from himself, and punched the jackhammering bit through Coleman's chest.

"You're starting to *bore* me," Tyler said, watching as Coleman fell over backwards. The drill was embedded deep in his chest, still running, pumping up a thick fantail of dark blood with every cycle, like an oil rig that's hit a mother-lode.

The other two men finally regained enough control over their misfiring neurons to bring their guns up. Unfortunately, Tyler had already grabbed the weapons from their hands while they were still watching Coleman fall.

"Oh, shoot," Callaghan muttered, unaware of the irony in that statement.

"Anything you say," Tyler replied, and twitched the trigger twice. The first shot shattered Callaghan's reflective face-plate, exposing his startled pug-face and the small, black hole that suddenly appeared in his forehead.

Hazelwood was praying wildly, slamming psalms and novenas together with the force of a super-collider. He was on his knees, unaware he had already been gut-shot. A black stain appeared on the front of his mining outfit, spreading like spilled ink.

"*. . . Lead me not into Penn Station . . .*" He was babbling, oblivious to what he was saying. "*And I shall dwell in the House of Pancakes forever . . .*"

Hazelwood's intonations suddenly stopped. He seemed to unhinge at the waist, and flopped over onto his back.

But Tyler hadn't heard him; he was already stalking down the long, narrow corridor. He kicked open the door to the Operations Deck, where various crewmen pored over their space charts and manned their computer stations.

"Class is dismissed," Tyler said, hammering back on the triggers.

Computer screens burst and imploded, sending showers of sparks onto the flammable paper charts stacked on the tables. Crewmen pitched sideways, throwing themselves from their chairs, trying to dodge that mad, deadly hail of bullets whipping past like angry hornets. Tyler moved methodically through the room, kicking over tables, exposing the workers huddled there, who vainly hoped he would pass them by. But Tyler was a man with a mission, and that kind of man is always thorough.

Within the space of a minute, the mining team had been whittled down to two members: Tyler, and the man now staring down the barrel of his gun.

"You're it," Tyler announced, and squeezed back on the trigger. The hammer fell with a dry click on an empty chamber. The madman glanced at the weapon and frowned. He looked like someone who had just been let down by his best friend.

"Honestly," he began in a perfectly reasonable tone, "this has never happened to me before. This is so embarrassing..." He shrugged. "I must be tired." Tyler turned then, as if to go.

The lone surviving crewman couldn't believe his luck. He was still running down a list of things he would do with this second chance when Tyler spun and delivered a fatal back-kick to his head. The man's neck broke with a dry, popping sound.

Tyler stepped over the jackstraw pile of corpses and moved to one of the undamaged computer work stations. His fingers danced across the keyboard in a box-step, and the obelisk tucked into his belt seemed to hum and sing in tune with his movements.

A few moments later, a small shuttlecraft left the dead asteroid and flew toward the *Cortez*.

Tyler was quietly, happily humming along with the obelisk when the ship docked.

Simultaneously, and far away, the guard, who has spent his life waiting for this moment and yet, had convinced himself it never would come, bursts through double doors into the vast underground chamber where the three high Elders sit before a large assembly of acolytes.

Before he speaks, they know.

"The key has been found," *he gasps, his eyes flicking nervously from face to face. He cannot long meet their gaze, and his eyes slide away.* "It will guide the one who possesses it to us! The Coming Back Time has begun!"

A startled murmur rolls through the hall, jumping from acolyte to acolyte like a curiosity being passed around. The three Elders try to mask their concern, their fear, but cannot. Only time-weathered and age-worn Odin is able to conceal his thoughts, but not before a flicker of surprise—and perhaps excitement—reveals itself on his stony face. But in the heat of the moment, no one has seen it, and who would understand it, even if they did?

The Main Elder rises then, arms spread, palms open, to face the crowd and try to restore order.

"The waiting is over," *he announces.* "We must prepare to defend the Chamber."

Aboard the Metal Mammoth Mining vessel *Cortez*, Captain Cameron sat in his command chair, elevated so he could see the whole of the bridge from this position. The walls and consoles of the bridge looked to be vaguely techno-organic, but dingy and sickly, as if they were grown from cancer cells and not healthy tissue, the men working at them little more than maggots crawling over the dying carcass.

Cameron turned to the ship's navigator. "Mister Sanders, have we received the read-out on the preliminary core samples from Tyler's crew?"

"Aye, Captain," Sanders answered, quick to please. "Reference file CS5039."

Cameron rested his elbows on the padded arms of his chair and laced his fingers together before his face, steepling them to rest against the small jab of his chin. "Mister St. Germain, has Lieutenant Tyler's prospecting detail in Section 15 checked in yet?"

From his science station, Germain St. Germain shook his head. "No, Captain. And they've been down there for twenty-six hours."

Cameron sat back, his palms resting on the arms on his chair. "Mister Lambert, signal a shift change. Those men must be going insane down there."

St. Germain checked his own instruments. A light on his board indicated a ship had berthed in Docking Bay F3 within the past few moments. He turned to inform the captain of this, when the doors to the command deck opened with a tired sigh, as if they were annoyed with having to do this menial, thankless job. Tyler's broad frame filled the doorway, and the light from the key, tucked into his belt, illuminated his crazed face from below.

To Cameron, his lieutenant looked like a salesman from hell. That thought would stay with the captain for the rest of his life . . . which turned out to be about five seconds longer.

"Lieutenant," Cameron began, "what are you doing here? Is something—"

Tyler took one step forward and shot Cameron between the eyes.

Now, St. Germain took quick notice of the handful of weapons Tyler carried. Obviously, he'd stopped at the ship's armory on the way from the docking bay to the bridge.

One of the crew members fumbled for the pistol he wore at his hip as Tyler casually, almost dismissively, turned, sighted, and fired. A bullet striped the air beside Tyler's head, missing his cheek by less than an inch, passing close enough that he could feel its heat. Tyler calmly craned his neck, found the would-be shooter, and fired two bullets in quick succession, so fast that they almost entered the same spot on the man's narrow chest, one atop the other.

"Apparently," Tyler said, turning to Lambert and St. Germain, "I've just been promoted. Any questions?"

Sarcasm and rhetorical questions were clearly lost on Sanders, because he actually stood up and halfway raised his hand, as if he were a student asking a question. "Excuse me, but may I ask—"

Tyler shook his head in disbelief, and emptied the clip into Sanders' jerking body. Tyler was six bullets down and the air around him reeked of cordite, but he couldn't remember the last time he felt this good.

"Are there any follow-up questions?" he asked the others, pointedly. "No? All right." He turned his cold eyes, like the windows to a haunted house, to St. Germain, who could feel his bowels turn to cold water. "A position seems to have opened up."

St. Germain stole a quick glance at Sanders' body, slumped comically in his blood-misted chair, then looked back to Tyler, who nodded his approval. St. Germain shoved the body from the chair, and it slipped like a bag of loose rags to the floor. He sat in Sanders' navigator's spot, trying very hard not to think that the warm wetness he felt on his back and the backs of his legs was another man's blood.

But then, that's the important thing, St. Germain reminded himself. *It's another man's blood, and not yours.*

When he looked at it that way, it didn't seem so bad. In fact, he was pretty sure he could live with that.

Beside him, Lambert was trembling violently, his Richter scale of mortal terror right off the chart.

But Tyler ignored them both, for the moment. He walked to a blank, gray screen on the console and jabbed at the keys. At once, the screen flicked to life and showed an exterior shot of the lifeless asteroid below them. Red, flashing type raced past the image on the screen:

ASTEROID TERMINATION CONFIRMED: 00:30, 00:29, 00:28 . . .

"Mister St. Germain," Tyler announced expansively, "you've got twenty seconds to get us out of here."

. . . 00:25, 00:24, 00:23 . . .

St. Germain and Lambert exchanged frightened glances, and bent over their consoles, throwing switches and firing the *Cortez*'s powerful warp-drive engines. Neither man asked about the crew still down on the asteroid. They both had a pretty good idea . . . and after all, it was still someone else's blood.

The huge mining ship turned in a half-circle, like some great beast in the tall grass, and shot away from the asteroid.

The mile-wide jetty of rock tore itself apart in a silent blast of light and debris, its shock-wave pushing the *Cortez* ahead of it. The ship trembled and yawed, but soon settled down.

And then it plunged ahead into the blackness of endless space.

TWO

The solemn birds sang their solemn songs, casting down a pall of dreariness as if it were a curtain descending, signaling the end of the first act in some existential play. A comedy? A tragedy? Who could tell? The playwright was fussy and undecided, and the story was still being written and fine-tuned even as the actors said their lines and went about their bits of business.

At least, that's how Julie would always remember that day, when she thought of it at all. Maybe there was nothing portentous about the birdsong, nothing ominous about the day. Maybe it was just another day, no brighter or darker than the ones that came before or followed after. Perhaps she was simply trying to find meaning and purpose where none existed. But they were Julie's memories, and if that was how she chose to remember that day, then that's how it was.

The Eden Commune was a remote colonial outpost in a distant sector of Federation Space. Few, outside of the Federation, knew of its existence, which suited its settlers fine.

Once, neither long ago nor far away, these settlers' forefathers were enslaved by the Arakacians and pressed into a brutal, bloody war with the Enlightened Ones. Most of the settlers were killed in that battle, but a few survived—enough, anyway, for the Enlightened Ones to help establish a new planet, a new colony, a new hope. They owed the Edenites that much, at least.

As generations of settlers unspooled, the memory of the past dimmed, and eventually went out. After a while, it was as though the past never happened. And if that was what the Edenites chose to believe, well, then that's how it was. The past, like the future, is always being written and rewritten.

The forest was deep and lush and pellucid, crawling with rumors and a promise they could keep lovers' secrets. Tendrils as big around as mooring cables unfurled and drooped from the exotic trees. A carpet of moss and fallen leaves covered the forest floor, dampening the already-silent footfalls of the hunters.

Sunlight bullied its way down through the interlacing of thick branches and foliage, falling in shafts as straight and narrow as pencils, creating pools of light that, on first glance, looked like a spill of gold coins on the ground. That always made Julie think of the story their mother told them when she and Julie's fraternal twin, Kerrie, were just little ones: A man followed a rainbow to its end, searching for his heart's desire, and found there a pot of gold. But when he got it home, he became worried and fearful someone would steal his fortune, so he hid the gold under his bed. Next morning when he woke, he looked at the pot and discovered what he had believed was gold was nothing more than yellow leaves.

Julie glanced back over her shoulder. She could just

make out, through the dense trees, the outer ring of the Eden Colony, and the modest farming activity going on within the encampment. Beyond that, although she couldn't see it, lay the small airstrip, and a handful of aging starships.

Julie smiled wistfully. *And Nathan . . .*

A sound of branches breaking somewhere ahead shattered Julie's thoughts. She snapped her head around, senses instantly alert to danger. Julie quietly admonished herself. Too much looking back over your shoulder could get you just as dead as not looking at all—their father, Martin, told them that, the day they buried Mom. Dad had been a lawman, bringing peace and order to this wild frontier of space, and had made more enemies than he realized. He was also a man who seldom looked to the past, preferring to look straight ahead instead. His steadfast refusal to look back—

"Julie—there." Off to one side, Kerrie was whispering with a sound like escaping steam. *"There!"*

Julie looked to where her tawny-haired sister was pointing, and spotted the armor-dillo rummaging for grubs in the thick, mossy blanket. The beasts weren't particularly dangerous, unless cornered, and then they could become fighters. Their thick, overlapping armor plating made them hard to stop, let alone bring down, but a few soft spots existed. For just a moment, Julie wondered why they had chosen to hunt this beast with bows and arrows, when she had a perfectly fine gun strapped to her hip. She shrugged. Sometimes, as Dad also used to say, the old hunting methods were still the best.

A hard winter had caused a food shortage for the armor-dillos, and they were becoming bolder, eating the crops necessary to Eden Colony's survival. Although their father had retired a long time ago, he was nevertheless the closest thing to law enforcement and game warden the planet had, so the task of containing dangerous wildlife fell to him. Martin didn't mind—what were the odds some armor-dillo's vengeful next-of-kin would come gunning for an old lawman's family?

The situation this time, however, was different. The armor-dillo the two sisters were tracking had been wounded by one of the farmers defending his crops, and its injuries had made it wild and dangerous.

Kerrie pulled ahead of Julie, leaving it to her sister to catch up.

The recklessness of youth, thought Julie. Kerrie was her junior by, perhaps, five minutes or so. *But, oh, the wisdom those five minutes more have given me.* She had to bite her tongue to keep from laughing.

The beast had moved deeper into the darkening woods. Ahead, Kerrie stopped and, with the specific hand signals their father had taught them, indicated *the beast is over the rise.* A hard wind—it was just a little too brisk to be called a breeze—rattled the leaves and branches, then stopped, as if the world was holding its breath in anticipation of some mortal blow.

The temperature must have dropped ten or more degrees as they moved deeper into the sunless woods, but now their blood was up, and neither Julie nor Kerrie noticed it. Julie had now emptied herself of all extraneous thoughts, focusing on the hunt and nothing else.

The wind kicked up again and shifted—the world exhaling its held breath—and blew the scent of the hunters to the sensitive snout of the armor-dillo. It knew the smell of man well, following the injuries it received, and that smell drove it mad with sharply-remembered pain. It bellowed a throaty cry of anguish and anger, and doubled back, charging through the brush, toward the sisters.

Julie still couldn't see the beast, but she could see the brush shaking. She brought her crossbow to eye level, preparing to fire.

Several yards ahead and to the side of Julie, Kerrie cried out and released her arrow. Julie could tell from the thunder of hooves still bearing down on her position that her sister's shaft hadn't done much more than annoy the armor-dillo. It was up to her now.

"Use all your senses," her father spoke softly in her ear. Julie started. She hadn't even heard him approach, and a hot blush of embarrassment colored her clear cheeks. "See with your mind. Your body will know when it's time to strike."

Julie took a couple of deep, steadying breaths and did as her father instructed. She closed her eyes, and listened to the ground-thunder coming closer. More than that, she could feel it in the hollow of her chest, the pit of her stomach, and she calmly released the arrow.

Just as the armor-dillo crested the slope of the forest floor, exposing its soft, unplated underbelly, the heavy shaft flew straight and true, impaling the maddened creature's heart. It let out a final shriek of pain and bewilderment, charged forward a few more yards, its brain apparently not connecting with the news that it was dead, and then finally crumpled to the ground. Its sides bellowed, drawing its last few breaths, and a thick, pink foam bubbled up from its opened mouth and nose. Its small, oil-drop eyes seemed to fix on Julie, and then whatever light was behind them just . . . vanished. One moment it was there, and the next, gone.

Julie had hunted game before, but this was different, somehow. That was for food. You couldn't eat one of these monsters, not even if you were starving. It was like trying to eat a tank. No, this was just killing, and the reasons didn't matter.

Her father understood the expression spoiling her lovely face. "You'll be all right, as long as you don't ever come to like it too much, Julie."

She shook her head absently. How *could* she? How could *anyone?*

Kerrie was larruping toward them, long, tawny hair flying out behind her, quiver hung over one arm, longbow slung over her shoulder. "Terrific shot, Julie," she called. "Hello, Father. Did you see? Did you see that shot?"

"Yes, I did," Martin answered.

"You weren't checking up on us, were you?" Kerrie asked, all suspicions now.

Martin smiled broadly and let out a small stream of laughter. "Of course not," he said. "But I thought we had a date, you and I."

Kerrie groaned theatrically and palmed her forehead.

"Oh, sweetheart, am I *really* that easy to forget?" Martin asked. "You are *murder* on an old man's ego!" He opened his arms wide and took both his loves to his chest. A lesser man might feel sorry for himself that he could hold all he held dear in just two arms. But Martin knew there were men who had nothing to hold, and he was silently grateful for this bounty, these fellow passengers who made the dark, confusing trip bearable.

"You two run on," Julie said, stepping out of the circle of her father's arms. "I have things to do at home."

"You sure?" Martin asked. But he was really asking, *Are you all right?*

"I'm sure," she lied, trying to push aside the disturbing thoughts that now ran through her head. Was it possible?

Could she reach a time in her life when she might actually *enjoy* killing? She smiled sweetly at Martin, trying to avoid direct eye contact—he could read her like a book when he looked into her eyes—as a slight shiver ran up her spine.

"Julie wants to see Naay-thannn," Kerrie quipped in a sing-song voice, and laughed. *"Naaay-thannn . . ."*

Five minutes, Julie thought again, smiling at her sister's teasing. She shook her head in exasperation. *But what a difference those five minutes make . . .*

"That's enough, you," Martin said, giving Kerrie a sideways hug. "Julie, you go ahead and be sure to give Nathan our love." To Kerrie, he added, *"Don't* say it."

Martin steered Kerrie around and ahead of him, setting her on her way. He followed her, and glanced back over his shoulder to see Julie.

It would be for the last time, as it turned out.

Julie enjoyed the walk back through the forest to the encampment, emptying her mind of everything, just going on auto-pilot. Sometimes, she reflected, you could think too much, analyze things to death. Sometimes, it was better just to strap in and enjoy the ride.

She passed the Daily farm, and watched for a moment as Mr. Daily fed the pigs. He raised a hand to wave it, was probably about to ask her how her hunting expedition went, but stopped as his son went racing past in his toy Spacehawk fightercraft. The pigs squealed in surprise and bolted toward every point on the compass.

"Hey, Dad, watch this!" the boy cried, furiously pumping the foot pedals. He wheeled his pretend starship through the muddy barnyard, kicking up a spume of dirty water. "I'm a Spacehawk—like Nathan!"

"Whoa!" Mr. Daily said, and laughed. "Slow down there, son. Those thrusters weren't designed for this kind of terrain!"

Julie watched the boy race his Spacehawk around the far wall of the compound, nodded her greetings to Mr. Daily, and moved on.

The small airstrip was near her home, and she walked across the tarmac, shimmery with heat, and into the shadowed coolness of the long, deep hangar. Julie first noticed, as she always did, the overpowering smell of oil and fuel that clung even to this vast area like some earthbound spirit. She stood in the open doorway for a moment, her eyes closed, allowing them to adjust to the darkness, then opened them. Not that it would have mattered; she knew every inch of this old hangar and could have navigated it blindfolded.

Outside, gleaming in the sharp sunlight, one Spacehawk sat ready to eat sky. Inside, another sat propped up on blocks, its engine suspended above it on a chain and hoist. It was ready to go, but Nathan had stopped working to prepare for that night's festivities. After all, who can think of grease pits and engine parts when you're about to announce your engagement to the most beautiful woman on the planet?

As she moved through the cluttered but orderly hangar, Julie shrugged the crossbow and arrows down from her shoulders and laid them on a fairly neat, long workbench. A few O-rings sat there, soaking in a small pan of oil; otherwise, it was devoid of clutter.

"Nathan?" Julie called, turning from the table and moving deeper into the hangar, toward the back, and the living quarters there.

Just past the dry-docked Spacehawk, she paused at a banquet table overflowing with party food and a large cake.

Atop the cake, drawn in blue icing, was a pair of crossed rings. Julie smiled crookedly, and wiped one long finger through the spill of frosting at the base of the cake. She popped her finger in her mouth, licked it clean, and entered the small living quarters.

She didn't bother to call for Nathan again; the little room wasn't big enough to hide a cat in, let alone her soon-to-be lifemate.

Clearly, though, he'd been expecting her. Laid across the narrow bed was the skimpy, skin-hugging dress Nathan liked her in. No, strike that: *loved* her in. Julie lifted it and held it up flat against her body, turning to admire herself in the full-length mirror next to the door. Above the low-cut neck of the dress, her face seemed to shine in the artificial lighting. A seductive grin played at her lips as she reached up with a free hand and worked the hair-tie loose. A thick, full shock of black hair tumbled like a raven-colored waterfall to splash against the white shores of her slender shoulders.

Not bad, she thought. *You clean up real nice, tomboy* . . .

Nathan grabbed her from behind and spun her around, burying his face in the sweet, musky smell of her hair, nuzzling the long, graceful curve of her neck. She giggled, and pressed her body against his, closer than mice in a shotglass. The dress was crushed between them. She inhaled him, the sting of his sweat, the musty, chemical odors of the hangar—man smells, all of them—and felt intoxicated.

At last she pushed away, gently and reluctantly. The dress clung to her body a moment, then slipped off and dropped to the floor.

"Where's your dad?" Nathan asked, guiltily glancing around.

She stooped to retrieve the fallen dress, stood, brushed

off an imaginary piece of lint it had picked up from the floor. Julie hung the dress on a clothes peg on the back of the door, next to Nathan's robe and spare jumpsuit.

"Relax," she said. "He's in town with Kerrie."

Nathan laughed and sat down on the edge of the bed, snagging Julie's hand in his as he sat. "She'll keep him busy. Does he suspect anything?"

Julie laughed, a sound both earthy and innocent, and allowed herself to be pulled down to the bed beside him. "He's an old law man. What do you think? He suspects *everything.*"

Nathan slowly moved closer to her, his hands on each of her shoulders, and placed light, flitting butterfly kisses on her nose, her eyelids, her forehead, her lips. "I wonder if he suspects what I want to do to his daughter right now?" Nathan murmured.

"I wonder," Julie replied, and Nathan laid back across the narrow bed and drew her down atop his chest. The springs sighed like hopeless romantics, and, in time, so did the hopeless romantics themselves.

Three

*S*pare *yourself this. Just tell me what I want to know and I'll leave you alone.*

Those words, over and over, planet to planet, like a catechism.

Tyler claimed the key was leading them toward the Waters of Immortality, but as far as Germain St. Germain could tell, it was only leading Tyler closer and closer to madness, and the men to total ruin. Their path was a pretty random crapshoot . . . not that he would have admitted that to Tyler. Certainly, St. Germain felt sorry—or as close to that emotion as he ever allowed himself to get—for the colonists on the worlds Tyler and his Psycho Crew ripped asunder, but as he constantly told himself: *It's somebody else's blood, and I can live with that.* But it got a little harder each time.

And the thing was, St. Germain had the odd surety that the Waters of Immortality *were* on all of those planets—or, at least, had been at one time. The key Tyler possessed was acting like some sort of dowsing rod, leading them to where the Waters were supposed to be, as if drawn by some ancient, mystic connection. Sooner or later, the key would home in on the real thing.

Always assuming, of course, that Tyler wasn't completely nuts, and that assumption got a little tougher to make with every passing day. Hell, every passing *hour*.

Tyler refused to let the crew of the *Cortez* rest, driving them onward, as if some unseen timer was running out on his frantic quest. So the men napped and nodded and dozed at their posts, in their seats, or standing on their feet. They had to grab whatever sleep they could, whenever they could, fast on their way to becoming zombies.

But Tyler never slept. *Never*. Whatever else that key he wore at his waist was, it had some kind of symbiotic relationship with its host, giving Tyler strength and taking ... well, St. Germain wasn't quite sure what the key took in exchange for what it gave Tyler. His sanity, perhaps. Not that there had been much of that to take to start with.

Then again, St. Germain thought, maybe it was just as well Tyler didn't allow him to sleep. When he closed his eyes for too long, he could see the faces of those on the planets they had invaded. Several worlds were dead husks to start with, although the *Cortez*'s mining machinery always unearthed traces of former civilizations, wiped out long ago. And the worlds which hosted colonists at all were invariably new, never older than just a few generations ... as if they were survivors of something terrible that had happened there before, something forgotten, or just never spoken of.

It was as if they were following an old trail, a course that had been charted by someone else looking for the same thing, someone who believed very strongly in the scorched earth policy. Someone almost as crazy as Tyler.

There was something to that thought, St. Germain was sure of that, and maybe he would have figured it out, if he weren't so tired.

He stared blankly at the bank of computer monitors mounted before him in his grim, dark cubicle, watching the stars scratch their chalky tails across the monitor. But at last the screens flashed and a stream of numbers and information raced across the bottom of the main viewscreen.

Lambert rose from his seat next to St. Germain and stood behind him, leaning over his shoulder. St. Germain studied the bitstream data and said, flatly, "Our next dead end, dead ahead."

Lambert glanced quickly, nervously over his shoulder. "Don't let Tyler hear you say that," he hissed sharply.

St. Germain sighed explosively and slumped back in his chair. He had seldom been out of it since Tyler commandeered the *Cortez*. It felt like an eternity had passed since that madman burst onto the bridge and shot Captain Cameron between the eyes. Not that St. Germain had had any great love for Cameron, either, but at least the man hadn't been a froth-jawed crazy.

"Well, judging by past experiences, my guess is the well's dry here, too," St. Germain ventured. He might not have been so free with his opinions if he had known Tyler was within earshot.

"This can't go on forever," Lambert said, hopefully, but it was clear from his tone of voice that he didn't really believe it. He was starting to think they would become space-born Flying Dutchmen, never reaching port, always searching for something that didn't exist. But he'd never admit that to Tyler.

"Oh, can't it?" St. Germain snapped back irritably, jabbing a finger at the screen and the information scrolling past. "Take a look at these readings. We've traveled halfway across the universe to a F.A.K.K.² planet!"

Lambert leaned in closer, studying the words that loomed above the planet on the screen: FEDERATION AS-SIGNED K. K.². He shook his head, upper lip slicked back from his teeth as if he tasted something unpalatable in his mouth. "What's that?"

"Worse than a dead planet," St. Germain said, his voice growing heated and angry. "*That* is a Federation Assigned Kitogenic Killzone to the second level...death to all carbon-based lifeforms."

But the planet certainly didn't look like a killzone. Even from here, Lambert thought it looked quite green and verdant, its vast oceans the brightest blue he had ever seen. "I don't get it," he admitted.

"What's to get?" St. Germain snapped back. "Tyler is nuts!" His voice kept climbing up in volume; he knew Tyler had to be hearing this, but he didn't care. "Look, even if all this immortality crap is true, why'd he bring us here?" He saw Lambert steal quick, bird-like glances back over his shoulder, trying to get his friend to rein it in before it was too late. "I'm tellin' ya, we'd be better off on our own. Even if we find it—"

"Germain—" Lambert choked, but there was no stopping him now.

"—even if we find it, how do we know he'd cut us in?"

"Germain..."

"We gotta jump ship...go our own way." He hadn't noticed that Lambert had slunk away from his place behind the chair, and that Tyler had taken it. "Next planet we get to, we gotta steal an escape pod and get out of here!"

Tyler's hand locked around St. Germain's throat and

jerked the man from his chair. Tyler held the would-be mu-
tineer before his face, gazing at him with his unblinking,
psycho eyes, like a snake staring down a cornered rat. St.
Germain wheezed for breath, but Tyler's grip was like a steel
clamp.

"You're welcome to leave—any of you—any time you
wish . . . in a body bag!" Tyler roared. He sounded like an
animal that had been taught to speak rather than anything
human.

Tyler had changed since assuming command, become
more powerful. His long hair was wild and unkempt, like a
lion's mane, and the key, always tucked into his waistband,
threw a cold, green light onto Tyler's hard-planed face from
below, making him look like something out of an old
horror-holo.

*Oh, God, why didn't we kill him when we had the
chance?* St. Germain wondered stupidly. *When he first
stepped through the doors to the command deck, after he
found the key, why didn't we shoot him then?*

"Tyler, please . . ." Lambert begged. The captain shifted
his unblinking gaze to include Lambert, who wholly expected Tyler to grip his throat with his other hand and simply mash his skull against St. Germain's. Instead, Tyler
smiled a smile that showed too many teeth, and dropped St.
Germain—whose face was now the color of a plum—to the
floor.

"Any time you want to take command, you let me
know," Tyler said softly, and that was somehow worse than
if he'd raised his voice in madness. "Now—scan for lifeforms."

It's a F.A.K.K.² planet, Lambert started to say, but did
not. Violence was never that far away with Tyler, and Lambert knew that calm in his voice was like the eye of the

storm. A step too far in any direction landed you dead-bang in the hurricane—the trick was to stay in the calm as long as you could, and hold onto something for dear life when you couldn't.

Lambert moved to Germain St. Germain's forcefully-vacated seat and punched in a series of commands. The sensors ran their scans, and reported back to Lambert on the screen below the visual of the planet.

"Well, I'll be . . ." Lambert muttered in open amazement. "Looks like we've got a colony, sir," he reported brightly. He was glad to give Tyler something like good news, because that kept the storm away a little longer. "The F.A.K.K.[2] designation must have been from an old registry."

St. Germain sat forgotten on the floor behind Tyler, rubbing his throat, pulling in gasping, reedy breaths through his nearly-crushed larynx. It was just as well he couldn't speak for the moment; anything he could say would only get him killed.

"Bio-scan," Tyler said. "Same compound."

Lambert did as he was ordered, and even St. Germain was curious. He found his feet, and stood looking over Lambert's other shoulder, watching the computer's screen. The look-down scanners zeroed in on a single colonist, who went ignorantly about his business of slopping the pigs. St. Germain, perhaps in a late attempt to smooth over his earlier faux pas with Tyler, entered a string of commands, and the image of the colonist froze, rotated, and zoomed in close. The image dissolved into a computer representation, then broke into a riot of colors as the scanners reduced the man to a chemical spectrograph. A green light, dead center in the imaged figure, began to blink excitedly, and the words SOURCE DETECTED scrolled across the screen.

St. Germain turned away, disgusted, but Tyler was too engrossed by what the scanners were showing him to notice.

"Well . . . how we gonna get it?" Lambert asked.

Tyler's smile was genuine, but no less chilling for it. "The old-fashioned way," he said.

"Oh, *now* what?" St. Germain groaned in dismay. The planet was still some distance away, but their path was blocked by the *Kobyashi Maru*, a ship from the Hidalgo Mining Corporation, a long-standing rival of Metal Mammoth Mining. The ship's commander, Captain Shintoho, warned the *Cortez* crew that they were entering a quadrant of space that Hidalgo had chartered.

St. Germain glanced back over his shoulder at Tyler, who sat in the Captain's chair, tugging thoughtfully at his lower lip as if he hadn't heard. "Sir?" he croaked. It still hurt to talk, so he swallowed and tried again. He did a little better this time. "The *Kobyashi Maru* is challenging us. What should I tell them?"

Tyler looked up from his reverie. "Tell them I'm coming over. I have something I want to discuss with their commander."

St. Germain conveyed the message, and turned to tell Tyler the *Kobyashi Maru*'s tractor beams would be ready to accept Tyler's shuttlecraft, but the madman was already gone. He returned a few minutes later and sat down in the command chair. Confused, St. Germain turned back to the giant viewscreen in time to see a small shuttle deploy from the *Cortez* and cross the airless gulf to the rival ship.

"I guess what I *meant* to say . . ." Tyler said, the sound

of his voice startling St. Germain so badly that his heart actually missed a beat, then raced to make up for it, "... is that I accept their challenge."

Lambert and St. Germain exchanged nervous, fearful glances. *Who* was aboard that shuttlecraft?

They watched with a sense of dread as the *Kobyashi Maru*'s tractor beams locked onto the little craft and drew it into its open hangar bay doors, like some gigantic creature devouring its prey. Except they both knew, somehow, that it wasn't going to turn out that way.

"Mr. Lambert," Tyler said, and for the first time, both men noticed the madman was holding some manner of electronic signaling device. St. Germain had a pretty good idea what it was—he'd seen the miners use ones like it sometimes when they were blasting through rock. "Radio the captain of the *Kobyashi Maru* and make this offer: any man who wishes to join our crew will be spared. They have one minute to make their decision."

Thirty seconds later, Captain Shintoho's badly frightened face filled the viewscreen. He was consumed with rage and bluster and indignation, but mostly fear. More than anything else, fear.

"This is an act of cowardice!" he thundered. "Callow, craven—"

Tyler interrupted him dismissively. "Yes, yes, but you're wasting valuable time. I suspect you're trying to jam my detonation device's radio frequency, but you'll never find the right wavelength in time. What's your answer? Do you join me, or—"

"We would rather die!" Captain Shintoho replied stiffly.

"Shoot yourself," Tyler said with a shrug, and thumbed the triggering device. "By the way, the detonator's frequency is the same as our ship's hailing frequency."

Barely a moment later, a white light blossomed in the center of the viewscreen and spread from side to side, filling the monitor with a blinding radiance from which Lambert and St. Germain had to avert their eyes. Tyler stared unblinkingly into the glare, watching as the last of it faded away, leaving only the blackness of space, like a negative image. The blast had vaporized everything of the rival ship, leaving no trace, no debris. Certainly, no survivors.

"That's gonna hurt in the morning," Tyler laughed, and added, "Prepare the men. We're going in."

The *Cortez*'s thrusters fired, and the ship moved through the darkness, bearing down on the F.A.K.K.² planet like the shadow of Death itself.

Four

"Why do I get the impression," Martin asked, "that you're doing your best to keep me busy? As if there's something at home you don't want me to see yet?"

Kerrie became instantly engrossed in a skein of silk samples on display before one of the small market stalls. "I don't know what you're talking about," she answered airily, briefly touching each of the samples, not really paying attention to any of them, but taking great pains to keep her face averted from her father. The old man said he could always tell when she was lying by the way she lowered her eyes. "I thought you'd like to get out of the house with your youngest daughter, that's all."

Martin laughed. "But that still leaves the matter of my oldest daughter... who is, at this very moment, I am sure, with my future son-in-law." He watched the set of Kerrie's shoulders for a reaction. They seemed to tense, for just a second, but that was enough for Martin. He laughed again, and put a hand on Kerrie's arm.

Kerrie turned to face him, worry in her eyes. "Julie's gonna kill me for telling you," she said.

"You didn't tell me, I guessed," he answered. In fact, he'd guessed it a long time ago, and it wasn't all that hard. Julie and Nathan were inseparable, and had been since they were kids. He'd been there for Julie almost as long as Martin himself had been. It's never easy for a father to let his daughter go, but Martin supposed it was a little easier to let her go to a good man like Nathan.

"Well, all the same," Kerrie said, a little petulantly, but they both know it was just an act at this point. "You be sure to act surprised when they tell you."

"Like this?" Martin asked, and mimed an over-the-top expression of surprise, hands thrown up on either side of his face, eyes comical and bulging, his jaw unhinged and gaping.

"No, no, no," Kerrie groaned, breaking into a laugh. "That's not surprise, that's mortal terror. Try again."

But something in the cloudless sky caught Martin's keen eye, and the look Kerrie read on his face was genuine. "That's better," she said. "That's real good."

"No," Martin said, watching as the shark-like shadow of the *Cortez* blotted out the sun, throwing the entire market-place into the unnatural chill of an eclipse. "That's real *bad.*"

The glue that strings moments together seemed to hold everyone fast, clogging the forward rush of time like sand in the gears of delicate machinery. The villagers and vendors stopped in their transactions, looking up, one after another, at the source of the ominous midday darkness. The massive, sun-stealing *Cortez* simply hung above them, like a dare, but no one could yet guess its deadly intentions. A murmur hopscotched through the colonists, skipping from one to the next: What is it? What does it want?

And then, the hangar bay doors irised open, and perhaps a dozen smaller, identical, darker objects tumbled from the breach in the hull. They dropped for a moment, like bombs; then, almost simultaneously, their dual burners all thundered to life, and the nature of the smaller ships became obvious.

"Fightercraft!" Martin shouted. "Take cover! Fightercraft!"

That was enough to shatter the frozen moment like delicate crystal, and the colonists scattered in all directions, like quail before hunting hounds. The shriek of the fighters' dual burners grew louder, and seemed to come from everywhere at once.

And then, carnage exploded all around.

The first assault of fighters buzzed close over the inverted bowl-buildings of the small village, like a flock of birds, unleashing a stuttering blast of high-caliber shells. Windows blew outward, showering down glass confetti. The ground kicked up in puffs of dust and chipped stone, and the knot of colonists still clustered in the village square seemed to burst like sacks of wet meat as bullets tore through them.

"Why?" Kerrie shouted. Receiving no answer, she cried again, *"Why?"*

Martin shook his head. "Go get Nathan!" he yelled to be heard over the harrying roar of the fighter ships. "Tell him to round up the others and get airborne, now!"

"What about you?" she shouted. "What are you going to do?"

But the old man just gave her a shove to get her going,

and stood facing the last ship in the first wave of fighters, like a sheriff of old calling out some high-tech gunslinger. The fighter strafed the ground on all sides of Martin, playing with him, but the old lawman refused to be frightened. He could feel the heat of the bullets as they scorched past him on either side, could feel the puffs of dust the shells threw up at him, but he squinted his eyes into narrow slats and, as if by magic, a gun appeared in his hand.

The pilot of the fighter burst into laughter. Who did this old fool think he was?

And then the Plexiglas of the canopy shattered before his eyes, a spiderweb of broken glass stitching out from a starpoint hole. A bullet hole, and the pilot felt a horrible, breathless burning in his throat. He tried to cough, and he felt a coppery liquid filling his mouth.

You shot me! he thought in angry wonderment. *You actually shot me!*

The pilot was dying and he knew it, but he'd be damned if he'd go down without taking that old fool with him. He angled the nose of his fighter toward Martin, bearing down on him, but Martin simply dived and rolled below the plummeting craft. The fighter's wings ripped through the walls of the drygoods store, spraying splinters of steel and shrapnel of stone in all directions. The nose of the craft hit the ground hard, gouged a long wound in the earth, and buried itself at an odd angle up to the leading edge of the fighter's canopy.

The impact of the crash peeled the canopy back, exposing the dead pilot sitting at the controls, his lifeless hands still locked around the joystick, riding the big one down to hell.

Martin studied the insignia emblazoned on the side of the crashed fighter and on the dead pilot's helmet: a Woolly

Mammoth, with gleaming, metallic, mercury-red eyes, terrifying tusks, and deadly, grasping teeth. Below that, the legend: METAL MAMMOTH MINING. Far from shedding any light on the attack, this just made it seem that much more senseless. Why would a mining company attack a peaceful colony?

Martin didn't have long to ponder the question, for the next wing of fighters began their run on the village. Incredibly, there were still people standing in the streets, those inside when the attack began, now come outside to see what was going on. Bare moments had passed since the first strafing run, but lives had changed drastically and forever in those few seconds.

"They're coming back!" Martin heard someone shout from above. He looked up and spotted a boy of perhaps sixteen or seventeen standing on the roof of the livery goods store. He had been up there repairing the roof with his father when the first assault hit, and now he was just standing there, watching.

Martin knew there was no time; he threw himself into the opened cockpit, onto the dead pilot's lap, and hit the ejector button with the side of his fist. The seat was blown out of the angled craft, and the massive G-forces slammed Martin back against the dead man. The ejector seat cleared the low edge of the rooftop, and Martin jumped free. The seat continued on over the building, over the next, and drove into the side of a great, sheltering tree at the edge of the village. A moment later, the parachute deployed, billowing out from the thick, leafy boughs.

Martin saw the boy's father lying in a pool of blood and spilled tar on the rooftop. The boy was either unaware this was the real thing, or he was in shock, because he was quite calm. Martin pushed the boy ahead of him and bolted for the door to the roof, taking the stairs two and three at a time.

Overhead, he could hear the scream of the fighters as they began their strafing run.

A moment later, the entire building shook as if it had been struck by the giant fist of some vengeful god, and the walls of the stairwell collapsed around Martin and the boy with a shriek and a bang.

On the streets, Tyler, Lambert, and other members of his Psycho Crew strode through the carnage, oblivious to the cries of the wounded and the dying. On the southern edge of the village, where the farming lands began their slow spread outward, several colonists had run out into the fields, counting on the tall grasses and crops to conceal them, but the fighters simply sprayed the fields with bullets. Later, the Psycho Crew would set fire to the fields, and those colonists who had survived the bullets would either die in the flames or flee, only to be cut down as they escaped the fire.

By now, several of the colonists had retrieved their weapons—guns, bows and arrows, knives—and were engaging Tyler's ground crew in a running battle. Bullets *whang*ed off the sides of buildings around Tyler, but he ignored them, and walked unconcernedly on, flanked by his murderous crew.

Tyler knelt beside a mortally wounded man; the hail of bullets had nearly ripped him in half, but he still clung to a tenuous life. Tyler grabbed a handful of the man's hair and jerked his head up to a level with his own face. "Where is it?" he demanded. "You can stop all this. Just tell—"

He realized he was talking to a dead man, and let the corpse's face drop into the slurry of mud and blood around them. Well, so what? There were others. Plenty of others. For now.

The Psycho Crew fanned out, and Tyler smiled as the sounds of gunfire and screams echoed and re-echoed off the walls of the marketplace.

"Remember back when we were kids?" Julie began, and propped herself up in bed on her elbow. Nathan traced small circles on her arm with his finger. "I used to wear that silly wooden pendant?"

Nathan nodded; he remembered. If it involved Julie, he remembered it all.

"Well, after that fire in our old house, I thought the pendant had been destroyed," she said, and laid back, her arms forming a letter V behind her head. "I was so upset, but you told me not to give up. And you found it in the rubble. There wasn't a mark on it."

"I remember," he said, and kissed the shelf of bone above her eye, the place that always made her tingle. She smiled and stroked his hair. "What about it?"

She shrugged with her free arm. "It just seemed a little strange . . . since there used to be a small nick on the back where Dad's knife slipped when he was carving it." She turned her face to meet his, and a lopsided smile tugged at her full, red lips. "Apart from that, it was an excellent copy."

Nathan groaned, rolled over onto his back, and wiped his hands down his face. "You *knew?* The whole time, you knew?"

Now it was Julie's turn to trace patterns and designs— interlocking rings, a Mobius strip, the symbol for eternity— on Nathan's bare chest. "The only thing I was never sure of was whether Dad was in on it with you."

Nathan raised one woolly eyebrow. "I'll carry that one to my grave," he said.

"I'm a cop's daughter, lover. We don't miss anything." She pressed in closer to him, and Nathan could feel the warmth and weight of her breath against his face. The tip of her nose touched his, and he had to squint to keep her azure eyes in focus. "And I feel it only fair to warn you, we've both had you under surveillance for quite a while now, and *you* are a keeper. So stop being so nervous."

"I know my rights," Nathan feigned protest. "And I want my lawyer."

"Well, okay, if you'd rather have your lawyer than me, then—"

Whatever Julie said next was drowned out by the boom of three fighters blasting by above the little hangar, chasing down the colonists escaping into the fields, and the wooded ravine beyond.

Julie and Nathan hit the deck running, quickly throwing on their clothes and grabbing weapons as they raced out of the dark hangar and into sunlight as sharp as glass. Even from here, they could see columns of black smoke rising above the treetops like giant spikes driven into the ground. A squadron of fighters began a descent on the town that lay beyond the trees, and below the rising columns of smoke.

"Get in the air, Nathan!" Julie shouted, fighting to remain calm. She buckled her worn gunbelt around her hips. "I'm going to town—Dad and Kerrie will need me!"

Nathan nodded, still unable to take his eyes off the signs of the disaster visible above the treetops. He tried to guess what the village must look like, but it was much worse than anything his mind could have conjured.

"Be careful!" Julie added.

"Love you!" he said, and kissed her quickly, and then he

was scrambling into the cockpit of the waiting Spacehawk. Within moments, he was airborne, but two of the three fighters that raced past moments earlier doubled back, and began strafing Nathan's Spacehawk. Nathan had practiced several hours a day with his fighter, and the Psycho Crew were not used to any real opposition.

Nathan took his Spacehawk up in a looping climb, leveling out behind the fighter that, a moment before, had been riding his tail. Now the black fighter was in Nathan's sights, and he thumbed the FIRE button on his controls. A stream of bullets poured from the Spacehawk's wing-mounted guns, and the fuel tanks of the enemy fighter burst. An umbrella of fire and smoke opened, and swallowed the fighter. It went into a screaming dive, and struck the airstrip. The nearest Spacehawk was caught in the spreading flames, and in a matter of moments, its fuel tank also ignited and blew.

Julie stopped, turned back to the airstrip, and began pelting across the tarmac to her own waiting Spacehawk. Much as she didn't like leaving Dad and Kerrie to their own devices in the middle of this mayhem, she knew she'd be of more help in her fighter.

Before she got a hundred feet, though, the ground buckled and ruptured around her. She fell to her stomach, and looked up to see one of the Psycho Crew ships bombing the airstrip. The shockwaves shattered the windows of the hangar, and the landing gear on one of the remaining Spacehawks twisted, threatening to send the fighter plunging down the side of the nearby ravine.

The Psycho Crew fighter banked, turned, heading back for a final pass. Julie sat up, but cover was too far for her to reach before the fighter would cut her down. She set her chin and grabbed the gun she kept holstered at her hip, unconsciously imitating her father's earlier showdown with another pilot.

Nathan looked back and saw the fighter swing around for another run at the airstrip and Julie, and broke off from his aerial fight with the second black ship. He pushed his Spacehawk, coming up on the tail of the ship bearing down on Julie, and thumbed the ammo button.

Nothing. Either the gate was jammed, or the magazine was empty. Not that it mattered, either way. Julie would still be just as dead.

"I love you," Nathan said huskily, and opened up the throttle on his Spacehawk. The tip of his fighter scraped sparks on the tail of the black ship as he overtook it. "Remember me."

And then his Spacehawk collided with the black fighter. They both vanished in a spray of fire and twisted, white-hot metal and glass. Instinct alone caused Julie to roll aside, out of the way of the falling wreckage as it slammed down on the ruptured airstrip.

"Nathan!" Julie cried. *"Nathan, noooo!"*

She screamed until her throat was raw, but it was still a small and insignificant sound for an event that heralded the end of her world.

Kerrie stood with her back pressed flat against one of the few buildings that hadn't been razed or set ablaze. There had been no sign of her father since the building he was in had been blasted by rocket fire. She had to assume he was gone.

He was gone, but the scum who caused his death was still here . . . for the moment. But if she learned anything today, it was how fast things could change in the blink of an eye. Kerrie had been playing hit and run with the Psycho

Crew, shooting them from hiding with her arrows, then breaking for another bolthole, working her way through the village in this way. But there were too many, and they were too well-armed and ruthless. She nocked her last arrow in her bow, and took several deep, steadying breaths, waiting until Tyler and his murderous henchmen strolled unhurriedly by her place of concealment. Then, she stepped out, raised her bow even with her shoulder, drew the heavy gauge string taut, targeted the crazed leader's neck, and gently released the arrow.

She would not have shot anyone in the back, but there was something about this madman that made her think she didn't want to look in his eyes.

The arrow whistled straight and true, bearing down on Tyler's exposed throat . . .

And his left hand whipped up and actually caught the arrow in mid-flight, mere inches from his neck. Tyler gingerly touched the tip of the arrow, his lips forming an "O" of mock surprise at its sharpness.

"My arrows all had rubber tips when I was a kid," he said, as he casually broke the arrow in half with one hand. He turned to face his assailant, a feral snarl like a mad dog's slicking back his lips.

Kerrie had been right—she *didn't* want to look in those eyes. It was like looking through isinglass into the fires of hell.

"Well, well . . . deadly *and* psychotic," Tyler said appreciatively, his wild-eyed gaze tracing the curves of her body. His smile grew wider still, until Kerrie was sure his face would split in half. "My kinda gal!"

He took a step closer, and she brought her bow up to use as a club. Tyler, Lambert, and Connor laughed at this, as if they were uncles who found the actions of a young niece precocious and endearing, not threatening at all. The other gathered members of the Psycho Crew joined in.

"Monster!" Kerrie hissed, and brought the heavy bow down in a deadly, whistling arc.

Tyler's left arm moved faster than she could see, and the bow broke in half against his upraised forearm.

"Will you marry me?" Tyler asked, and now there was not just madness burning in his eyes, but something worse ...something just for her...just for Kerrie.

She gripped the ends of the broken bow in both hands and lunged forward, trying to impale this creature on the jagged edge as if he were a vampire, but Tyler was, once again, too fast. He jerked the bow out of her hands and threw it over his shoulder. Lambert and one of the crew moved quickly, seizing Kerrie's arms to hold her fast.

Tyler traced the edge of a splintered fingernail against her soft, pale cheek. "Are there any more at home like you?" he asked, head tipped to the side, like a dog listening to a high frequency only he can hear. Perhaps madness was like that, a note so high and rarefied that only a certain few responded to its siren call.

"As a matter of fact...there are!" Julie said, stepping into sight at the edge of the rooftop.

She fired her gun, punching a hole through the first henchman who had his hands on Kerrie. The others grabbed their weapons and blasted at the rooftop, but Julie had already launched herself off of the building, aiming for the thick canvas canopy fronting the shop. She hit, trampolined up, somersaulted gracefully off, and landed lightly, firing off two more rounds at Tyler's Psycho Crew.

Kerrie watched her sister's movements with awe, saw the fires of unbridled hatred burning in her eyes. But there was something else to Julie's heated expression, beyond the feral snarl and dagger-like gaze—a haunted look that spoke volumes.

Had something happened to Nathan?

God, no, Kerrie thought. *Not him, too . . .*

She struggled fiercely, wanting to join her sister against this madman and his evil crew, but she just wasn't strong enough to break free.

Lambert, meanwhile, had both arms around Kerrie, trying to ignore her savage kicks at his legs as bullets *spang*ed around them. He dived for cover, dragging her behind an overturned wagon full of barrels. The girl was nothing to Lambert, and he would have happily let her go, but Tyler obviously pegged her as a keeper, and, unlike Germain St. Germain, who seemed to have some inexplicable deathwish, Lambert wasn't going to get on the captain's bad side.

The sounds of gunfire brought other members of the Psycho Crew running, guns chattering angrily. A chunk of stone from the building behind her struck Julie's cheek and laid it open. She turned and dived through the broken window, looking for cover inside the shop.

She glanced around, her eyes already adjusting to the darkness. She could hold them off in here, she thought, maybe even separate them, pick them off one at a time. Julie stood up in the window and fired her pistol, but felt her heart freeze when she saw what Tyler held: a rocket launcher.

And it was pointed right at her.

Tyler waved cheerily and jerked back on the trigger. The recoil of the weapon barely shook him. Julie cried out in alarm and dived for the floor as the shell struck the wall and detonated. Wood and stone rattled down atop her, and that was about the time she and consciousness parted company for a while.

Kerrie saw it all from where Lambert held her prisoner, but she refused to give these monsters the satisfaction of tears. She closed herself off, knowing there would come a time later—how much later, she couldn't guess—for tears and rage and grief, but that time was not now.

Tyler chuckled to himself, and pried a weapon from the hands of one of his dead goons. He raised the automatic rifle to his shoulder and fired the gun at the only remaining upright wall in the village square. The bullets blasted the soft plaster, and spelled out the word "F.A.K.K.²."

Tyler pitched the empty rifle aside, then stepped back like an artist admiring his handiwork.

"Now it really *is* a dead planet," he roared, and laughed.

After a moment, when they were sure it was what Tyler expected, the rest of his men laughed, too.

Five

J ulie was having the strangest dream.

Through the ruins of Eden, moving as silently as the ashen smoke that drifted over the rubble, a gnarled, ancient looking man with a face like a skull—death's simple, unlovely geometry—slowly walked toward her. He did not stop to check his way, but came surely to where Julie lay, buried among the stones and timbers. Now that he was closer, she could see he was no more substantial than the oily smoke from the countless fires pocking the landscape.

And yet, despite his opaqueness, his shadow crept across Julie's face, as tentative as a small, frightened animal, and she knew he was real.

She opened her eyes

(weren't they open already? How could she have seen him if her eyes had been closed?)

and lay gazing torpidly up at the man. She felt no fear, just a strange calm and curiosity.

"Are you Death?" she mumbled through her mashed and bloodied lips.

"To some," he answered.

"What are you to me?" she managed.

As she spoke, he drew his sword, but Julie didn't read it as a threat. The wizard—for that was what he most reminded her of—raised the rune-carved blade high above his head, and vines of green, mystic energy crawled along the sword, crossing, twisting, interlacing over and over.

"I am the bridge," he answered.

She could feel the small hairs on her neck prickling with the growing charge of mystic energy contained in the sword, and she felt the liquid behind her eyes begin to bubble and boil.

"There is nothing more for you here," the wizard said, running his bare hand along the cutting edge of the blade; where it passed, the dancing energy simply disappeared. When his hand reached the end of the weapon, it was once again just a sword, nothing magical about it. "Your destiny awaits you in Neo-Calcutta."

Julie had been wrong about one thing: the energy from the sword did not disappear, but now resided in the hand that had stroked the blade. The old man raised his green-glowing appendage, studied it with practiced disinterest, then made a fist and slammed it into the rocks beside Julie's head.

She opened her eyes with a start, and pain flowed like a liquid through her skull, down her spine, and spread through her bruised and bloodied body. The acuteness of her injuries forced Julie's dazed mind into sharp focus, and she wasn't surprised to find the wizard had been part of a foolish dream.

He was a messenger from your subconscious, telling you to wake up and get in gear, she thought. No supernatural communiqué there—just her mind telling her she had work to do.

Julie had been lucky in one regard: the cross-timbers of the collapsing building had fallen in such a way as to slough the falling stones away from her, leaving her relatively unharmed. With a good, strong piece of lumber, she was soon able to roll the stones back from the tomb caging her.

For a moment, she thought she might still be dreaming her fever dreams, because the sight that greeted her was like a nightmare superimposed over her safe, familiar world. The colony was awash with thick, greasy smoke which the wind momentarily shredded long enough to reveal the twisted wreckage of the homes and buildings. Weapons lay in the streets where they had dropped from dead hands, but the only bodies she could identify wore the black hazmat jumpsuits of the Psycho Crew. A few of the dead were prickled with arrows Julie recognized as belonging to Kerrie. For a moment, her heart surged with hope, and smashed against the bars of its cage like a trapped bird—could the others have survived somehow?

It didn't seem likely, but then, *she* had survived.

Julie shook her head. She sensed her survival had been some divine intervention, a destiny that wouldn't allow itself to be thwarted so soon. If anyone else survived, it would be a miracle, and miracles didn't fall from the sky like rain.

On the helmet of the dead man closest to her, she could see the odd insignia of the Metal Mammoth Mining company, the beast's pinpoint red eyes glowing like blood.

"You came a long way just to die," she told the dead man.

Something mirrored in the helmet's polarized faceplate caught her attention. She studied it, the letters printed backwards on the glass, then turned to look at the wall on which the letters had been stitched by bullets.

F.A.K.K.².

The name for a dead world.

"I shall be the instrument of your vengeance," she said to the lifeless planet, then set her sights on home . . . for the last time.

Tyler looked up from the key laid across his lap at the sound of a knock on his cabin's door. He was never far from the obelisk or its silent counsel, and he suspected—he knew—it would soon impart more wisdom to him. He supposed the obelisk doled it out in bits and pieces, aware that too much information too fast could blast out Tyler's cerebral cortex.

Not that the key cared for Tyler's well-being. No, he was as much a tool to the key—a means to an unguessed-at end—as the key was a tool to him. On those occasions when his thoughts cleared—and you could see it happening in his eyes, like looking at a frozen lake and seeing a body bump by just below the icy surface—Tyler, the *old* Tyler, was mortally frightened. But then the corpse would be carried away on a relentless current, and Tyler's eyes were only a frozen lake once more.

"Come," Tyler ordered. His fingers absently stroked the cuneiform symbols engraved in the obelisk's frictionless surface. The cabin door opened and St. Germain entered, bearing before him, like a butler, a small, silver tray, on which sat a single, capped ampule holding a liquid the color of rust.

St. Germain's face was drawn and bloodless, as white as a virgin bride on her wedding night, and his eyes looked as raw as two eggs. He offered the tray to Tyler, who picked up the ampule, popped its top, and waved it beneath his nose, inhaling its piquant aroma, like a fine old wine. And in a way, that's what it was—just wine, and don't dare to think about what horrible crop yielded this drink. St. Germain felt the gorge rising in the back of his throat, but he knew better than to allow Tyler to suspect. No, it was somebody else's blood, and he could live with that, and it was just business as usual aboard this star-prowling, world-devouring madhouse.

"Interesting body," Tyler said, and laughed at his own gruesome pun. "What's the vintage, would you guess?"

St. Germain shook his head, his lips pursed. "Nineteen years, maybe twenty."

"Nineteen," Tyler said wonderingly. "As young as that."

He put the capsule to his lips and splashed the thick, rust-colored liquid into his mouth. Tyler wiped his mouth with the back of his hand and felt the liquid trace a burning thread down his throat, igniting a bonfire in his stomach. He sat back in his chair, gripped the key with both hands, and smiled at the things it told him.

"We're gonna need a jump port," he announced to St. Germain, although the latter had the odd feeling that Tyler wasn't much more than a ventriloquist's dummy voicing the key's commands. "Set a course for Neo-Calcutta."

The path to her home was only a road that led to nowhere in particular now. Only a road, and the home only a set of walls which held a few memories that might or might not be relatable to key points in her life. Remarkably, the house had not been damaged by the black fighters.

But no miracle, she reminded herself. *Just remarkable.*

Julie dressed with quick, efficient movements, putting on her skin-hugging flight suit. She paused for just a moment at her dresser, and opened the small jewelry box that sat there. She rummaged through the real jewelry and handful of rare coins and stones, and found the wooden medallion Nathan had counterfeited for her when they were both a lot younger.

Say it, she thought bitterly. *When you were both* alive.

Julie returned the medallion to the box and closed the lid. That part of her life was over and gone forever. There was no room for it now. Books, pictures, trinkets—all junk belonging to a dead world, and she was alive. She was not a part of the dead, but she would avenge them.

At the foot of her bed was an oaken hope chest, but it looked more like a small coffin sitting there—a coffin to hold her dead hopes and murdered dreams. She left her room and her youth behind, and moved to her father's study, where he kept the weapons. Julie was surprised by her lack of emotion upon entering the room, but she was secretly glad for it. The great clock in the corner ticked off the minutes as serenely and casually as ever. She unlocked the weapons cabinet, selected the ordnance she thought she would need, and stopped herself from locking the remaining firearms back into place. It wasn't as if a neighbor's kid was going to wander in here and help himself to a handful of semi-automatic death. Not anymore. Not ever again.

And that thought, that conscious break with tradition and the unconcerned ticking of the old clock, slammed home the reality of the situation with all the force of a bomb blast. Everyone in Eden was gone. All of them, really gone. Not just hiding in a closet to jump out and yell "Surprise!" at her and Nathan at the wedding announcement they had planned for tonight. The guests had stepped outside for a moment and accidentally locked themselves out. They weren't getting back in again. There was no one to open the door for them.

She had to hold onto the back of her father's favorite

old chair for a moment and wait for the feeling of drowning, of overwhelming hopelessness, to pass. Then she was good to go.

Julie left the room, left the house and the clock that would continue to count away the minutes and hours and days until it finally wound down, unattended, and left her old life behind like a snake shedding its skin. She made her way to the shattered airstrip, where the blackened wreckage of Nathan's Spacehawk lay in scattered pieces—forcing herself to not look back, only ahead—and moved to the only undamaged fighter she could find: the craft Nathan had been working on. Julie had to lower the engine back into its housing and re-connect it. No big deal—her father had taught her how to take apart engines and put them back together before she even had her first serious kiss.

She taxied the craft over the blast-heaved pavement, hit the VTOL lift button, and watched the world drop away beneath her. Julie flew her Spacehawk over the ruins of the village, looking for signs of life she knew she would not find, then hit the dual burners, and got on with it.

She activated the navigational computer. "Set coordinates for the closest spaceport that can handle a class-C vessel."

"Searching, searching, searching," the computer replied in a friendly, helpful voice. "Confirmed: Neo-Calcutta, course set. ETA 93.7 hours. Ready to engage on your command."

Neo-Calcutta? Julie had difficulty drawing breath into her lungs, as if she had just stepped into a pool of freezing water.

Your destiny awaits you in Neo-Calcutta. The voice of the wizard echoed in her thoughts. Had it *really* been a dream, or . . . ?

Julie shook her head. No. She refused to believe in visions and scriers. She had taken a blow to the head, and her senses couldn't be completely trusted yet. Her subconscious knew that Neo-Calcutta was the only likely spaceport a craft that size could possibly jump from, that's all. Or maybe that shot to her head had scrambled her sense of time, giving her a false sense of deja vu. But it was not a vision. Those things didn't happen, and certainly not to her.

"On your command?" the nav-com repeated. Julie knew it wasn't possible, but she thought she detected just a hint of annoyance and a whiff of condescension in that synthesized voice.

"Engage," she ordered. The nav-com thanked her in almost gushing tones. Julie settled back in her chair, and watched the darkness of space wrap around her.

She closed her eyes, and slept—deeply, and without dreams.

The nav-com was speaking to her in reproachful tones, telling Julie her destination was dead ahead. There was a brief, panicked moment of disorientation, when she couldn't recall where she was, or why, or how she got here, but it all came back in a wave, like air rushing to fill a vacuum.

She rubbed her eyes, a child waking after a long trip to find herself at grandmother's house, and blinked Neo-Calcutta into sharp focus. The Spacehawk was approaching a cluttered section of the huge, rotating space station, a domed central cluster of skyscrapers in the hub, all other arms of the spaceport spread like spokes on a wheel. Julie watched as dozens of spaceships descended in a choreographed ballet onto the docking platforms. From below these platforms, departing spacecraft left the great, domed city. A ship—its shape like that of a beaming, happy face—moved across the endless, horizonless sky in front of Julie.

She fired the Spacehawk's reverse thrusters, slowing the speed of her fighter.

"Requesting incoming docking coordinates," she spoke into her helmet's communications link. A filtered, artificial voice responded (without artifice or sarcasm, she noted): "Please continue holding pattern, lock in approach H-A-L 3000."

"Confirmed," Julie said, watching as the nav-com programmed this into her craft's guidance system.

"State the nature of your visit."

She replied simply, without considering. "Revenge."

There was a pause as the SYStems OPerator ran this reply through its checklist of acceptable responses. It was not among them. Not officially. "Processing ... Invalid entry. Resubmit."

"Business," she answered, strained.

"What is the nature of that business?" the SYSOP asked; its tireless and unperturbed tone made Julie long for the acerbic nature of her nav-com.

"Family business," she said, and hoped that would end it.

It did. "Confirmed," the SYSOP answered. "Forty-eight hour visa, file number VK-120. Pilot, identify yourself."

Julie started to give her name, but caught herself. *If a tree falls in the forest and no one hears it, does it make a noise?* she thought. *And if no one who once knew you still exists, are you still that same person?*

She didn't think she was, or ever would be again.

"Pilot, identify yourself or permission to dock will be refused," the SYSOP warned with all the patience of the damned.

"F.A.K.K.²," Julie replied, remembering the odd graffiti that had been shot into the stone wall. "My name is F.A.K.K.²."

"Confirmed," the SYSOP replied almost at once. "You are cleared for docking, F.A.K.K.², Quarantine Level 6, Platform 9B. Thank you for visiting Neo-Calcutta, and remember to visit our duty free gift shop in Sector 12."

"I'll remember," Julie said to no one in particular. "I promise, I'll remember."

The Spacehawk continued its slow and graceful spiral to the surface of the docking platform, guided by bursts from its retro-rockets. Even as it descended, the small craft's main thrusters had already begun cooling, fading down from a weak red glow to a black as cold as any broken heart.

Six

The sign above the door read CLUB DEAD–WHERE THE DAMNED COME TO MINGLE, but that was already pretty widely understood on Neo-Calcutta. The legend was not meant to be a selling point, but more of a warning that this was not a place to bring your family . . . unless your family was a pack of murdering, back-stabbing, brain-damaged thugs.

Tyler and a core contingent of his men headed for the club as soon as the *Cortez* berthed, waiting for the next available jump port to open. Club Dead was an experiment in relative dimensions, in that it was actually much bigger on the inside than it appeared on the outside. It was not done with mirrors, although in a way that was correct: the science that allowed the interior to occupy more room than the exterior measurements was based on infinite recursion, the odd effect one gets when placing a mirror directly in front of another mirror. In this way, the club owner was able to get around several hidebound zoning ordinances and pack the bar with even more of the galaxy's undesirables.

Better they should be here, drinking until they passed out, instead of wandering through the streets of Neo-Calcutta.

The only potential downside—and this depended on with whom you spoke, as to whether it was a minus or a plus—was in the same science of infinite recursion. Theoretically, should these mirroring engines fail, there would follow a dimensional implosion, trapping the patrons between the planes of reality like specimens between the sheets of glass in a microscope slide.

Along the wall and near the entrance to this great, open, multi-level, neo-Goth cavern of a club, stood something resembling a traditional bar, crammed with every conceivable alien form of lowlife and, stocked behind this bar, every conceivable form of hard drink, ranging from simple skull-cracking liquor to something just shy of hazardous materials.

On stage at the opposite end of the room, a hard-driving, pulse-pounding heavy metal band clanged out its three chords. In fact, it was not a "live" band as such, but rather larger-than-life, three-dimensional holographic projections. These holo-musicians could be supplanted by the programmed projected video images, and occasionally these images bore some vague relation to the song they illustrated.

The area from the main entrance to the distant stage was a maze of drinking pits, private booths, and gaming tables, and each of these stations was densely packed with drinkers and gamers. Beautifully exotic women with equally exotic appetites moved from table to table, pit to pit, man to man, sometimes just looking for a dance, sometimes looking for something more, and always finding either.

As much for safety's sake as expediency, there were no waitresses as such, but a computer-generated image of a traditional, interlac-speaking barmaid that appeared on small videoscreens set into each of the tables. This inter-active waitress would receive orders and relay them back to the barkeep, who would then identify the patron on her screen—TYLER; CAPTAIN; CORTEZ; METAL MAMMOTH MINING—and deduct the appropriate amount of credits from the patron's account. After which, bottles and glasses would be sent via a small transmat pad built into each of the tables.

Tyler turned away from the girl dancing on his party's table to watch with some faint amusement as Lambert frisked Morroc, a prissy little businessman with whom Tyler had arranged a meeting. Satisfied Morroc was not carrying a weapon, Lambert nodded, and allowed the businessman to sit at the table across from Tyler. Between them, the woman continued her erotic dance, but Tyler had already lost interest in her. Her presence was now just an intrusion.

"Let's not waste one another's time, shall we?" Tyler said to Morroc. The threat could not have been much more ev-ident.

"We're both busy men, eh?" Morroc offered, hoping to ingratiate himself to his client. He placed a small, flat laptop computer on the table, but was unable to open it because of the woman dancing next to it. "We can do *without* the laptop dance," the businessman said huffily. The woman just smiled and continued dancing.

"Am I getting to you?" she asked, smiling coyly.

"Not really, no," Tyler answered, clearly bored. "You're just getting old."

He stood and roughly shoved the dancing woman off the table and onto the raised floor surrounding the drinking pit. The dancing girl picked herself up, looking at Tyler in sur-prise, ready to give him a piece of her mind, but the coldness in his eyes silenced her protests. That look told her she was getting off light with just a skinned knee and a couple of bruises. She hurried off, certain that, at any moment, she would feel a bullet slam into her back between her shoulder blades, amazed with every moment that she didn't.

Morroc laughed. It was easy to laugh at your own misfortunes, but it was a rare man who could laugh at the sufferings of others. Tyler liked that in a potential business partner.

"You were inquiring about some arms?" Morroc began, opening his laptop computer. "And some men?"

The Commercial Zone of Neo-Calcutta looked as if someone had taken the absolute best, most remarkable qualities of Bangkok's red light district, New Orleans' French Quarter on a particularly drunken, garish Mardi Gras, and the Las Vegas Strip back when the underworld ran the show, and threw them away, leaving only the worst traits in their place.

It was through this hyperactive marketplace that F.A.K.K.², wearing a long, black cowl and cloak over her form-fitting flight suit, moved with a purpose none of those around her could have imagined. The Zone was an assault on her senses, born and reared as she was on a green and wooded world. But this was a jungle, of sorts: narrow, garish, neon-lit, complete with predators that could also disguise themselves to blend in with their surroundings, or lay their traps for unsuspecting victims.

A few isolated pockets of passersby stopped to listen to the various street vendors hawking their wares, flinging their garbage. It was like a bad, burlesque caricature of Eden's own market, but it was hard to see how an all-out, both-barrels-blazing attack by Tyler and his Psycho Crew could make this bazaar any worse than it already was.

The smell was overwhelming; it was as if the streets were

open sewers, but it was even worse than that, somehow. Over the smell of rot hung the humid air of despair and desperation and, worst of all, the stink of hopelessness, as if the walls and streets of this place sweated it.

As bad as the smell was, F.A.K.K.² thought the sound, the clang and pound and white static of street noise and vulgar conversation, was worse. It was as if these buildings and lights vibrated at a certain pitch, like a struck tuning fork emanating a continuous cacophony that went past the ears and hummed in the nerves and cells and fiber of her being.

"How much?" someone at her side was asking.

She glanced over, saw the toad who asked the question. He was a small, fat man, with bad teeth and an even worse complexion, as if he'd lost an acid fight, gone home, thought about it, went back out, and lost another one.

"How much *what?*" she replied. She kept walking, hoping to leave the man behind, but he moved his short, stubby legs faster to keep up.

"You," he said. He was ahead of F.A.K.K.² now, walking backwards so he could see her from the front. It was a great front. "How much? Whatever it is, it isn't enough."

"I'm not for sale," she answered, and broke eye contact, hoping that would end the matter. If anything, it only intensified the man's desires, and sharpened his longings.

"Everyone and everything is for sale," he countered, stepping directly in front of F.A.K.K.², forcing her to stop or walk right into him. Either way, he would have been happy. "You're magnificent. Where have you been all my life?"

She studied the ugly little troll for a beat, and said, "Well, for the first thirty years or more, I wasn't even born."

He laughed. "A woman like you could really hurt a man ... if he's lucky."

"Hurt him?" F.A.K.K.² replied. She sneered. "I could *kill* him . . . if he's lucky."

"Done . . . and done," Morroc said brightly, tapping on the keys of his small laptop computer. He hit SEND, and waited for the familiar tone that told him the deal had been transacted in full. "My men will meet you at your ship with the merchandise."

Tyler had already disconnected from the scene, sitting back like a dour-faced emperor, fingering the cuneiform engraved into the obelisk. Morroc closed the cover on his laptop and slipped it into his jacket pocket, but he had noticed the key, and something in his mercenary brain began to jingle and hum.

"That's . . . an interesting little souvenir," Morroc said slowly. "Did you pick it up in the duty-free zone?"

The men surrounding Tyler laughed at that. Morroc did not like being the object of humor, but he could bear it a little longer, if he could only get this buffoon to part with the obelisk. Morroc didn't know what it was, exactly, but something inside the key seemed to be talking to him, downloading things into his mind. Whatever it was, he knew he had to have it.

Tyler said nothing, but continued to trace the runes with his fingernails. His silence was beginning to annoy Morroc and make him uncomfortable.

"Tourist fodder, of course," he tried again. "Completely worthless. Something like that is available at any number of—"

Tyler moved faster than thought. He grabbed Morroc around the back of the neck with one huge palm and pulled the merchant's narrow face closer. Morroc could smell the stale stench of liquor and insanity on Tyler's breath, but he refused to flinch. Tyler held the key up with his other hand, waving it slowly, hypnotically, back and forth before Morroc's eyes.

"Are you sure?" he asked the smaller man. "Absolutely sure?"

Morroc opened his mouth to answer, but the light inside the obelisk was flickering like a pulsar. Whatever this thing was, it was not available in the Commercial Zone.

"Here," Tyler said, releasing Morroc and offering him the key. "Take a good, long look."

Morroc's eyes flicked to Tyler's, looking for some sign of duplicity, but he saw none, or chose not to notice if he did. The key was talking to him, and he had to answer. Morroc reached for it as if a man in an underwater dream, and Tyler placed it in his hand. Morroc smiled—but not for long.

He felt his blood begin to boil, as if he were being microwaved from within, and smoke began to roil forth from his mouth and nostrils in thick, oily tendrils. He tried to talk, to beg Tyler to take the key, take it now, but all he could manage was a liquid, strangling sound. His eyes orbited up into the top of his skull, and he slammed back into his chair. Morroc's feet jittered and scuffed like pistons on the littered floor beneath the table, his head nodding up and down as if he were keeping time with the hard-pounding music.

Blisters formed and exploded on Morroc's exposed flesh as the liquid in his body reached the boiling point. He began to slide beneath the table, and Tyler reached over and plucked the key from Morroc's blackened fingers, breaking the circuit.

"Negotiations got a little heated there," Tyler said to no one in particular, watching as Morroc's body disappeared beneath the table and hit the floor with a wet thump. "But we came to a satisfying agreement. This calls for a celebration, and I'd say that calls for a drink . . . a very *big* drink!"

The men roared their approval, and Tyler leaned back once more into his seat, a king in royal repose.

F.A.K.K.² almost walked past Germain St. Germain without a second glance, but something tickled at the back of her conscious thought, and she turned around for a better look at him. He was haggling furiously with a fat, disheveled street vendor in the Commercial Zone, just one of many prospective buyers as far as F.A.K.K.² could tell, and she would have dismissed him, had it not been for the Metal Mammoth Mining insignia she saw emblazoned on his black hazmat jumpsuit. Behind her wraparound, polarized glasses, F.A.K.K.²'s eyes narrowed, and her breath caught in her throat.

She moved closer to hear what the man was saying; it was pretty much what she might have guessed, given the business district they occupied.

"She's high-grade, silicone rubber flesh," the fat man was saying. To F.A.K.K.², he looked quite a lot like the troll who had tried to buy her—before she had been forced to break one of his legs, of course—or at least enough so to be his brother. And that was a creepy thought, to think a woman would give birth to another one after seeing how badly the first turned out. The vendor was pointing to a cyber-woman, so realistic that F.A.K.K.² for a moment took her to be a real woman. So realistic, she was drawing a crowd of seedy, shifty men, along with a handful of indeterminate other sentient beings.

F.A.K.K.² stood near enough St. Germain that she would

be sure not to lose him in the crowd, but she didn't think he was going anywhere yet.

"Skeleton's PVC with plastic ball-and-socket joints, and she is fully customizable with a choice of seven synthetic hair colors and lengths, and eye colors."

St. Germain was trying hard not to seem eager, but he had already fallen in love and planned his entire future with this cyber-woman. He would do the honorable thing and marry her, of course. A bride like this—and at these prices—didn't come along every day.

"Even better, she's loaded up with all the latest micro-sensor massage technology," the vendor continued, reeling his fish in a little more with each word. "Imagine how these long fingers would feel on the kinks in your neck after a long, hard day."

St. Germain had already imagined it; he'd jumped straight past that to the number of cyber-children they would have.

"She comes with an expandable vocabulary of over two thousand words," the man said.

St. Germain whistled softly through his teeth. All that, *and* she could talk? The cyber-woman shifted her weight from one well-proportioned hip to the other, and placed her hands firmly on either side of St. Germain's head and pulled him close to her breasts.

"How . . . how much?" St. Germain managed, his face buried in pendulous synth-flesh.

"Only two thousand, and I'll call you a bandit," the vendor said.

"Whoa, I don't . . ." St. Germain said, backing away from the cyber-woman. "I mean, two thousand . . . that's an awful . . . I don't have . . ."

But Venus, the cyber-woman, struck a pouty pose and didn't bother to hide the fact her feelings were injured by St. Germain's indelicate dickering over a few thousand credits. St. Germain felt his heart sink, and knew he was the worst cad who had ever lived, not at all the sort of man who deserved such a wonderful cyber-wife. But, deserving or not, he had the credits, and sometimes that was all a man like St. Germain needed to land a wonderful wife like Venus. The universe continued to make sense.

With Venus safely compressed and tucked away in her carrying case, St. Germain hurried through the Commercial Zone, late for his meeting with Tyler. His thoughts alternating between love for Venus and fear of Tyler, St. Germain failed to notice the dark-cloaked figure that followed him from a distance.

There was nothing of love in *her* eyes.

Club Dead, she thought. *Fitting name.*

F.A.K.K.[2] stood back in the mouth of an alleyway, her dark cloak making her just one more shadow among many, and watched as St. Germain talked to the club bouncer at the entrance. From here, it looked like little more than a simple door carved in the featureless wall, and her man would be easy to spot once inside. But, moments from now, she would realize how wrong she was.

An empty cab rattled past where she stood; she glanced at its logo emblazoned on the passenger door: HARRY CANYON TAXI SERVICE. When F.A.K.K.[2] looked back in the direction of the Club, St. Germain had gone in. After a moment, she followed.

St. Germain made his way to the drinking pit, where Tyler was hoisting a keg of liquor off the table. Flamboyantly, he punched his fist against the cork, knocking it into the barrel, then lifted the keg above his tilted head, and poured the contents into his open mouth. The Psycho Crew and Tyler's new recruits urged him on at a manic pitch: "TYLER! TYLER! TYLER!"

Finished with his drink, Tyler threw the empty keg aside, narrowly missing one of the dancing girls. She opened her mouth to scold him, then realized it was the madman from earlier, and decided to say nothing.

Tyler let fly a long, rattling belch, to the amusement of his men. "Better an empty house than a bad tenant, eh?" he joked, and laughed drunkenly, although he was not drunk. It seemed no matter how much liquor he consumed, he couldn't get drunk.

He had a pretty good idea why. Tyler removed two of the small ampules from his pouch, and placed them on the littered table. After a moment of ceremony, he picked up one, popped the cap, and threw it back. Seated now, St. Germain reached for the remaining ampule, assuming it had been placed there for him.

He was wrong.

Tyler grabbed him by the neck and slammed his face down into the tabletop, hard enough to make the surface star with cracks.

"Nobody touches those poppers 'cept me!" Tyler roared.

Lambert shook his head at St. Germain's folly. *Stupid idiot,* he thought, then called for a bar towel to clean up the mess. *I'm one to talk, though. It's going to take more than a towel to clean up the mess I'm in,* he reprimanded himself. He had gone from first officer aboard a ship with one of the universe's biggest private mining concerns, to first officer for a lunatic bent on spreading genocide from one end of glory to the other. Probably *not* the life his parents had envisioned for him.

Still, it could be worse. He could be a telemarketer.

A bus-bot came over at Lambert's command, and plopped a leech the size of a barn cat on the cracked table-top to sop up the blood that had spewed from St. Germain's nose and split lips. As the leech went happily about its task, the bus-bot clamped a pair of pincers around the semi-conscious man's head, pulled him out of his seat, and dragged him across the floor toward the exit.

F.A.K.K.[2] had been standing near the bar, disoriented by the sheer size of the club's interior, unable to spot the man she had followed or the madman who had plundered her planet. One of the bar hounds had been chatting her up, although she barely noticed, intent as she was on not losing the trail.

The man was big, clean-cut, and lantern-jawed, wearing a captain's uniform that looked more like a costume you'd expect some actor on a kid's show to wear. He exuded a smarmy sense of self-confidence, and he assured her, at every chance, "Don't worry—I got an angle."

At last, F.A.K.K.[2] looked directly at the big man, and asked, "What, exactly, are you a captain of?"

His smile, as big as a jack o' lantern's, seemed to double. "Why, my own destiny, of course, pretty thing!"

"Then, you're a very lucky man," she answered. She looked back toward the club's interior, and noticed the bus-bot dragging St. Germain along behind. He was waking up now, and trying to slip out of the calipers clamped around his head, but the harder he struggled, the tighter the spring-action made the pincer arms grip. F.A.K.K.[2] noticed the di-rection from which her man had been dragged, then disengaged herself from the increasingly annoying "Cap-tain" Lincoln Sternn and followed St. Germain's blood trail back to its origin point.

F.A.K.K.² felt a wave of adrenaline as big as a tsunami wash through her system at the sight of Tyler, seated in his drinking pit, laughing like a college boy during a night on the town.

How, she wondered, *could anyone wipe out a whole world and then go out for a round of drinks with your pals? "Why, because wiping out whole worlds is thirsty work, sweetcheeks,"* she imagined the madman answering. And she supposed that *would* be his response, if she asked him.

Tyler tapped the keypad under the table, and the image of the waitress appeared. When he ordered more drinks for himself and his men, the waitress cautioned him he was running up quite a tab.

"Never mind," Tyler answered. "Just keep 'em comin', and tell the barkeep to pour one for herself."

A moment later, a variety of drinks and bottles of liquor materialized on the table in front of Tyler. He grabbed the bottles and glasses and started tossing them at the mangy assemblage seated and standing near him, as if he were dealing cards.

The drinks distributed, Tyler raised his own glass—the second ampule—popped the top with his thumbnail, and said, "To life everlasting."

"Nobody lives forever," F.A.K.K.² said, stepping forward. As she did, she cast off her black cloak, revealing the bandoliers crisscrossing her chest, and the grenades that hung from the weapons belts. She drew the guns holstered at her hips, and brought them up, walking deliberately toward Tyler and his men all the while.

Tyler sat where he was, too surprised for the moment to react, and then F.A.K.K.² squeezed off a round from each gun, the bullets striking Tyler squarely in his barrel chest.

The force of the bullets picked him up from his seat and threw him out of the drinking pit.

"This is for Nathan!" she cried.

Tyler's henchmen were already diving for cover and drawing their own weapons, but F.A.K.K.² wasn't concerned with them. In all the world, there was only herself, her world's killer, and this moment. After this, whatever happened, happened. Incredibly, Tyler sat up where he lay sprawled on the floor, his feet still dangling down into the drinking pit. He looked at F.A.K.K.² and smiled, runnels of blood dribbling from the corners of his mouth.

"Lemme guess . . . Scorpio, right?" he said.

"Not even close," she answered dismissively, and popped off another round of lead. "This is for my people!"

Tyler's body jerked back, driven into the legs of the gaming table behind him. Cards and credits flew like leaves in a hurricane, and despite the gunplay, several gamblers scrambled for the scattered riches, crawling over Tyler's body to retrieve the wealth.

F.A.K.K.² stepped closer to the edge of Tyler's drinking pit, her guns raised and ready to put two more holes through the madman, but she recalled her father's words: *Just don't come to like it too much.* Reluctantly, F.A.K.K.² lowered her weapons and turned from the drinking pit.

Unless one of Tyler's Psycho Crew decided to avenge their captain—and F.A.K.K.² frankly didn't think he inspired that kind of loyalty—the fight was over. That just left her to find purpose for the rest of her life. No problem. And dying is only death. No big deal.

Behind her, rising like some hideous jack-in-the-box, Tyler sat up, his bloody, gaping chest as ragged as a ransom note. He shook his groggy head, fumbled another ampule from his pouch, and crushed the contents into his mouth.

"And there's no mediciny after-taste," he commented to himself, then called after the departing woman, "I'll tell you this one for free: When you kill someone, make sure they're really dead before you turn your back on 'em!"

F.A.K.K.²'s jaw fell open in shock. He couldn't *possibly* have survived that, could he? But she didn't have long to wonder, because even over the thunderous music, she could hear the sound of a pistol's safety being thrown off, and she was diving for cover behind an overturned table even as the bullet striped the air where she had stood.

And now the Psycho Crew and other bar patrons began returning fire. The patrons didn't particularly care one way or the other about Tyler, but it was a chance to shoot something, and sometimes you just have to settle for whatever comes along.

Bullets *whang*ed off the metal table, whirling white-hot into the air, embedding in the ceiling or splintering the floorboards. F.A.K.K.² pushed the table ahead of her, staying behind it for protection as she did. She stopped, raised up, and fired back at the killers.

Tyler watched as his wounds healed, like a film shown in reverse; shattered ribs knitted themselves together once more, and traumatized muscle and broken veins and arteries rejoined. Moments after the sub-structure was healed, the flesh grew back, hiding what had been, seconds earlier, mortal injuries.

On stage, a stray bullet hit the holo-projection mechanism, and the band fritzed, buzzed with static and, images wavering, vanished into oblivion. The lack of a live band, though, did not do much to diminish the sounds of chaos in the club.

F.A.K.K.² pushed her table forward once more, but she was moving blindly and didn't realize she was at the edge of a drinking pit. She and the table both pitched forward, into the pit, and she landed hard, striking her temple on the corner of the table. Her vision filled with kaleidoscopic splashes that strobed in time with her heartbeat. F.A.K.K.² tried to force herself up, but her limbs refused to understand what her brain was telling them—apparently, they were just visiting from another part of the galaxy and didn't speak that language.

Tyler was moving surely closer, his healed chest still smoldering from the bullets. He knelt beside F.A.K.K.², who lay sprawled across the table that canted halfway into the pit, and stroked her long, raven tresses with a surprising gentleness.

But nothing was ever what it seemed with him, for the next moment, he gripped a handful of her hair, jerked her head up, and slammed her face-first into the underside of the table. She was already teetering on the edge of unconsciousness, and Tyler drove F.A.K.K.² down into the dark and dreamless waters.

Behind him, the gunfight was winding down, as if everyone had already lost interest in it. Tyler hauled F.A.K.K.² out of the pit and threw her, like a fish he had caught off the side of his boat, onto the floor. He stood over the unconscious figure, studying her face, but she was a cipher to him. He'd already crushed a lot of worlds, driven several civilizations into extinction, and after a while, all victims started to look alike to him.

His eyes slid from her face to her chest, and the bandoliers that formed an X across her breasts. He smiled when he saw the grenades that were magnetically secured to the metal ammo belt. "Well, what red-blooded male could resist putting his hands on *those* babies?"

He reached down with both hands, slipped his fingers

through the safety pins of the grenades, as if he were trying on rings in a showcase, and jerked them all free from the primers.

The grenades began beeping as they counted down through the seconds to explosion.

Tyler casually stood and began moving for the exit, and the bar patrons all stayed well back, watching without really understanding what had just happened. "You might want to join me," he called back unconcernedly to his Psycho Crew. "And quickly."

That was enough for them. They began their march for the door—the only exit in the entire cavern—shoving other bar patrons out of their path, shooting some dead where they stood.

"Hey!" the barkeep shouted after Tyler as he passed the bar near the door. "Who's gonna pay for this mess?"

Tyler stopped, turned to her with a smile. "This should cover it, with a little something left over for you," he answered, and tossed her something. She caught it on the fly, and as she examined it, Tyler and his Psycho Crew left. They were twisted metal rings . . .

Realization seemed to come in stages, like stairsteps that get bigger with each rise, reaching levels of comic-opera proportions. Her eyes bugged and her mouth worked without forming words.

The word she was looking for was almost certainly *grenade.*

Any other words she might have been searching for are probably best left unguessed.

Seven

These sounds, these words, filtering down through the pain and the darkness:

BEEP BEEP BEEP

"... grenades ..."

"... out of here before ..."

BEEP BEEP BEEP

"... explode!"

F.A.K.K.² had never been knocked unconscious in her entire life. In the past few days, though, she had not just explored that dark territory, but been driven deep into those black woods and left there, like an unwanted animal.

There was no wizard this time to help her find her way back to the light, but there was a persistent beeping in her ear that some part of her knew to be a very bad sign. She woke with muddy senses, her eyes pulled to the source of the timed beeping: *the grenades slung on her bandoliers were primed!*

F.A.K.K.² didn't waste time trying to disconnect the grenades. Instead, she unhooked the bandoliers' clasps and flung them, grenades and all, away from her and deeper into the club.

She bolted for the exit door on legs that felt too long and too rubbery even as the grenades detonated. The bombs imploded first, sucking everyone and everything within the blast vicinity—tables, people, bottles, glasses, lighting fixtures—into an intense central mass, as if someone had just pulled the plug on the universe and the contents were rapidly funneling down the drain.

Then, the blast. Whatever the implosion had drawn in, the blast hurled away twice as violently. The bombs harnessed the kinetic force of the implosion, then expelled it, like held breath.

The shockwaves slapped F.A.K.K.[2] from behind, catching and lifting her off her pumping feet, shoving her along like an unseen, giant hand. She cleared the buckling doorway just as the worst of the blast struck. The interior of Club Dead was incinerated by the force of multiple explosions, the blast seeming to grow like a fractal. Even worse than that, the blasts destroyed the transdimensional warp engines, causing the various dimensions, stacked side-by-side like books on a shelf, to rip jaggedly apart and separate from one another.

Anyone unfortunate enough to be standing in one of the overlapping dimensions when they shut down was immediately pulled into that plane of existence. The really unlucky ones who stood on the spot where the dimensions actually overlapped were torn in half and sucked into both realities.

The concussive force of the grenades was siphoned into the closing dimensions, which was all that kept the entire outer structure of the club from collapsing into rubble on the streets outside. As it was, the jolt ripped the sign off the wall above the door, and scattered the letters into the streets and alleys like oversized tiles in a Scrabble game.

A few dozen yards away from the carnage, Tyler and the remnants of his Psycho Crew moved on through the wicked mecca. None of them bothered to turn back to observe the destruction Tyler had initiated. It had gotten to be an old sight by now—if you've seen one building collapse, killing all of its patrons, then you've seen a hundred buildings collapse.

The yodeling cry of sirens in the distance did not add haste to Tyler's step; what did he have to fear? Immortals fear nothing, and Tyler knew now he had joined a very special and exclusive clique. These lickspittle fools who attended his every word and moved to fill his every need thought Tyler might be gracious enough to reward them by holding open the back door to that secret club of immortal beings and letting them in, but it seemed to Tyler godhood wouldn't be such a big deal if *anyone* could do it. It wasn't like Club Dead, where just any scumbag could walk in off the streets.

F.A.K.K.² dragged her beaten body into the alley across the street, and collapsed below a slowly dripping drainpipe, huddling among bags and boxes of garbage. A fragment of the Club Dead sign—the word DAMNED—lay next to her, but she refused to acknowledge the irony. She refused to acknowledge much of anything, until she gradually became aware of someone trying to rouse her.

F.A.K.K.² expected to find Tyler standing over her, ready to finish the job, but the puzzled face of Germain St. Germain swam into hazy focus instead.

"Eden Colony," he was saying, reading the identi-badge on her blast-tattered flight suit. "Hunh. Never thought I'd see one of you people alive again."

She recognized him as one of Tyler's Psycho Crew, and that added a snake-like quickness to her reaction. F.A.K.K.² grabbed him by the throat and flipped him off of her and flat onto his back in the litter-strewn alley. Then she was on top of him, the tip of her knife dimpling the soft flesh on the underside of his jaw. St. Germain was still trying to understand how he ended up on his back even as F.A.K.K.² was delivering her ultimatum.

"You've got three seconds to convince me not to kill you. One . . . two . . ."

"Tyler!" he gasped, afraid to say much for fear the movement of his jaw might make the knife punch through his throat. He hissed the words through gritted teeth. "I know how to kill him!"

"Tell me . . . now!" she growled.

St. Germain could feel the pressure of the knife against his throat increase. He expected at any moment to see a thick red geyser of blood fountain past his eyes, and when he did not, he knew he had her, even if she didn't yet realize it.

"First we catch him," he said, almost smugly. "Then I'll show you how to kill him."

In fact, he wasn't all that sure he knew any more about killing Tyler than this woman did, but that was for later; right now, he just wanted to get this lethal lovely off of him. St. Germain reckoned he couldn't lose, for once: if he convinced her he was indispensable, he'd live long enough to find a way to escape or kill her, or she'd actually find Tyler and he'd kill her. If it was the latter, St. Germain might be able to weasel his way back into Tyler's good graces. But if, wonder of wonders, this bloodthirsty babe actually *did* manage to kill Tyler, well, even better.

Although the only duplicity she had encountered, until

now, involved nothing more serious than a counterfeit wooden medallion, F.A.K.K.² nevertheless recognized the stink of a lie on this man's breath.

"Wrong answer," she said, and leaned a little harder on the shaft of the knife.

"Easy, easy!" he cried, close to a panic. "I was there... saw what he did to your colony!"

She knew that, but to actually hear it made her loosen the grip on her knife, just a bit, enough that the man was able to barter for his life a little more easily.

"Look, lady, we were forced into it. Tyler took over our ship..." St. Germain sniffed the air like a drug addict in need of a fix, or an animal detecting the scent of approaching danger. "He's found some key... to immortality, he says. It tells him where to go." He sniffed again, and raised his chin. He wasn't trying to avoid the blade, just show F.A.K.K.² the vivid scar that adorned his throat like a necklace. "He tried to cut me out... see?"

She saw, and he took advantage of her momentary hesitation to press on. The key to success for any good salesman is persistence—when you're bargaining for your life, you can be pretty persistent. "I ask you, is that any way to treat a partner? I should be the one with the key, not him!"

F.A.K.K.² sighed heavily, as if she were trying to expel the weight of her dead world and the world of the living off her shoulders. "Where is he?"

"There," St. Germain answered, pointing a finger up toward the distant dome above them, indicating the vast void beyond. "He's gonna make a hyperspace jump!"

She sighed again, but not as heavily; it was more a sigh of weary resignation. She sheathed her knife, but not before warning St. Germain: "Let's just say you're at T minus 2 and holding."

*   *   *

The *Cortez*'s hour of jump time was fast approaching, and the men were going about their duties in preparation. But it was routine work, and the talk turned, as it did more and more frequently, to Tyler.

"Did you see the way he took those hits?" one of the new sign-ons—Slag—asked for what was almost certainly the hundredth time. "That power's for real!"

"Yeah," Conner complained from his work station next to Slag's. "Tyler took the hits, but what if that'd been one of us? We could've gotten our butts blown off back in the bar! When do we get *our* share?"

"St. Germain tried. Look what happened to him," Lambert answered. "He was stupid and so are you—both of you." He was standing behind the two men, making sure the jump-coordinates were entered correctly. He did not relish the idea of bunging out of hyperspace smack in the middle of a sun or a cloud of anti-matter. "Just shut up and wait ... if you want to live long enough to get a taste."

The men returned to their tasks, and their brooding silence.

Like a hermit crab shedding the trappings of an old life and wrapping itself in the clothes of the new, Tyler had cast off his former existence of a dangerous but petty thug toiling away in anonymity at a job he despised, and embraced his new incarnation as a man ascending to godhood. He stood, stripped to the waist, in his new quarters—formerly Captain Cameron's modest chambers, now bedecked with trinkets and weapons from a dozen conquered worlds—gazing at his reflection in the full-length mirror before him.

Ostensibly, he was admiring his perfection, but deep

down, next to the bone, where truth lives, he was checking himself for any evidence of the fatal wounds he had been dealt by that lunatic woman in the Club Dead. The wounds were healed, of course, but still . . .

"What more could the universe want in a ruler?" Tyler asked his reflection. "Perfect body, perfect mind."

"Try perfect psycho!" Kerrie suggested, hotly.

He let his eyes wander away from his own reflection to that of Kerrie. She was imprisoned in a spherical cage—also an artifact of a now-dead world—that looked like a giant version of a play-ball in which small rodents could walk and thereby move their spherical prisons around the floor. But no doubt about it: it was still a prison.

Badly incongruous with the high-tech surroundings, the room was decorated in the archaic trappings of an ancient alchemist: complex distillation devices, strange chemical experiments, oversized specimen jars holding perfectly preserved bodies of strange, now-lifeless creatures, floating like worms in giant bottles of Tequila. If he'd bothered to look at the memorabilia he'd surrounded himself with, Tyler would have seen he had built a shrine to death, not life everlasting.

And, like a necromancer of old, he lit his quarters with candles of all shapes, and sizes, and colors.

"And speaking of perfect bodies . . ." Tyler began, turning away from the mirror to study Kerrie directly. There was an air of animal magnetism about him.

"Why didn't you kill me, like you did all the rest?" she asked, gripping the bars of her cage.

Tyler steepled his fingers together before his face, as if in prayer. "Sometimes horrible, unexplainable things happen. No one knows why. Some chalk it up to fate, others, karma. Me, I like to think of this all as a test." He opened his arms expansively, to take in the room and the enormity of all creation beyond these walls.

"A test?" Kerrie spat, unable to believe what she was hearing. Did this madman think the entire universe was put into place just to vex him?

"You've heard the old saying: 'Whatever doesn't kill us . . . makes us stronger.'" Tyler gripped the bars of her cage and shook it, trying to make her lose her balance. There were spikes jutting from some of the bars on the inside of the cage, and Kerrie had already been cut by these spikes several times. She grabbed the bars, and held firm.

"Then, why don't you see how strong you've made *me?*" she growled with pure hatred. But instead of provoking him, Kerrie only managed to elicit a chuckle from Tyler.

"I have such delicious plans for you," he said. "So delicious . . ."

"Don't even *think* about it," she warned him. Before she would allow whatever he was planning to happen, she would throw herself on the deadly spikes within her cage.

"Time to come out and play," he announced. He reached for the cage door.

But before he could unlock it, Lambert's voice interrupted over the ship's P.A. system: "Hyperspace jump in two minutes. Repeat: hyperspace jump in two minutes."

Tyler cursed under his breath, and turned from Kerrie. He pulled his shirt on over his bare torso in quick, punchy movements, and paused at the door. "Don't be disappointed, my love. I'll be back."

He left her there, alone in that ossuary, assuming her helpless, but Kerrie was never helpless. Her sharp eyes found once more what she had earlier espied, but had given Tyler no indication she had noticed anything but him. Draped on a chair near the door were Tyler's ragged and bloody clothing from his gun-battle at Club Dead. He had thrown his dirty clothes—his "play clothes," he had called them—on the chair as he changed out of them, and had gotten distracted by the sight of himself in the mirror, the way a bird is drawn to something shiny. When he left, he had forgotten his belt.

And his gun.

Perhaps she could shoot the lock off her cage. She'd prefer to shoot his head from his shoulders, but Kerrie would, for the moment, settle for freeing herself.

Cautiously, she shifted her weight forward, and the cage began to roll slowly, precariously forward. . . .

The jump ports were really little more than clearings in the jumbled tangle of abandoned spacecraft that peppered the central dome of Neo-Calcutta. Overflowing storage sheds radiated from the towering central launch tower, and numerous lights, now dim with cataracts of dirt and grime, dotted the domed roof, shining what light they could manage to the launch pads far, far below.

A dozen hyperspace portals were set into the groundward bell of the dome, and the *Cortez* sat on the roundabout that wheeled it around to face the appropriate portal. When the wormhole engines cycled up and opened the gate, the *Cortez* would blast down the short runway, enter the door, and be instantly inside the hyperspace corridor.

On a waiting platform above the *Cortez*, the ragtag Spacehawk sat waiting its turn to jump. Since F.A.K.K.² had not known where or when Tyler would jump, or even that he would, the Spacehawk was not scheduled for departure, but the dark-haired warrior would not allow something that trifling to stop her now.

She and St. Germain, burdened with a bulky duffel bag, raced through the cramped and cluttered corridors of the station leading to the platforms.

"We'd make better time if you got rid of that thing," F.A.K.K.² snapped over her shoulder.

St. Germain thought he could probably just drop out of the picture, disappear behind a tangle of rusting machinery; if she was so desperate to catch Tyler, she wouldn't waste time looking for him, would she? He didn't think so, but she was as crazy, in her own way, as Tyler was. And besides, Morroc's men were combing all of Neo-Calcutta, searching for Tyler and his Psycho Crew. Even if St. Germain escaped this suicidal woman, he doubted he could long elude Morroc's paid killers.

And there was also the matter of how he'd get off this domed planet without a ride. He bit his lip, and hurried a little harder to keep up with the woman.

"You're crazy, you know," he puffed, breathless from running with a full pack. "You'll need an army to kill Tyler, even if you do catch him!"

F.A.K.K.² stopped so suddenly that St. Germain almost ran into her. She turned and regarded him with eyes as cold as the eyes of the dead. "You're talking yourself right out of any usefulness you might have to me," she warned him. "Especially if you don't know how to kill Tyler."

"Oh, I know, all right," St. Germain shot back, hoping he sounded like he meant it. How did things manage to keep getting worse? They had to level off sooner or later, didn't they?

St. Germain was once again astounded by how wrong he could be, when the lift they rode deposited them on the level on which the Spacehawk sat. He felt his stomach clench like a fist. "Your ship's right behind this piece of junk . . . right?" he asked, hopefully.

But F.A.K.K.² entered her code into the access panel of the Spacehawk, and the hatch opened with a grinding sound like a bad transmission. "It got me this far."

St. Germain shook his head. "This is hopeless," he moaned. "How can we make a jump in *that* thing? We're dead already!"

"You *will* be, if you don't know how to kill Tyler," she repeated.

"So you keep reminding me," he said.

She studied his face for signs of deception, but found only despair. F.A.K.K.² cursed to herself—there was no way to know for sure what this odd little man knew, and what he only pretended to know. "All right, let's go. And stow the bag."

F.A.K.K.² swung her long legs over the side of the open cockpit and dropped into the pilot's seat. She threw a series of start-up switches and the engines whined like spoiled kids. A moment later, the dual thrusters boomed to life, and a fierce, white glow issued from the rockets. St. Germain studied the Spacehawk, then looked back across the huge enclosure. He saw other men walking in and out between the waiting spacecraft on the floor below, and thought again of Morroc's thugs.

He told himself this woman had somehow managed to live through Tyler's raid on her planet, but he couldn't decide if he felt better because she was obviously a survivor-type, or if he was more concerned because she was clearly living on borrowed time.

Oh, screw it, he thought. *It's all borrowed time after that first breath.* He clambered into the passenger seat behind hers.

F.A.K.K.² closed the hatch and cinched the straps across her lap and chest. St. Germain wedged his duffel bag under the seat, and began buckling in. As ragged and dangerously driven and—put a nice face on it—*psychotic* as she was, F.A.K.K.² was also the most exciting woman he had ever met, even more than his cyber-wife.

And thinking of Venus, stowed just a few inches beneath him while he was this close to another woman, made St. Germain's blood race. He leaned forward, forgetting to finish belting in, and sniffed F.A.K.K.²'s wild mane of hair. "Look, maybe when this is all over, you and I could . . ."

"Forget about it," she answered sharply. "I'm *not* your type, I'd *never* massage your back after a long, hard day, and I know *more* than two thousand words."

St. Germain sat back, deflated. Bad enough she'd rejected him flat, but she also knew about Venus. He wondered if he should feel insulted by the crazy woman's backhanded comment about his future wife.

The Spacehawk began to taxi to the edge of the platform. Below and ahead, the *Cortez* began its dart toward the hyperspace portal.

"*Cortez* to Jump Control," Lambert spoke into his communications panel. "Set lock-in for Uroboris."

A moment's pause; then, "No preset lock-in. Request coordinates."

Lambert looked back over his shoulder at Tyler, seated in the Captain's chair. The first mate was completely lost. "There are no—"

Tyler fingered the obelisk with one hand; with the other, he rubbed small circles on his temple. He said, "Quadrant 90069, sector 4013 . . . in the Terackian system."

The SYSOP replied, "Searching . . . downloading outer star charts . . . location verified. Warning, no return jump port. Please confirm lock—"

"Confirmed!" Tyler snarled. For a man who had just discovered all eternity, he was quite impatient.

The SYSOP acknowledged the confirmation, thanked them for visiting Neo-Calcutta, and told them to brace for the jump. Lambert didn't really hear what the artificial intelligence was saying—he was too concerned with what it had said in regard to a terrible paucity of return jump ports.

"It'll take us forever to get back," he informed Tyler. He felt the skin tighten across his belly, as if it wanted to slither off of his bones and stay here without him.

"Forever won't be a problem," Tyler answered. "Once we get there."

A series of lights flashed on the giant Hyperspace Ring. The gate opened, revealing a shimmering curtain of colored lights, like an aurora borealis. The light reached out, as if to embrace the ship, and the *Cortez* bolted for the jump corridor, like a rabbit in the shadow of a bird of prey.

The Spacehawk zipped after it.

"Wait!" St. Germain cried, buffeting back and forth against the sides of the narrow ship. He was still fumbling with his straps. "What are you doing?"

"I'm not going to lose him now," F.A.K.K.² said, and added more thrust to the dual burners.

The door of the space portal slammed shut a moment after the Spacehawk cleared it, and the little ship raced faster up the side of the huge mining ship. F.A.K.K.² brought her ship up to a point just below the *Cortez*'s bridge.

The pulsating lights accelerated, whisking the *Cortez* and its stowaway along into hyperspace at geometrically-increasing speeds. In mere seconds, they would be in the long, tortuous throat of the hyperspace corridor itself.

"You can't just piggyback their jump!" St. Germain cried.

F.A.K.K.² toggled a switch on the control console before her, and a small door opened on the instrument panel. A spring-loaded lever rose from this recess, and F.A.K.K.² depressed the handle.

"Is that a tractor beam?" St. Germain cried with a suspicion bordering on frank paranoia. "It *is*, isn't it? Are you *insane?* We're gonna rip to *pieeee—*"

And then the *Cortez* and its barnacle of a guest were blasting down the hyperspace highway with the throttle flat out. Psychedelic lights strobed intensely past the view ports, stitched through with shorter, then longer, bursts of colored lights, like a Morse code. The lights almost immediately resolved themselves into amorphous globs of glowing, stretching bursts of fiery blooms, and the lights raced together in whorls to form a super-structure to support the walls of the hyperspace tunnel.

The lights were humbling, breathtaking, as they stretched past the cockpit's glass canopy. St. Germain gasped in awe, craning his head back to see the tunnel behind them. F.A.K.K.² didn't notice. She studied her instrument panel, and tightly gripped the stabilizer joystick in both hands, her fingers laced together for extra strength. The big muscles in her arms were shaking crazily already from the effort of keeping the ship on track.

"So far, so good," St. Germain said, afraid to jinx it by admitting things were okay. "We'll track Tyler to wherever they end up ... wait 'til they're in orbit. Then, you ... I mean, we—*we,* I mean ... sneak on board and kill 'em all."

F.A.K.K.² replied through gritted teeth. "Don't you think it's time you told me how to kill that slug?"

St. Germain smiled. For once, he was in charge of a situation. "Uh-uh. You'll just have to let me do this my way."

She said nothing; she was fighting hard to not lose control of the ship. It was like riding a wild, bucking horse in the vortex of a hurricane. St. Germain didn't like the silence. He had a pretty good idea why F.A.K.K.² was so quiet. He placed a comforting hand on her shoulder, and found the muscles there wound tight as mainsprings.

"We gotta be smart," he cautioned. "You saw what he's capable of—"

"Whatever it takes to end it," she managed. *"Whatever."*

And just like that, St. Germain felt events spiraling out of his control all around him. He sniffed nervously, a look of displeasure on his face as if he had smelled something quite disagreeable and overtly offensive to him. Perhaps he had smelled which way the wind was really blowing for him. His words were laced with panic when he spoke.

"We gotta be *smart*. Look what happened when you tried it your way—almost died, didn't ya? We got time. Right? Let's stick to the plan, right?" He sniffed again, as if he would inhale all the recycled air aboard the Spacehawk. "Right? Stick to the plan? Huh?"

Lambert punched another string of coordinates and stabilizing equations into his navigation console. Their trajectory seemed slightly skewed for some reason, as if Lambert had failed to factor in some crucial element, some shred of information that adversely affected the *Cortez*'s performance in this twisting, racing tunnel.

He glanced at his sensor screen, and shook his head in disbelief at the blip that appeared there beside the *Cortez*. Behind him, sitting with his legs outstretched at the helm,

Tyler leisurely allowed the contents of yet another popper to dribble into his open mouth. More than immortality, it was like a wildly addictive drug.

"We've got company," Lambert said. There was no good way to say it, so he just said it.

Pulled out of his repose, Tyler was standing at Lambert's work station in two quick strides. "Excuse me . . . but, 'company?' "

Lambert tapped the blip on the screen with his fingernail. "See that? It's like somebody just hitched onto our jump."

"That could change our trajectory," Tyler said in dead earnest, and added, with equal gravity, "Nobody gets a free ride off of me. Destroy them."

Tyler's face was close to Lambert's. He looked up at the Captain, and wondered why he didn't take St. Germain's advice and jump ship when they had the chance. "In hyperspace?" he questioned.

"Yes! In hyperspace!" Tyler growled, turning his face from the screen to glare into Lambert's eyes. "Is that a problem?" he asked, significantly.

Lambert looked away, and busied himself with carrying out the Captain's orders, insane as they were. "It's just that I never heard of anyone firing on another ship in hyperspace before," he tried to explain rationally. But you may as well reason with a flood, or fire, or earthquake. Tyler was a natural disaster, but certainly not an act of god.

"Just . . . do . . . it," Tyler commanded.

Lambert grimaced; there was no real way of guessing what would happen if he fired the lasers, although he had a pretty good idea what would happen if he didn't. He flipped up the small safety cap, exposing the recessed firing button. He locked the laser's targeting system onto the hitchhiker, and depressed the button.

The exterior lasers sparked to life, and a brilliant, ruby beam sizzled out of the firing tube. The laser burned straight and true for a moment, then warped and bent, as if it were something solid melting on a hot griddle. The laser struck the swirling wall of the hyperspace corridor, sending a rippling shockwave dancing along its length, accompanied by a shower of colorful sparks.

Tyler watched all this from the helm. "Would you care to explain that?" he growled.

Lambert shrugged his eyebrows, helplessly. "Well, we're traveling faster than light, and a laser is light . . . we're moving too fast for the laser to work."

"Then send two DD40 fighters," Tyler ordered. "Now."

It was a suicide run, but Tyler was able to convince two of his pilots that he would share his poppers with them the moment they returned. Having seen the way Tyler had eaten lead and walked it off back in Club Dead, the men were a little more willing to do this mission, if that was their reward. To prove his good intentions, Tyler removed two of the ampules from his belt pouch, and placed them on the console.

"They'll be waiting for you, when you get back," he said.

The two men—Slag and Lud—were in their fighters in moments, and the two craft detached from the docking bay of the *Cortez*. The second they left the hangar, both craft were sent spinning helplessly away into the vortex. The first black fighter plowed into the curved wall of the corridor, sending shockwaves up and down the length of the tunnel, then ricocheted back to ram into the other fighter. They were both out of control now, pinwheeling end over end, slamming off the walls, into one another, and were soon gone down the unforgiving highway.

"We lost both of them," Lambert reported, unnecessarily.

Tyler put the poppers back in his pouch. "Waste not, want not," he said to himself, and ordered Lambert, "Send my bomber out, then."

"But—"

"One more word, Mr. Lambert," Tyler warned, "and I'll send *you*."

St. Germain was almost shrieking now—loud, sustained bursts that sounded like a bat trapped in a closet.

The muscles in F.A.K.K.²'s arms were like carved marble, and the veins in her neck and forehead stood out in blue relief. She was having a tougher time keeping the Space-hawk stabilized, with all the trauma the unpredictable hyperspace corridor was suffering.

"Release the tractor beam!" St. Germain cried. "You wanna destroy both ships?"

"I told you—whatever it takes!"

St. Germain tried to stand in the cramped, narrow cockpit and reach over F.A.K.K.²'s shoulder to disengage the tractor beam. "Look, I admire a good psychosis as much as the next guy, but not when it affects my well-being!" he said, and lunged across the back of the seat.

F.A.K.K.² took one hand off the joystick, long enough to backhand him hard across the face. He dropped back into his seat, checking his mouth and nose for blood.

In that brief second, an uncertain world spun once more on its unsteady axis.

Tyler's bomber, twice the size and firepower of the fighters, appeared in the *Cortez*'s open bay doors and, like the fighters before it, was immediately slipstreamed into the eddying hyperspace corridor. But this time, the bomber slammed into the Spacehawk and ripped off its right wing, leaving it with all the aerodynamic soundness of a thrown brick.

F.A.K.K.² powered the little Spacehawk up to maximum, and put all her might into holding the joystick steady. She and St. Germain were thrown violently from side to side.

"We're hit!" he cried, watching in terror as the last of the right stabilizing wing was peeled off by the corridor's unbelievable forces. Inside, sparks danced across the command console, stinging F.A.K.K.²'s exposed flesh. But she refused to cry out, and she would not let go of the joystick, or her single-minded mission. "I knew this would happen! This is all your fault! Am I bleeding?"

The epileptic throes of the Spacehawk shook the duffel bag free of its place beneath the passenger seat, and the cyber-wife unlimbered to her full size in the cramped quarters.

"What about *me?*" Venus asked, her face directly before St. Germain's, as if she had heard his whiny protests about perceived injuries. "What about *my* needs?"

"Ohohohoh, do something! Pull out! No, no, not you, her!" St. Germain was babbling, his attention divided between his overwhelming desire for Venus and his even-more overwhelming desire not to die. "Lower! A little more to the left! Dive! Dive!"

Incredibly, the bomber had managed to hold its course in the swirling tunnel for a few seconds, long enough to lock its firing systems onto the Spacehawk. Fortunately, the missiles it fired were sucked away in the backwash, but the bomber again smacked against the smaller ship, the impact crimping the canopy and starring its glass.

The bomber and its full complement of weapons exploded against the curved wall of the corridor, and this time, the integrity of the tunnel began to break up. Lights strobed like pulses of lightning within the vortex, and cracks like great veins formed in the walls of the corridor. The vortex behind the two ships began closing, a cave-in racing up as fast as the ships were traveling.

If they didn't get out of this death-trap in the next few seconds, the hyperspace tunnel would collapse upon them like a crushed drinking straw.

With the precise and delicate structure of the tunnel grossly violated, the *Cortez* began to buck and yaw. In calm and measured tones, the onboard computers warned the crew they were all about to die. The ship's designer had believed there was no point instilling panic in a crew.

"The tunnel's breaking up!" Lambert cried, adding a fitting pitch of hysteria to the situation the computer clearly neglected. "We're not gonna make it!" He wheeled to face Tyler. "You've killed us, you ba—"

With equal calmness, so calm that the message was initially overlooked as more of the same, the computer announced, "Hyperspace travel sequence successfully completed. ETA Uroboris: 32 seconds. 31 seconds. 30 seconds."

The tunnel end frayed apart like old yarn as the two ships exploded out of the collapsing corridor, emerging in the stratosphere above Uroboris. But the damage was done, and the two ships began spiraling out of control. The planet appeared to race to meet them at greedy, dizzying speeds.

Tyler stood, calmly studying the giant viewscreen as the scarred face of Uroboris filled it. "The power's there," he said, and reached out his hand as if to touch the planet. "Mine for the taking."

In Tyler's quarters, Kerrie had managed to roll her cage to the seat holding the pistol, but now the sharp dive of the ship caused the ball to roll backward, toward the far corner. She cried in alarm and gripped the bars, trying to keep from being impaled on the spikes inside the cage.

Somewhere in her mad scrabble to stay upright, she lost her grip on the gun.

"Break off!" St. Germain was shrieking in F.A.K.K.²'s ear. "You're going to kill us all!"

"Then I've won," she said with grim determination.

The heat of re-entry was rising in leaps and bounds, and the damaged Spacehawk was handling hard, now that it had entered the atmosphere with only one wing. The violent torque of the atmospheric stresses were too much for the Spacehawk's systems, and the overload caused the tractor beam to fail. The *Cortez* began its planetfall, tumbling farther and farther away from F.A.K.K.².

"Nooooo!" she screamed. "Not now! Not now!"

The awful forces caused the small crack in the Spacehawk's canopy to widen, and the entire panel of Plexiglas exploded. Everything that wasn't bolted or strapped in was instantly sucked out through the opening. Venus was wedged in the breach for a moment, her arms and legs thrust out before her, imploring for help.

"Venus, baby!" St. Germain cried, and made a mad lunge for her just as she was ripped out through the hatch. Seeing her like this made him realize she was the one he loved. The vacuum tore at St. Germain now, and pulled him halfway out and headfirst. F.A.K.K.² grabbed his booted foot with one hand, while with the other she tried to maintain some semblance of flightworthiness in the Spacehawk.

But the outer pressures were just too great, and St. Germain was sucked out of his boot. He tumbled away into the cold void, in eternal pursuit of his beloved.

F.A.K.K.[2] cast the boot aside, and it was instantly pulled out the broken canopy. She fumbled an oxygen mask over her nose and mouth.

"Nathan," she said softly, but the air was too thin to support even this one word.

And then she was watching the planet rush up to claim her.

Eight

To the surprise of no one, Tyler was first man up, like some sugar-hopped kid on his first day of school vacation. He made his way up the inclined deck, where Lambert sat in his operations chair at a steep, sixty degree angle. The first officer's crash harness had cut grooves in his flesh where the straps cinched fast and tight upon impact, and he thought he'd probably sunk a floating rib, but he was alive.

Not that that was any consolation. They were stranded now on a planet that looked as if its highest level of technology might be the wheel—someday—and the *Cortez* was a smoldering ruin, torn in half by the violent impact of its rough landing.

Around them, the men who had survived the crash tried frantically to salvage their consoles and equipment. Pools of fire lit the bridge in fitful brushstrokes of red and orange. Black smoke columned up from the ruptured computers and sprung deck plates.

"Lambert, damage report," Tyler barked. "How's the lab?"

Lambert checked the lab link-up; it was still on-line, but operating on reserve power. "One hundred percent operational," he answered.

"Did any fighters survive?"

"Well, we found a wheel . . ." he answered sarcastically.

"Good work. Keep looking. Personnel?"

Lambert shook his head. "Seventy-eight percent dead or missing."

"Flight status?"

Lambert laughed like a loon, and flipped on the outside monitor. The great viewscreen filled with a smoky image of the crash site. It was taking a whole lot of power to maintain the image, but Lambert was trying to drive home his point. Anyway, once the power failed, so what? Where was this thing going, ever again?

The debris of the huge spacecraft lay scattered across the stark, rock-strewn plain, leaving a marker of wreckage all the way to the horizon. Seen from the remote camera, the Cortez's shattered hull looked almost like a broken Christmas ornament. All around the point of impact, huge, white-hot pieces of metal spiked the ground. A few bodies dotted the landscape, lying torn and twisted as scarecrows that have come down from their crosses for a nap.

Tyler shrugged. "Lick of paint here, patch there, I think she's good to go," he said. "How about you?"

"Sure," Lambert said, feeling a mad laugh building in the back of his throat. He had to jam his fist into his mouth to keep the laugh from exploding out, because he had a bad feeling once it got started, he wouldn't be able to stop. "Why not?"

Tyler regarded his first mate as if the man were crazier

than he was. He continued, "Scan the immediate area. I want visual and lifeform readings."

Lambert unbuckled his crash harness and felt his ribs and organs shift back into place. He grimaced, reached up and punched up another set of coordinates. The cracked, failing viewscreen sputtered and wavered, but finally another image—this time, a geographical map—filled the screen.

"Looks like we've got some live ones," Lambert said, the insanity turned from his door for a little longer, at least, by the routine of survival. "Two locations. Closest one has a couple hundred thousand of them ... approximately ten kliks north-east of here."

Tyler looked around the darkening bridge. The fires were filling the cabin with smoke, and the emergency generators were cycling down to extinction. He spotted a crewman lying impaled on a sharp piece of metal jutting up from the deck plates; the man gripped the spike, and tried once more to heft himself free, and, once more, failed.

"Well, that's good news," Tyler said, nodding. "We could probably use a few new recruits to replace these unreliable layabouts. Mr. Lambert, gather the weapons, assemble what's left of our men, and, oh, let's just shoot the injured, what do you say? We're moving out."

The man nailed to the deck gasped his horror. "Shoot us?" he cried. "Can't you just give us some of your ampules?!" He tried for a sincere, hopeful expression, hoping to impress upon Tyler that the injured could be rehabilitated, no need to go looking for replacements, but his expression only looked more like that of a man who's fallen off a cliff and hasn't hit the bottom yet.

Tyler knelt beside the spiked crewman, nodding. "Well, yes, I suppose I could do that, but the problem is ... then there isn't enough for me. That kind of talk is insubordination . . . mutiny. And do you know what the penalty for mutiny is?"

The impaled man didn't believe that strictly applied to a commercial vessel, such as the *Cortez* once was, but Tyler held his hand out, palm up, to Lambert, who reluctantly placed his sidearm there. Tyler shrugged and tipped his head to one side, indicating he'd like to help, but there was nothing he could do. Tyler placed the barrel between the man's eyes and jerked back on the trigger.

Word quickly spread throughout the ship that the injured were to be eliminated, and the Psycho Crew moved to carry out that order. But Tyler's madness seemed to be some form of communicable disease, for his men took uncommon glee in fulfilling their duties. Some cases, such as the impaled man, were actually mercy killings, but the Psycho Crew, caught up in the bloodlust, decided to arbitrarily extend the definition of "injured" to include those crewmen who were merely shaken up by the rough landing. Informed of this, Tyler laughed, and allowed the murders to go on. It might do the men some good to let off a little steam. The injured had other ideas, and those at all capable of holding a weapon fought back. The whole thing quickly degenerated into a gun battle.

"You've got to stop this!" Lambert shouted at Tyler. "Or there won't be any men left!"

Tyler reluctantly intervened. As he moved farther away from mortality, he had also moved farther away from clear, rational thought.

Across the horizon and toward the far side of the settlement the *Cortez*'s sensors had detected, the Spacehawk sliced sharply through the thick, mud-colored clouds, shielding al-

most gone, and hull glowing as bright as a charcoal bri-
quette.

Although power had failed, F.A.K.K.² manually wrestled
the nose of her fighter up, skimming the ship just above the
tops of the deep, shadow-haunted canyons that formed a
series of interconnected mesas. Needles of stone thrust up
like accusing fingers, and F.A.K.K.² just managed to guide
her ship between this narrow passage.

But it was really just a matter of degrees: she would
either strike the side of a mesa and instantly disintegrate,
or plow nose-first into the hardpacked earth, spin end over
end, and *then* disintegrate.

F.A.K.K.² gritted her teeth and pulled back on the
fighter's controls, trying to slow its forward momentum with
the remaining wing's foil. The fighter rose, dipped, leveled
off, and continued its mad dash across the landscape.

"Oh, sh—" she gasped. A few hundred yards ahead of
her, the ground simply dropped away, and a vast canyon
lay beyond that, its opposite side so far away as to be impossible to see. If she didn't bring the Spacehawk down here,
now, she'd go plunging into that grand abyss. Grimly,
F.A.K.K.² leaned forward on her throttle, and the ship started
down.

The belly of the fighter scraped the ground, bounced,
rose, wobbled, and went down again, screeching over the
sandy terrain as if in mortal agony. The edge of the cliff
was rushing up fast. F.A.K.K.²'s hand reached for the ejector
lever, and jerked it back.

The detonation charges blew the pilot's seat up and back,
away from the ship as its nose skidded up to the edge of
the canyon . . . and stopped.

The seat reached its apogee, seemed to hang in the air
for a moment, then began its quickening descent. And still

the parachute hadn't deployed. F.A.K.K.² thought it would be a pretty sad fate that would allow her to come this far to die because Nathan had forgotten to do something as simple as repack the 'chute on the ejector chair. Of course, she was coming to think fate was doled out by some blind, dysfunctional moron, and she had seen little in the past few days to make her think otherwise.

Suddenly, with a loud popping sound, the 'chute unfurled behind her—billowed, filled, caught the wind, and checked her stone-like plunge toward the desert floor. The safety harness jerked tightly across F.A.K.K.²'s chest, squeezing the air from her, and the chair seesawed toward the rough terrain.

She leaned her head back against the padded seat, thinking she would only rest her tired, grainy eyes until the chair touched down. That was the last thing she remembered for a while.

The approach of the two ships did not go unnoticed.

Odin watched the flaming contrails of the doomed ships as they blazed their way across the reddish sky. The larger object, he could tell by its trajectory, would land near the settlement of Shantaar. But it was the smaller of the two craft that interested him.

"The Convergence has begun," he whispered to himself. "We must depart at once."

Kerrie couldn't believe her luck.

The bone-rattling impact of the crash had violently thrown her cage against the wall of Tyler's cabin, and the force of that had actually sundered the bars. The bars themselves had protected her from serious injury, but she was still dazed and groggy. Kerrie checked herself, making sure nothing was broken, no organs hanging out, and, reasonably sure everything was where it was supposed to be, she wriggled free of the torn and twisted metal.

The numerous distillation jars had been flung against the walls and floor and ceiling, and shards of broken glass reflected the dim cabin lighting like a sea of diamonds. Pools of foul-smelling juices lay at Kerrie's feet, and somewhere, she knew, must lay the perfectly preserved body of the odd alien creature she had seen imprisoned in its glass display. She really didn't want to see it outside of that environment, because then it would be a little too real. While still encased in glass, she could pretend—just—that the body was nothing more than a cunningly-crafted fake, like the ones in the sideshows of the traveling carnivals she and Julie used to sneak into town to see when they were children. Mother didn't like them going to such freakshows, but how could anyone resist those dark and foolish delights?

Kerrie smiled as she recalled the sideshow attractions Julie used to make up to amuse her: See the rare two-headed armor-dillo, born with only one head! Marvel at the average-sized giant! Gasp at nature's cruelest mistake, the two-eyed Cyclops! Come for the freaks, stay for the reasonably-priced, all-you-can-eat buffet.

Julie, she thought, and realized she hadn't come through the crash undamaged at all. Kerrie thought her heart might be broken.

The cabin doors were twisted from the crash, and Kerrie had to lever them open by slipping her fingers between them and working the doors apart. She glanced out into the corridor, but could see no one. In the distance, she heard gunfire and screams, and looked back into the cabin for the gun she had dropped. But everything lay scattered and bashed about, and she could not immediately spot the gun. She supposed she might be able to find it, but probably not before Tyler or one of his Psycho Crew found her.

Better just to take her chances, unarmed, with whatever lay outside these walls, than risk capture once more by Tyler.

Kerrie crept out into the darkened corridor, pressing against the walls and keeping to the shadows as best she could.

At a T-junction in the main corridor, opening onto the great mess hall, Kerrie stopped for a moment, unable to believe her eyes. She had assumed the sounds of pitched battle to be between Tyler's Psycho Crew and this planet's inhabitants, but now she saw it was all-out war between the crewmembers. A stray bullet splashed off the steel wall next to her head, and that got her moving.

The far end of the corridor simply ended. The ship had been torn in half by the crash, and the ragged plates and exposed girders made Kerrie think of the rotting carcass of some great sea creature, washed ashore to become prey to scavenger birds.

She stood at the edge of the shattered deck and looked down—it was quite a drop to the ground. Exposed circuits in the wall buzzed and sparkled next to her. She tested the vertical cross-girder, found it still secured to the hull, and shimmied down hand over hand, until she was near enough to the ground to jump the rest of the distance.

She sprinted through the flaming piles of wreckage—twisted engines thrown from the ship's bowels, shorted circuitry boards, and charred bodies—and reached the rocky ridge she had spotted from above. Keeping low, she clambered up the scree, fat pebbles click-clacking down the slope as her bare feet sought purchase. Hidden in the chine, she sat down in a small ball, one arm wrapped around the other,

her long legs drawn up to her chin. She shivered, although the day was not cold at all.

Even as she was planning her next move, a stone cudgel came whistling down in a hard, vicious arc and cracked against her temple, putting Kerrie's plans for the immediate future on hold for a while.

The high desert air began shading into the color of rust as the sun slipped down farther on the horizon, dragging night along behind it to lay over the world like a blanket. A few wishing stars, all foreign and unfamiliar in this remote quadrant of the universe, began to burn through the darkness, and the cold rind of a moon, sharp as a fishhook, appeared over a butte. A second moon, nearly full, rose in another corner of the darkening sky.

F.A.K.K.² still lay strapped into the ejector seat, sitting at an odd angle on the hardpan floor. The desert around her slowly showed signs of life, for the night creatures had begun stirring at the first indication the ground was cooling.

A small, bristling ball of matted fur, more claws and fang and slavering mouth than body—like some mad scientist's idea of a tumbleweed—crawled onto F.A.K.K.²'s lap, moving to her soft, unprotected throat, and the warm, pulsing highway of veins and arteries it smelled there.

It spread wide its drooling maw to clamp about her throat, and the foul, stygian stench that wafted from its fetid insides acted as smelling salts to F.A.K.K.². Her eyes jerked open to the sight of a hundred dagger-sharp teeth inches from her face, the sound of the creature's stentorian breath roaring in her ears, like wind in a tunnel. Reacting purely on instinct, she backhanded the creature away from her.

The desert-piranha spun in the air, before it even hit the ground, rolled like the tumbleweed it resembled, then raced back toward F.A.K.K.², who was still strapped down to her heavy ejector seat. She grabbed her knife from its sheath on the side of her calf, flipped it around, and threw it at the creature as it leaped to cover the distance between it and its prey. The tumbleweed opened its mouth to defend itself from this threat, and the knife gouged into the soft roof of the creature's mouth, punching out through the top of its skull.

Its momentum carried it forward, and it landed in a graceless heap at F.A.K.K.²'s feet. She watched it cautiously, alert to any signs of movement, but her knife had struck true. F.A.K.K.² unbuckled her straps and tried to stand, but her legs felt as steady as quicksand. She pitched forward, and a chain of coughs racked her body. She shook her head, trying to clear it, but the pain that suddenly exploded in her shoulder brought her thoughts into crystal clarity.

A hyena-lizard, watching F.A.K.K.²'s encounter with the desert-piranha from its place on the warm rocks overhead, had decided she was easy prey, after all, and leapt down onto her back, driving its teeth into her shoulder. Her pauldron kept the teeth from breaking the flesh beneath it, but another such bite would surely do the job.

She threw herself backward, landing on top of the creature. It yipped in pain and alarm, and let go of her arm. F.A.K.K.² grabbed a fist-sized rock from the ground and spun around, smashing the rock down onto its sloped skull. The hyena-lizard, gore dripping from its cracked head, tried to push itself to its feet—food was forgotten, and all that remained now was revenge. F.A.K.K.² could have understood that.

She slammed the rock down once more onto the thick skull, and the beast grunted, its limbs folding beneath its weight. It regarded F.A.K.K.² through bloodshot, hate-filled eyes—the eyes the slain have for a killer—and that was how it died, carrying that animus with it to wherever it is hyena-lizards go when they are turned from this world.

F.A.K.K.² sat down, breathing hard, wary, cautiously checking the surrounding desert rocks and shadows, alert to more danger. It seemed the whole desert was one vast killing bowl, and she had unwittingly found herself introduced into that hostile environment. For the moment, however, she seemed safe, and she hefted herself to her feet. Her legs were still as wobbly as a newborn colt's, but she managed to start walking for the Spacehawk, sitting on the crest of the bottomless canyon.

As she walked, she removed the pauldron and looked at it; the hyena-lizard's gnashing teeth had crimped it, and one broken tooth jutted from it at a crazy angle, like a spent bee stinger, but it had kept her from serious injury. F.A.K.K.² traced her fingers gently over the raised numbers stamped into the shoulder protector: 1-4-3.

"Nathan," she said softly, like a prayer. It had been his pauldron; he had given it to her for good luck, and it had done its job. If only . . .

No. She refused to open that door yet. Grief, she knew, was like the desert predators, hiding in a hundred shadowed places, or just below the surface, ready to come larruping out and bear her down, biting and clawing until every inch of her was raw and flayed and exposed, just one more victim.

She fitted the pauldron into place, and moved ahead. F.A.K.K.² climbed carefully aboard the Spacehawk, its nose cantilevered out over the sheer precipice, and began salvaging what she could.

*   *   *

Kerrie had gone from a bad situation to an even worse one.

When she woke, she found herself sitting on the rough ground with her arms spread-eagled and tied quite snugly to the spokes of a cart wheel. From the ache in her arms, the swollen knot on the side of her head where she'd been bludgeoned into unconsciousness, and the angle of the evening shadows, she reasoned she'd been out of the loop for quite a while.

Her captors were reptilian creatures, with armored and pebbled skin, and the long, webbed fingers of lizards. They walked upright, like men, and wore the furs of mammals, and carried pouches and belts and wore boots—also made of mammals—but they were clearly cold-blooded creatures in every sense of the word. Kerrie had the idea they were scavengers, taking castoffs where they could find them and stealing goods when they couldn't.

The smallest of the creatures paced over to where Kerrie sat. He stood over her, twitching the tip of his long, powerful tail, and squeezed the meat of her arm and shoulder between his long, cold fingers, as if he were testing her for ripeness. And, as Kerrie thought that, the lizard licked his lips, and she understood that was *exactly* what he was doing.

"Get away!" she screamed, the lump on the side of her skull throbbing painfully from the effort. She leaned forward, straining, the scratchy ropes cutting grooves into her soft flesh. "Stay back!"

The lizard scampered back, looking at her with nictating eyes. He backed away, dragging his tail behind him, and returned to the campfire. The lizard-thing sat down in a huff, as if offended by the idea of talking food, and gazed across the fire around which the other scavengers sat, waiting for the joint of meat sizzling on a spit above the flames to finish cooking.

Kerrie shivered, wondering what would happen next.

"Me hungry," the small creature said. The smell of cooking game caused him to slobber uncontrollably.

"Me, too," the bigger creature answered.

They looked from the spit to the face of their leader. He had two brains, one in his skull, and one in his tail. By virtue of this, he was doubly as intelligent as the others; therefore, they looked to him for the answers.

"The question is, do we eat her or sell her?" he asked.

The small scavenger could wait no longer, and grabbed the half-cooked joint from the spit. The others tore off their share, and descended upon their raw and bloody food, grinding bone and gristle between their powerful jaws and jagged teeth.

"We won't eat her," the lizard with two brains said, jerking his clean-picked meat bone in Kerrie's direction. *"We'll sell her in Shantaar."*

The big creature belched loudly, ragged bits of meat still wedged between his teeth. He sucked at them, and said, *"Not worth much. What if no one buy her?"*

Two-brains' smile was as cold as his blood. "Then *we eat her.*"

The salvage work on the Spacehawk didn't take long because there was not much that could be salvaged. It was only made slow because F.A.K.K.² didn't like the idea of her weight aboard the damaged ship causing the unstable ground beneath it to crumble and give way, pitching the little fighter into the chasm.

The communications radio was a mass of melted circuitry and wires, fit for little more than a future as a doorstop. A few combat accessories survived—a handgun and some spare ammo, rations, telescopic glasses—but the rest of it was blackened with smoke and fused into unrecognizable globs by the intense heat of re-entry.

Whatever else that might have survived had been pulled out the broken canopy, along with Germain St. Germain and his cyber-wife. Funny, she didn't have any trouble killing other people; it was only Tyler who gave her a problem. And St. Germain took a high-dive into an empty pool without telling her how to kill the bastard . . . if he ever really knew.

F.A.K.K.² laughed thinly at that; her dry lips hurt, but she had to laugh. What difference did it make, whether or not St. Germain told her how to kill Tyler? She didn't see how that sociopath could have survived the crash.

But then, you *did,* she thought. You *walked away. Why couldn't* he?

Because . . . well, because that would mean everything that had happened so far had still been for nothing, and everyone who died so far had died for nothing. Could fate be that blind?

Yes. Yes, of course it could. If she learned nothing else from the horrible end that befell Eden, she should have learned that.

F.A.K.K.² carefully swung her leg over the side of the cockpit, the bag of salvage slung over her shoulder. The Spacehawk trembled under this shifting of weight, and the nose began to tilt down. The sandy ground beneath the ship was giving out, and F.A.K.K.² jumped onto what remained of the fighter's wing. She raced along the wing until she could see ground beneath her once more, and she leaped off the sagging ship just as the earth gave way.

The ship dipped forward, its nose below the rim of the canyon now, its rear rising higher. Its belly scraped and screamed against the precipice, falling slowly at first, and then, the weight of the Spacehawk caused the ground to crumble and disintegrate. The ship went over with one last, fearful scream, and F.A.K.K.² lost a little more of her tenuous link to her dead world and buried past.

She sat for a while, waiting for the final sound of impact that would tell her the ship had finally hit bottom, but every time she thought she'd heard it, a few moments later, and much farther away, she would hear still another bang. She knew then some falls never end. Once you get started, it's only by the grace of whatever gods there be that you don't fall forever.

F.A.K.K.² decided not to waste any further time or effort philosophizing; what was done, was done. She found her telescopic binoculars in the bag of salvage she had filled, removed the caps, flipped the battery pack on, and fitted the lenses over her eyes. She told herself she was looking for some sign of civilization, a spaceport from which she could make her way off this hostile world. She told herself this, but she knew better. F.A.K.K.² knew what she was really looking for.

She turned her head slowly, panning her binoculars across the far horizons. This whole planet, from what she could tell, was nothing but fuming volcanoes and fused rock, so rough-hewn that some angry god must have hacked the mountains and canyons into creation with a dull ax. The binoculars revealed a rising cone of black smoke. F.A.K.K.² reached to her lenses to adjust the magnification, and as she did, something huge and hideous filled her vision. It had an elongated, drooling proboscis centered on its rough, cratered head; but occupying most of its face were rows and rows of honeycomb-shaped eyes. F.A.K.K.² cried out in alarm, stepped back, and drew her weapon. She swiped the glasses from her face and looked for the creature, but could not find it.

F.A.K.K.² raised her binoculars and looked at the green-glowing lenses; there was a small, alien blowfly walking across the electronic viewfield. She laughed, felt the steel-spring tension flood from her body and cool relief rush in to fill the void. She shooed the fly away, holstered her gun, and fitted the binoculars back over her eyes.

And now she could see there were several thick plumes of smoke, clustered together like a black forest. Even with the amplification, F.A.K.K.² couldn't make out the source of those fires; they were unlike the fires of volcanoes. She watched the rising stacks of smoke laddering up and up, finally climbing so high the winds shredded them. She had a sense they were caused by the wreckage of the *Cortez*. She wanted to see Tyler's twisted, ruptured, fire-blackened, sun-bloated corpse up close.

Except, she just didn't believe it was over yet. It didn't *feel* over.

She took her glasses off, and tucked them carefully back into her kitbag. All she really knew—and she knew this in her gut to be true—was that Tyler was somehow still alive.

F.A.K.K.² stood on the rim of the canyon, the night filling it with deep, clotted shadows. Some falls, she knew, were endless. This one hadn't even begun.

Even as Odin had seen the ribbons of fire that stitched the red skies and heralded the arrival of the agents of light and

FAKK2

•THE MAKING OF A LEGEND•

A woman always has her revenge ready.

—MOLIÈRE

The Metal Mammoth Mining Company starship Cortez *in orbit around the* "F.A.K.K.²" *planet Eden.* Art by Simon Bisley.

Often an entire city has suffered because of an evil man.

—HESIOD

Tyler: the madman responsible for the destruction of Eden and the murder of its inhabitants.
Art by Simon Bisley.

On the Neo-Calcutta space station, F.A.K.K.² confronts Tyler and his men at Club Dead.
Art by Kevin Eastman.

In revenge and in love, woman is more barbarous than man.

—FREDERICH WILHELM NIETZSCHE

Following the destruction of Club Dead, F.A.K.K.² "persuades" Germain St. Germain to help her in killing Tyler. Art by Simon Bisley.

The naked hull alongside came,
And the twain were casting dice;
"The game is done! I've won! I've won!"
Quoth she, and whistles thrice.

—SAMUEL TAYLOR COLERIDGE

Traveling through the hyperspace tunnel, F.A.K.K.²'s Starhawk fighter collides with the Cortez. Art by Simon Bisley.

. . . for where we are is hell, And where hell is there must we ever be.

—CHRISTOPHER MARLOWE

A difference of opinions: After crashlanding on Uroboris, Tyler confronts a barbaric warlord . . .

. . . then uses the warrior's head for a crown after defeating him and taking control of his army. Their next stop: The Holylands. Art by Simon Bisley.

**The only secret people keep
Is immortality.**

—EMILY DICKINSON

F.A.K.K.², Odin, and Zeek survey the wreckage of the Cortez. *Soon enough,
they'll discover the dark secret behind Tyler's regenerative powers.*
Art by Simon Bisley.

The Promised Land always lies on the other side of a wilderness.

—HAVELOCK ELLIS

F.A.K.K.^{2} and a group of acolytes journey to the Holylands to defend it from Tyler and his army of warriors.
Art by Simon Bisley.

We stand at
Armageddon,
and we battle
for the Lord.

—THEODORE
ROOSEVELT

The siege of the Holylands begins, with Tyler leading the charge.
Art by Simon Bisley (top) and Kevin Eastman.

The final battle: F.A.K.K.² and Tyler fight to the death as chaos reigns.
Art by Simon Bisley.

**O dark, dark, dark, amid the blaze of noon,
Irrecoverably dark, total eclipse
Without all hope of day!**

—JOHN MILTON

Endgame: As the battle rages for control of the Waters of Immortality, the skies above the Holylands darken ominously. Only F.A.K.K.² stands between a madman and the destruction of an entire world.

In war there is no substitute for victory.

—GEN. DOUGLAS MacARTHUR

If I cannot bend Heaven, I shall move Hell.

—VIRGIL

Genesis of a warrior-queen: Initial sketch of Eden colonist Julie; final F.A.K.K.² design; Julie Strain as the real-life F.A.K.K.².
Art by Kevin Eastman.

Photo: John McInnis

All evils are equal when they are extreme.

—PIERRE CORNEILLE

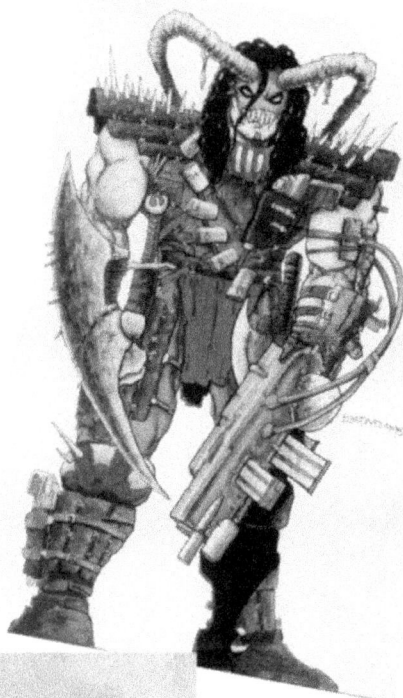

Man-made monster: Initial sketch of Tyler in Cortez *uniform; Tyler in warlord gear; final design of warlord Tyler.*
Sketches by Kevin Eastman; painted art by Simon Bisley.

Zeek, Odin's rock-like servant, who ultimately holds the key to F.A.K.K.²'s success against Tyler. Art by Simon Bisley.

Odin, the enigmatic wizard who enlists F.A.K.K.²'s aid. But is he truly a friend . . . ?
Art by Simon Bisley.

. . . the comrades who fight and fall . . .

—NICOLA SACCO

The Keeper of Time:
Ruling elder of the Holylands, he turns to the warrior-woman to lead the defense of his realm.
Art by Simon Bisley.

Germain St. Germain: The unfortunate Cortez officer who winds up caught in the middle between F.A.K.K.² and Tyler. Art by Simon Bisley.

Lambert: Tyler's right-hand man during the madman's quest for immortality— and who has his own plans for attaining life everlasting. Art by Simon Bisley.

A man cannot be too careful in the choice of his enemies. —OSCAR WILDE

Grinner: A former soldier for the warlord of Uroboris, he quickly throws in with Tyler once the madman takes control of the army. Art by Simon Bisley.

O tiger's heart wrapp'd in a woman's hide!

—WILLIAM SHAKESPEARE

dark, so had the planet's more warlike inhabitants. Unlike Odin, they did not know—nor would they have cared—that the fate of the universe would soon be fought for on this planet of fire, or the part they themselves would play in that battle.

The barbarians knew only that something the size of a small planet had fallen from the sky and disgorged dozens of wounded and dying meatsacks. The bloodbags were frail things, not plated like the lizards that roamed the desert. Sometimes, the barbarians would capture one of the meatsacks from the gated city when one wandered too far from safety, but they had never seen so many, all in one place. The smell of fresh blood and burned flesh caused the lizards to throw what caution they possessed to the wind, and drove them into a murderous frenzy.

The Psycho Crew had the superior weapons, but the lizards had the home court advantage and the numbers.

But then, the Psycho Crew also had Tyler.

"Well, isn't this always the way?" Tyler complained. "As soon as you get in the tub, company drops by!"

The Psycho Crew had taken cover behind the huge, jagged slabs of metal that had been torn from the hull by the impact to ring the outer perimeter of the crash site, and they were able to turn back the first wave of reptilian attackers. But the barbarians were fresh and thrived in this hellish heat, while Tyler's men were worn from their endless push across the universe, and the oppressive heat sucked the life from them.

Lambert knew it was just a question of time, and from his place near Tyler, he thought of putting a bullet through the madman's brain and claiming the liquid for himself. He hadn't come all this way and survived all they had just to become lizard chow, had he?

How did that old anagram go? "Desperation: a rope ends it." Well, a bullet would do the job just as surely. If not, then Lambert would be sure to save one for himself.

Before Lambert could raise his gun, though, his eardrums were pierced by the shrill cry of the giant, bat-like creature that came swooping down through the heavy black pall of smoke that hung over the battle. He looked up and watched with a sense of disassociation as the bat dropped lower, finding its way through the wreckage with its horrible, soul-curdling sonar. As the bat circled ever closer, the reptilian warlord that had been riding it leapt off his mount and landed within the *Cortez*'s ring of defense.

The warlord let out an ululating screech and charged across the distance, bearing down on Tyler. The creature was huge, heavily plated, horns jutting from his back and skull. Several were broken, injuries sustained in countless past battles; the remaining horns had been filed and sharpened into murderous spear-points. The lizard carried comically huge battle-axes in each hand, but there was nothing funny about them. As he charged, he swung the axes, chopping down Tyler's men and never breaking stride.

Tyler stood with his back against the outer hull of the ship, watching the warlord hack his way closer. He pointed at the lizard's thick, twitching tail, and said to Lambert, "See all those different shades in his tail? Like geological strata? Well, that's where he's lost the tail and it's grown back."

Lambert couldn't quite believe he was hearing this. Maybe the bat's sonar had damaged his eardrums, or maybe he was just having trouble grasping the language today, because Tyler was calmly lecturing him about the regenerative powers of lizard tails while a monster twice Tyler's size came charging through flame and gunfire straight at them.

"I was just telling my friend here about—" Tyler said to the warlord, but the lizard swung the first ax. Tyler was able to duck beneath it, the blade shattering against the hull of the *Cortez*. But the second ax drove down into Tyler's massive shoulder, splintering bone and shredding veins and arteries. He grunted and dropped into a sitting position.

The warlord turned away from his vanquished opponent and faced the field of battle. He raised his stumpy arms high, and let forth a victory cry, which was returned a hundredfold by his warriors.

Tyler calmly wrenched the heavy blade out of the shattered bones of his shoulder with a sound like nails being torn from old wood. Blood fountained down his tunic, flowing freely with the obstruction of the ax removed. The blood burbled once, and ceased. Broken bones grew back together with a clicking, skittering sound, like knitting needles fretting on some spool of yarn, and the ragged lips of Tyler's wound closed with a wet, muddy smacking sound.

"Let's see you regrow this!" Tyler roared, and swung the broad-ax.

The warlord grunted something that sounded like *"Huh?"* and started to turn his head in Tyler's direction. The blade cut cleanly through the lizard's thick neck, and his horned head struck the ground and rolled, jaws gnashing and snapping stupidly, trying to take one last shot at his killer. The lizard's body staggered around in a half-circle, black blood jetting up like an oil gusher from the severed stump of his neck, then tripped over its own feet and collapsed in a twitching heap, blood still squirting, but much more slowly now. In a moment, when its heart ceased beating, the bloodflow would stop altogether.

Tyler lifted the lizard's head—it had stopped snapping now, but there was still the slightest light of life and cunning in its glazing eyes—and scrunched it down onto his own head, forming a grotesque crown. Black ichor streaked down his temples and cheeks like warpaint, and Tyler meaningfully lifted his arms out from his sides, then slowly hoisted the bloody battle-ax above his head. He gripped its thick shaft with both hands, and cried out in a deafening voice: *"I—am—Tyler!!"*

A long beat; Lambert wasn't sure if the lizards were rallying for one last, all-out charge to avenge their fallen warlord, or if their brains were so small it took a moment or two for this new information to sink in. And then, the rest of the warriors roared their approval as one mad, frenzied mob. They raised their weapons—axes, spears, arrows, maces—over their heads in a gesture of fealty, and chanted, "Ty-lor! Ty-lor! Ty-lor!"

Tyler glanced back over his shoulder—now completely healed—at Lambert and the ragtag survivors of the Psycho Crew. The blood from the dismembered head had almost completely painted Tyler's face now, and only his intense, insane eyes were clear and bright. Lambert understood what Tyler expected, and, after a beat, raised his pistol above his head and joined the chant. Before long, the rest of the men were shouting as well: "Ty-lor! Ty-lor! Ty-lor!"

"Can I get an Amen?" Tyler roared.

F.A.K.K.[2] walked on through the night, putting her mind on auto-pilot and just setting one foot down in front of the other. She knew she would have to find a way around the great stone gash in the earth—it would take too long to climb down and then scale the far side, even if she could do it—always assuming it didn't girdle the entire planet. But there was nothing to do for it except keep walking, and keep hoping.

The first action was easy enough, but hope was a tough commodity to come by, and there seemed a particular shortage of it on this violent, barren world.

The nights on Uroboris were short, and the sun rose too soon, quickly burning away any coolness the morning may yet still hold. F.A.K.K.² could find no shelter, no wall of rocks to shade her from the hammerblow heat of the sun, and she probably wouldn't have stopped that long, even if she had. Not while there was still a chance her world's killer was alive; one hour she delayed finding him was one hour longer he was allowed to live. One hour longer than he deserved. One hour longer than the Eden Colony got.

She trudged on, and the sun rose, and the air was still and breathless.

F.A.K.K.² stood atop a pile of boulders, looking down into the dry riverbed that cut through the narrow valley spread out before her. This world seemed to be nothing but wounds and tears, as if the volcanoes that pocked the landscape vomited up the molten core of the planet and left nothing underground but honeycombs and tunnels that could no longer support the weight of the surface. The planet was collapsing in upon itself.

She might not have noticed the buggy sitting next to the empty riverbed, had the sun not heliographed off its metal frame at that moment. F.A.K.K.² squinted her eyes against the arrows of sunlight, and fitted her binoculars. She zoomed the magnification in on the gleaming anomaly—everything else around here was dull, flat red rock—and was surprised to see it was indeed a cart of some kind. She dropped her field glasses into her kipsack and scrambled down the gradual slope of the rock face. Loose stones rolled and tumbled ahead of her, kicking up a choking cloud of red dust.

F.A.K.K.² reached the bottom of the arroyo and approached the buggy; it looked more like a rickshaw, with a set of handles tipped forward and resting against the ground. Whoever had pulled it here was nowhere to be seen. She looked into the passenger's seat—nothing of interest.

She took out her water bottle, unscrewed the cap, and took just enough to wet her mouth. F.A.K.K.² reluctantly swallowed the little she allotted herself, looked at the bottle, which was all the liquid that survived the crash, and capped it again. She sighed, smeared the sweat off her brow with the back of her arm, and sat down heavily on a nearby rock.

"I can't breathe!" someone gasped in a muffled voice. It sounded like it was coming from her butt. "Get off my face! Get off!"

F.A.K.K.² sprang to her feet, looking around for the source of the voice. And then, the rock on which she had been sitting began to unfold itself until it stood before her as a small, stout creature carved of stone, studying her curiously with its row of bright, cabochon-cut, gemstone eyes.

Her gun was in her hand and trained on the rock man before she was even aware of having reached for it.

"What the hell are you supposed to be?" she demanded.

"I am Zeek," the rock man answered simply, its rows of eyes shining with bright wonder.

"What the hell are you?" Clearly, he thought that was her normal expression of greeting, and was simply being polite. Zeek leaned forward and touched F.A.K.K.²'s leg. "Ooooohhh, whatever the hell you are, you're so *soft*," he marveled.

F.A.K.K.² smiled lopsidedly, and returned her weapon to its holster. "I'm harder than you think, little stone man," she answered.

Zeek seemed perfectly content to spend the rest of his days just staring at this amazing, new, soft one, his multi-faceted eyes sparkling in the bright sunlight. But F.A.K.K.² was not content to be stared at so openly, and she turned from the stone man and began walking toward the buggy once more.

Zeek gasped in alarm, compacted himself into a ball of stone, and rolled himself into her path, intercepting F.A.K.K.² before she could reach the buggy. He uncoiled, quick as a snake, and stood before her, his stubby arms upraised. "Please ... you must not touch my master Odin's property," Zeek told her. "He has left me with the responsibility of guarding it."

"Relax," she said. "Your ... thing is safe with me." F.A.K.K.² looked around, up and down the length of the river bed. The valley floor wound around a curve some distance farther on, but she could see no sign of this Odin. Whoever— or whatever—that was. "Where is your mas—"

"Please excuse my little friend!" a warm and booming voice called out from behind her. "He takes his duties very seriously."

F.A.K.K.² spun to face the speaker, startled. The man had not been there before, she was sure of that.

"I do," Zeek admitted.

"I am Odin," the man continued, walking closer to F.A.K.K.². She saw he carried a bag slung around his waist, and a long, ash-wood walking staff. His face was shaded and hidden by the wide brim of the hat he wore, jammed down over the top of his head to the tips of his eyebrows. But as he moved nearer, F.A.K.K.² had the oddest feeling she knew that face, anyway. "I can tell Zeek likes you. What are you called, child?"

She bristled at that. "I am not a child," she answered.

"My name is F.A.K.—" she began, and stopped herself. That was not her name. That was a lie—a designation given to a cold, unfeeling angel of death on a mission of vengeance. The antithesis of the gentle, caring woman who had laughed and loved an eternity ago. It was only the title of her duty, and she would be glad to be relieved of it.

"Julie," she said softly. "I'm Julie." It was suddenly vitally important that someone else know her given name. After all, it was about the only thing she had left of her old life, the one that made sense right up until the moment the giant *Cortez* blocked out the sun above Eden.

"Julie's soft," Zeek added. If it was possible for stone to blush, he would have. "Very soft."

Odin chuckled. "You are not from our world, are you?" he asked.

It was Julie's turn to chuckle now, but it was a sound as barren as the sighing desert winds. "Hardly. What is this place?" She spread her arms to indicate the planet she was quickly coming to think of as a tumorous growth on the galaxy's back-side.

"Uroboris," Odin answered, unslinging his pack and storing it in the seat of the little buggy. "Some call it home ... others are less generous, and call it hell." He turned to her then, and she could see his face and its hard, geometric planes clearly. She felt a chill whipsaw through her so violently she feared it would cut her in half. "Why have you come here?"

She continued staring at him, but couldn't answer. The lines into the town called Julie's Mind had been cut, and no incoming or outgoing messages could be received. *I dreamed you*, she heard her mind saying, but all that came out was, "Uh ..."

"My master says you have come from the sky," Zeek

interjected, tugging on Julie's dangling hand, as eager as a clever child for this woman's attention. "Do you have it? Do you have the key?"

"I don't know anything about a key," she admitted; she was speaking to Zeek, but looking at Odin. How was it possible she had dreamed this man? Was this whole thing just a dream, then? Was she still strapped into her busted Space-hawk, her fevered mind unspooling these images behind her unconscious eyes? Julie touched her shoulder, the one the hyena-lizard had mauled, and the pain there was genuine enough to convince her this was real. "I crashed here, trying to kill a madman who won't stay dead."

Beneath the shaded brim of his hat, Julie thought Odin's eyes grew momentarily wide. "I did see *two* fireballs . . ." he ventured. "The other was headed in the direction of a city called Shantaar."

Thoughts of dreams and deja vu were immediately el-bowed aside by this news. Her back stiffened, lips pulling back in a snarl as a dark cloud passed behind the girl's eyes. Julie was gone again, her place taken once more by F.A.K.K.², her dead world's avenger. The soft one, the woman she was before, had been forced into the dark re-cesses of her mind. But F.A.K.K.² knew she was still there. She could still find her, when this was all over. *If* it would ever be over.

"I have to go there!" F.A.K.K.² exclaimed, grabbing the old man's biceps in her hands. His arms felt like steel, and some eldritch power seemed to hum through his veins in place of blood. "Can you show me?"

"Yes, I can show you," Odin said, fixing her with one eye, his head slightly inclined. "In fact, we'll take you there. But it will cost you."

She stepped back, anger flaring, her cheeks hectic with

color. "Cost me *what?*" she demanded fiercely. "Tyler already cost me everything I have! I'm torn down to absolute zero! I don't have any more left to give!"

"That's not entirely true," Odin said, and he raised his hand. At first, F.A.K.K.² thought he was reaching for her, that he had found the one thing she had left to give, but he was pointing at something past her. She turned her head warily, and then laughed when she saw what Odin was trying to indicate.

Zeek had grown bored with the conversation and had begun rummaging through F.A.K.K.²'s rucksack. He stood there now with her old Discman held gently in one limestone hand, the earphones plugged into the tiny boreholes on the sides of his head that served as ears. His rows of eyes were closed, and his squat little body was swaying back and forth to the sound of music only he could hear. With his free hand, Zeek tried to snap his fingers in time with the beat, but it sounded like rock striking rock.

F.A.K.K.² laughed, and it was so sudden and honest that the sound of it startled her. "Okay," she said. "I can live with that."

Odin tapped Zeek on the head. His shining eyes opened slowly, reluctantly. Odin gestured to the buggy, and Zeek nodded. To F.A.K.K.², Odin indicated "after you," with a bow and a raised arm.

"Doesn't this thing need an engine?" F.A.K.K.² asked, looking at the cart.

Odin chuckled and pointed at Zeek. "You're looking at it," he said.

Once the pair was seated, Zeek picked up the bearer handles to pull the cart. F.A.K.K.² was at first concerned that the little rock man wouldn't be powerful enough for the task, but he set off at a strong, even gait, nodding his head to the tinny music.

"Don't worry yourself about Zeek," Odin told her, reading the look on her face. "He's tougher than he looks. Now ... why don't you tell me about this madman?"

F.A.K.K.² sneered. "A bastard named Tyler killed everyone I ever cared about," she answered. She thought she would be able to state these bare facts, the bones on which the tough skin of this new life grew, but she heard the hitch of raw emotion in her voice, and regretted having said this much. "The only thing I care about now is seeing him dead!" *Finish strong,* she thought. *Dad always told you that.*

"I am sorry," Odin offered at length. She had to turn away. She was used to hard times, but simple kindness was more than F.A.K.K.² could bear. "I sense your sadness. It's hard to be the last of your people."

The little buggy rattled across the stony, arid terrain, the wind blowing its lonely song across the alkaline flats, as the sun began its slow, welcome descent into the west.

Even as the humble little rickshaw carried its passengers toward the city of Shantaar, Tyler was also being borne there, albeit in a somewhat more ostentatious manner. He sat comfortably in the covered Captain's chair, torn from the bridge deck of the downed *Cortez* along with a palette made of the same deckplate to which it had been bolted. Heavy iron bars were welded to the sides of the palette, and the lizard warriors carried the platform on their shoulders as if Tyler were some king, and they his royal entourage.

Tyler was furious to discover his prize—the woman from Eden—had escaped her cage and the ship. He had raged and roared like a spoiled demon, and punched his bare knuckles through a steel hatch. The broken bones in his hand and wrist began healing almost at once, but he didn't care. He had been thwarted. For once in his life, since ascending to near-godhood, he had been denied something, and he did not accept it graciously. He vowed to spend the rest of his endless days tracking down that little witch and making her suffer. He had offered her his love, as rough as a stone, but all that he had to offer, and she had rebuked him. What was the point of being a god, of ruling the universe, if you couldn't make someone love you?

Some things never changed.

At the peak of his anger, Tyler attacked one of his lizard-warriors and tore out the creature's throat with his bare teeth. "If you hadn't chosen that moment to attack," the madman ranted through a mouthful of lizard meat, "I would have been here to stop her escaping!" It was the demented, circular reasoning of a child, blaming his own shortcomings on the world at large. Tyler neglected to take into account the fact that Kerrie had been his unwilling captive in the first place. And that he had wiped out her entire race in the span of an afternoon.

While Kerrie had been his prisoner, Tyler had been able to wax poetic about the wheel of karma, and how its impartial turnings always put one traveler down, while it raised another traveler to the top. But that was when he was on top, and Kerrie on the bottom. The problem was, the wheel of karma always made a complete rotation. It was hard to remember that when your own destiny was on the rise; it was impossible to believe your time would ever come when the great wheel was grinding you beneath it like chaff.

The warrior sank to the floor, making liquid gagging sounds, and slumped sideways.

Tyler spat out the gobbet of flesh from his mouth.

"Hunh!" he muttered to himself. "It really *does* taste like chicken!"

Now, the madman stood tall on the palette to address his assembled troops. "We march on Shantaar!" he cried, arms raised above his head. The men and monsters all began to chant as one: "Shan-taar! Shan-taar! We march on Shantaar!"

Tyler smiled. Immortality. Limitless power. And unswerving loyalty from legions of barbaric, half-witted lizard-things that tasted like Mom's Sunday night dinner.

The perks of godhood were getting better all the time. . . .

"You ride," F.A.K.K.² told Odin. "I'm walking."

She had seen the oasis sitting on the horizon like a shimmering vision of heaven; F.A.K.K.² palmed her scratchy eyes and looked again, but the oasis was still there. And now, as the stale breath of the desert shifted, she could smell the cool, slightly mineral aroma of the pool of water and the too-sweet scent of exotic flowers that erupted in colorful chaos around it.

F.A.K.K.² jumped over the low side of the buggy and patted Zeek on the head. He was still lost in his music, listening to the same disc for the fifth or sixth time. Zeek looked at the soft one as she pointed toward the greenery, and then she was sprinting on her long legs ahead of him. Zeek tried to run, too, but his own stumpy legs were not built for speed, only endurance. He would never win the race, but he would always finish.

F.A.K.K.² was too intent on reaching the pool to notice the breathtaking rock formations and the lush, tropical vegetation. She began peeling off her clothes and boots even as she ran. At the edge of the pool, she leapt and her sleek body knifed through the shimmery, electric-blue waters. She dived deep, so deep even the glare of the sun was dimmed and the blue of the waters grew indigo.

She could not find the bottom of the pool; the waters grew steadily darker and colder, and reluctantly, she pushed back toward the air. F.A.K.K.² looked up, toward the sun-burnished surface of the water, where golden coins of sunlight lay scattered about, like yellow leaves. She broke surface, and breathed deeply, shaking her plastered hair away from her face.

F.A.K.K.² saw Zeek, drawing the wagon behind him, approaching the oasis. He spotted her, and raised a hand to wave. She returned the greeting, and rolled over onto her back. F.A.K.K.² floated away from them and toward the far end of the pool, where a small, stone archway rose out of the waters. A stream of water dribbled down from the stones, a lovely, natural fountain, and there were dozens of small, beautiful rainbows hanging in the air on the mist like party decorations.

Why not? she thought. *There are always rainbows after rain, and, eventually, laughter after tears.* The water buoyed her, and she closed her eyes and continued to drift along, floating under the small waterfall. The water rained down on her lithe body, and she let her mind drift away from its tight, careful moorings, the way a boat will sometimes break away from shore. As she emerged from the other side of the arch, the light took on an unnatural color, making everything seem dreamlike and ephemeral.

And then Nathan was there, in this little corner of heaven walled off from the rest of hell. His spirit had fled the flames of Eden and come here, to wait for her. How and why didn't matter. Julie and Nathan swam together in the waters, as playful as porpoises, leaping high, then diving deep below the surface.

Nathan drew her close and held her as only lovers can. He brushed his lips softly over her slender throat, and nibbled her ear, and kissed each of her eyelids, and gave her small, flitting butterfly kisses all over her body.

"I will always love you," he said. "I will love you forever."

She wanted to warn him, *don't promise forever, you don't know what that means.* But how could she tell him that when even she didn't know yet what it meant?

So, what she said was, "I love you, Nathan, and I will love you as long as I live."

Perhaps that wasn't forever, but how could she tell him that nothing, not even love, lasts forever, when every other word still seemed to rhyme with moon and spoon? And would he have believed her back on Eden, when the only deceit the universe held came in the forms of counterfeit wooden medallions and surprise engagement parties?

And yet, he was here just as surely as she was, so perhaps some things did survive, even if the form changed. What was change but survival, after all?

Nathan opened his mouth to say something, but all that he could manage was a hideous, blistering scream. There was raw terror in his eyes, the kind of terror a man can feel only when he is about to die and knows it.

F.A.K.K.² opened her eyes.

Nathan was gone.

But the water around her was tinged a bloody red.

Nine

The burning city in the desert was a place of dark wonder.

Shantaar was carved of igneous rock and hardened molten lava, but, as unusual at that may have been, it was hardly enough to warrant a second look. After all, there were few other raw materials on this desert world with which to build homes or villages, let alone cities. But Shantaar was a bizarre apparition, because it seemed to float on thermal updrafts that bellowed out of the live volcanic crevice in which the city had been built.

Veins of lava, funneled through stone aqueducts, heated and illuminated the city. The ends of the aqueducts sloped away from the hovering city and descended into the volcanic crevice, and disappeared below the face of the bubbling magma. As the lava grew hotter, it climbed up the leg of the aqueduct, flowed through the city in its carved destinations, and poured back down the other leg of the stone canal. Giant, curved exhaust tubes all around the base of the floating city vented the explosive volcanic gasses which, in the cold heights, became ice crystals and fell like snow onto the city's central icy peak.

This city in the clouds—or at least, city in the clouds of deadly volcanic gasses—allowed its inhabitants to thrive by night as well, for the lizard creatures grew dull and sluggish in the desert cold, easily conquered. Here, in a city heated by the violent forces raging beneath the planet's shattered face, the reptiles never had to worry about forced hibernation.

And the gates of Shantaar were easily defended from most attacking armies.

Tyler had expected to have to battle his way into the floating fortress, but the lizard warriors visited the city often on leave, and were able to gain them safe entry. The immortal madman was vaguely disappointed, and promised to treat himself to some good old-fashioned, home-grown mayhem the first chance he got. He had a feeling it wouldn't take long to find in this place.

Shantaar reminded Tyler of a funhouse-mirror reflection of Neo-Calcutta, with its narrow, chaotic alleyways populated with arms dealers, drug pushers, flesh peddlers, palm readers, tattoo artists, and body-piercing stalls.

The heat here was stifling and brutal, and sat on your chest like a grade school bully. No surprise, really, considering the open spouts and troughs of lava that crisscrossed the city. Hideous stone statues, carved on the corners and fronts of buildings, stood vigil like gargoyles, and poured lava from their eyes and noses and mouths instead of rainwater. The lava spilled from these statues, sputtered and hissed into stone troughs and gutters that carried it through the streets and through homes and buildings.

The city was lit with the fitful, dancing light of the flowing magma, reminding Lambert of the old paint-print depictions of hell. Despite the massive heat, he shivered coldly. It was hell, all right, and Tyler seemed right at home. They'd followed the devil all this time, bartered their souls away for the promise of eternal life, and now the devil had brought them home to meet the folks.

Tyler turned to face the men; his face was even more demonic in the guttering, diffuse red light.

"I love this place!" he said, and smiled a smile fitting a lord of darkness. "I'll take it!"

The scream came again, and F.A.K.K.² shook the last of her mirage-dream away. The red in the water was not Nathan's blood, but merely the reflected glow of the setting sun filtered through the scarlet skies.

But that scream was real enough.

She swam back to where she had left her clothes beside the pool, and was dressed and ready in moments. Zeek and Odin had arrived at the oasis, but had kept a respectful distance from her as she bathed. F.A.K.K.² could see Zeek, standing atop a creeper-covered wall of stone, looking at something in the desert, in the direction of Shantaar. Zeek climbed down the creepers, hand-over-hand, and ran to Odin, saying something F.A.K.K.² couldn't quite make out.

Still, judging from his obvious excitement, F.A.K.K.² decided it would be best to expect anything. She unslung her gun, but Odin shook his head in a small, barely noticeable arc. "Let me handle this," he said, and seemed to walk up the interlocking ropy tendrils of the creepers covering the wall as if they were not vegetation, but steps.

F.A.K.K.² felt the flesh on her arms rash out in a wave of goosebumps. She had no use for sorcery, and she wanted to run into the desert and leave Odin and his little golem far behind, but she needed them. And hadn't she herself told

St. Germain she would do whatever it took to bring Tyler down?

She became aware Zeek was watching her with his round and unblinking eyes. Impossible as it seemed, the gemstone eyes contained far more humanity than she had seen in Tyler's . . . and even her own, of late. Zeek was watching her with trust, and perhaps something like a schoolboy crush.

"Soft one?" he asked, almost shyly.

F.A.K.K.² nodded. "Lead on, Zeek," she answered, and followed him over the wall.

Now she could see what had made those hideous, inhuman screams. Lying in the distance, little more than a shapeless lump in the gathering twilight, was some manner of giant lizard mount. It had been ridden hard, as evidenced by its numerous wounds, and had died within meters of the oasis. She noticed a shallow trail leading away from the dead mount, across the parched, cracked ground, approaching the oasis.

Her eyes followed the dented earth, and spotted Odin kneeling beside a man lying in the trail at the edge of the greenery. She jumped down from the wall and sprinted over to them. As she moved closer, she recognized the man's tattered and bloody clothes as belonging to Tyler's Psycho Crew. F.A.K.K.²'s hand dipped for the pistol at her hip. If she'd been a little more objective, though, she would have realized the man was more in need of a hole in the ground than a hole in his head.

". . . marches on Shantaar," the dying man was saying. F.A.K.K.² moved closer to hear the rest of the conversation.

"Who marches?" she demanded.

The injured man tried to locate the source of this new voice, but his eyes were swollen shut and crusted with desert grit. It wouldn't have mattered—his vision was failing like the light.

"Tyler," he said, and coughed. It sounded like something had broken loose and was rattling around inside his chest.

"Tyler," she hissed, bristling with anger. What did it take to kill that monster?

Odin gestured for Zeek to bring the dying man water from the oasis, and the little golem hurried off to do as he had been ordered. F.A.K.K.² had the feeling Zeek was making a wasted trip. Now that she was beside the man, she could see it wasn't a groove in the parched earth he had made—it was a trail of his own blood and entrails, like slime left by some ghastly garden slug.

He was dying, and F.A.K.K.² regretted it was not at her hand. *Just don't come to enjoy killing too much,* she heard her father telling her. But how much was too much? If it was true you could never be too rich or too thin, if there was no such thing as having too much fun, then how could you ever enjoy killing too much?

But she knew she was rationalizing, and disgracing her father's memory. It seemed whatever Tyler didn't destroy outright, he twisted and ruined.

"Did Tyler do this to you?" Odin asked the man.

He coughed again, and was silent a long time before answering. F.A.K.K.² thought he had died, but at last he said, "Ordered the injured shot ... but I wasn't dead. When the Igua-nomads attacked ... I escaped ... stole a mount while Tyler was making plans to attack Shantaar ..."

Up close, F.A.K.K.² could see he wasn't much more than a boy. Had this young fool any idea what he was getting into with Tyler? Had he even had a choice?

The setting sun backlit F.A.K.K.² in a corona of red, unearthly light, and the man saw her for the first time. "Are you . . . are you a messenger of death?" he asked weakly.

She sighed. "No. Not for you," she answered, and, despite what part this man may or may not have had in the burning of Eden, she gently brushed his matted hair from his face.

"Wish I could see you," he said, his voice trailing off. F.A.K.K.² had to strain to hear the rest. "Don't think I'll be seeing anything pretty again . . . where I'm going . . ."

Wherever it was the man thought he was going, he left for it a moment later. To her surprise, F.A.K.K.² felt sorry for the dead man. He was surely some mother's adored son, the great love of some woman's life. Somewhere. Here, he was just one more nameless dead man.

"This Tyler is a cold, ruthless creature," Odin ventured at last, trying to draw F.A.K.K.² out of her reverie.

She nodded. "That would be one way of describing him."

"And yet, you're still alive," Odin continued. "I'm impressed. Perhaps there is hope yet."

F.A.K.K.² looked across the vast, arid desert, where the moons were rising, and the stars were shining, and where Tyler wrapped the darkness between the stars around him like a cloak.

"I don't understand," she said.

"There is yet much you do not understand," Odin said, flatly. Her anger flared for a moment, but cooled again. He was right. No point getting angry about that. "Be patient. Time is the key to your survival. To everyone's survival."

"Everyone?" she spat. "You make it sound like I'm part of some big galactic chess game! Look, I want revenge on the creature that killed my family and wiped out my planet! End of story. Don't you—don't *anyone*—try to hang a 'savior' sign around my shoulders, because I don't want it.

There's not much job security in that career. Everybody who's filled the office before ended up dead."

But Odin pressed on, as persistent as a salesman. "You have been born twice—once by your mother, and once by forces beyond your ability to understand. You may not realize it yet, but you have within you the potential for power so great . . . you can stop worlds from being destroyed."

F.A.K.K.² jerked her head around to face Odin. "The only world I cared about saving, I couldn't!" she said hotly.

Before the wizard could say anything more, F.A.K.K.² stood and turned on her heel, returning to the cool nightshade of the oasis.

Tyler and his men spent the night in drunken carousing in a pub called The Dewlap. The original Psycho Crew drank very little of the foul, viscous brew the pub served, but the Igua-nomads regarded it as ambrosia. Lambert once expressed concern to Tyler that even with these new warriors, it may not be enough to storm the Holylands.

Tyler dismissed the idea. "That's the good thing about our new footmen—even if they die in battle, we can always eat 'em later."

Lambert laughed perfunctorily and thought about excusing himself from this noisome den, but knew the air outside was just as foul and stifling. There was also the matter of crossing the room without stepping on one of the lizards' tails that lay all about the floor, like unwound firehoses. In his present state, Lambert was less certain he could safely navigate the obstacle course, and he didn't want to try to talk his way out of trouble with these bruisers. No, better just to stay put, he decided.

He shot nervous glances around the darkened pub, afraid to make eye contact with any of the patrons. But he did notice there were several castes of reptiles in Shantaar. There were the more warlike lizards, the Igua-nomads and the Kimo-nomads, both desert wanderers. The Salvage-manders were scavengers, bartering whatever re-useable junk they could find for food and drink. Lambert could just pick up a trio at a nearby booth celebrating a sale (although he distinctly got the impression that one of the three said something about "should have eaten her instead."), but there was so much noise, and the lizards' dialect so varied and sibilant, it was hard to tell much of anything. Monitor lizards watched everything, and served as bar bouncers.

To Lambert's surprise, the barkeeps were some form of mutant frog or toad, but then, he supposed that made sense; the amphibians would be badly equipped for a life in the hostile, waterless desert, so they evolved a sense of business instead. Cunning, he thought; very cunning.

But as for the rest of the lizard-things, Lambert couldn't guess. They appeared to be some sort of evolutionary offshoot of their own. Possibly the sun's radiation, unfiltered by much of an ozone layer, bred mutations such as Lambert guessed these to be; perhaps they were the progeny of unlikely couplings.

"See anything green?" Tyler asked his first mate, and laughed. There was nothing but green all around them.

Lambert's head was starting to pound. The bar-band was awful, mostly percussion—rock against stone, or femur against skull—with some manner of screeching vocals that sounded more like a challenge than lyrics to a ballad.

Tyler had insisted on wearing the crown made of the reptilian warlord he had slain in the attack on the *Cortez*, and it was attracting several unwelcome looks. A couple of the lizards seemed to recognize the face, but couldn't quite place it. Of course, in the desert heat, decay had set in almost at once, and the head was bloated and flyblown. Still, the horns were almost as individualistic as dental records, and in time, someone would be sure to recognize it.

Lambert was just glad there were no Thesauruses drinking here tonight. If anyone could place the face, it would be one of them. Those shifty little know-it-alls were nothing but trouble.

Lambert started chuckling to himself, and knew he was drunk. Anytime he demonstrated a sense of humor, he knew he'd had enough. He was surprised to realize he had drunk so much; at first, he didn't like the wretched drinks they served here, but after a few sips, the drinks numbed your natural gag reflex and made it easy to knock them back.

A grossly obese lizard waddled into the pub and sat down heavily on two of the stools at the bar. Several of the regulars recognized him and all called out his name: "G'Norm!"

Tyler had taken the poppers out of his pouch and lined them up in a neat little row on the table before him. He alternated drinks with poppers, like shooters. Lambert eyed the last of the vials covetously, but knew it was still too early to make his move.

He had accepted it as fact that Tyler would not share the waters of everafter with the men; if he was going to drink of immortality, Lambert knew he would have to help himself. But not yet. A brave man may die but once, and the coward a thousand deaths, but Lambert didn't mind that. At least the coward kept coming back.

He smiled at Tyler, and ordered another drink.

Early the next morning, with the sun still just a violent smear on the far horizon and the sky around it a chiaroscuro

effect, Zeek cheerfully woke Odin and F.A.K.K.². He motioned at the sky as F.A.K.K.² rubbed the sleep from her eyes.

"Time to go," he told them.

Zeek pulled the little buggy to a halt before a low, stone hut
covered with shreds of dried moss. The windows of the hut
were shuttered against the miserable high-noon heat, and a
few chicken-like creatures scratched listlessly in the dust.
They were just going through motions, not really expecting
to find anything edible. Frustrated, they pecked angrily at
one another.

A broken cart wheel sat half-buried in the sand before
the house, and the curved black handle of a water-pump
stood at attention. A fat drop of liquid hung suspended from
the pump on a long, jiggling thread of water. A bucket sat
empty and dusty beneath the spout. Next to the house ran
a wide and deep fissure through which flowed a stream of
lava.

"You aren't trying to tell me this is Shantaar?" F.A.K.K.²
asked Odin, sarcastically.

The old wizard stepped out of the buggy. He offered her
his hand, but she refused it, and stepped over the side herself.

"No," Odin answered, moving closer to the hut. F.A.K.K.²
followed Zeek, and she could feel the enormous heat rising
from the crevice the nearer to it they came. "But it's one
way in that Tyler should know nothing about."

She stood on the rim and peered over the edge. Zeek
stood beside F.A.K.K.², holding her hand gently in his. She
wasn't sure if he took her hand because he was protecting
her, or if he was drawing courage from her touch. Both,
perhaps. She held his hand a little tighter, but, being stone,
Zeek didn't notice.

"Molten lava?" she asked the little golem. "We have to pass over molten lava?"

He nodded, his tone serious. "Yes. Shantaar lies on the other side." He looked at F.A.K.K.² and made her his conspirator. "I hate this place," he confided.

"How do we get across?"

From the rough-hewn hut (to F.A.K.K.², it looked as if a small volcano had grown up here and solidified in the more-or-less shape of a hut) stepped a decrepit old desert dweller. It resembled a skinless toad, dripping some manner of gelatinous secretions from its pores. It wrapped its squat and rotund body in damp moss to stay moist, and waddled unsteadily on flat, splayed feet, wincing painfully at the bright sunlight and heat.

"I am Chartog, guardian of the red river," the creature croaked, and F.A.K.K.² watched with revulsion as its dewlap expanded and contracted as it spoke. "I know the way across . . . and I will tell you . . . if you pay my price."

"It never stops, does it?" F.A.K.K.² asked. "No matter how much I pay, it's never enough."

"I ask little," Chartog said, harrumphing its throat. "Just a kiss. What's one more to a pretty little thing such as you? How many have you squandered on faithless loves? How much would it mean to an ugly little thing . . . such as me? Don't you find me . . . attractive?"

Even as F.A.K.K.² tried to brace herself for the inevitable, Chartog opened its lips. A worm-like tongue slithered out of its mouth, and seemed to sense the air. It flicked in F.A.K.K.²'s direction, and she stepped back, a hand over her grimacing mouth.

Chartog stood erect and pulled open its robes of damp moss. A swirling green mist rose from beneath the thing's clothes and parted to reveal a transdimensional vortex swirling hypnotically within. It was as if Chartog was a living gateway, and the wet slime was all that held the creature together and kept it from discorporating.

The stench of the mist was overwhelming, and F.A.K.K.² took another step back. She nearly fell into Odin's arms, but he held her steady, and moved forward.

"The surest way to Shantaar is through me," Chartog coaxed, and the tongue hovered like a cobra, waiting for its moment to strike.

Chartog took Odin's hand, and the old wizard leaned down to kiss that hideous, suppurating sore of a face. The toad-creature sighed and, after a beat, opened wide its green mossy robes once more. Odin simply stepped within their folds and vanished.

"You shall never cross, my sweet," Chartog said dismissively, and closed its robes against F.A.K.K.². The creature began shuffling back to the eruption of a hut, and F.A.K.K.² called after it.

"Whatever it takes to kill Tyler," she said, and stepped closer to the creature.

The toad-thing hissed and grinned at her through toothless, slobbering gums. Holding Zeek's hand in hers (and she knew this time with a certainty they were each drawing faith and strength from the other), F.A.K.K.² took Chartog's veiny, skinless arm in her other hand. She could feel the gelatinous secretions actually ripple beneath her fingers, but she was in for the long haul now. She slowly leaned down, and, with great reluctance, kissed the creature deep and long.

When she dared open her eyes again, F.A.K.K.² was in the vortex, and Odin was waiting for her and little Zeek. She smeared the goo away from her lips, and looked at Zeek. His eyes—each and every one—were full of trust and faith in her. So many eyes, so much faith.

What was power without faith to temper it?

Why, it was Tyler, of course.

And faith without power was Germain St. Germain and the rest of the Psycho Crew. That ragtag lot of losers followed Tyler because he was the only one who offered a vision, however warped, that gave them hope, a chance at being something other than just a nameless drone working for one of the faceless corporations. And they were so desperate to believe in his vision that they would do anything, kill anyone, that Tyler ordered. The dead man at the oasis was just a boy who died blind. That happened, sometimes, to those who allowed others to see for them.

The trio floated lazily and dizzily through the void, falling sideways and up, crossing over six magnificent landscapes as effortlessly as the shadows of clouds. And these mystical horizons all seemed to share one vanishing point, joining together to form the Seventh Bridge of Shantaar. The light that rose from it was dazzling, but it was more than that. It was too big to look at, and F.A.K.K.² had to turn her head and shield her eyes or be struck blind.

The three gracefully tilted, zoomed down, and landed on the Seventh Bridge. F.A.K.K.² felt its sensible, reassuring weight beneath her feet, and she ventured opening one eye, just a bit, to look. She saw they were standing on a barge of heavy metal pipes, pulled by a gigantic cable. The barge floated like some otherworldly hovercraft on the clouds of noxious gas rising from the magma. She looked down again, farther this time, and saw they were crossing high above a moat bubbling with hot, roiling lava.

F.A.K.K.² looked behind them, and saw they had crossed through a buzzing waterfall of living energy. It was like the hyperspace portal, but had less truck with science than it did sorcery. She looked ahead again, and saw the smoke—

which she had mistaken for steam from the magma, but now realized was still all part of that living energy they had passed through—clearing to reveal the dark wonders of Shantaar.

"But, these aren't the Holylands," F.A.K.K.[2] spoke as much to reassure herself as to confirm her deduction.

Zeek chuckled and clapped his hands together. Even *he* knew that!

"No," Odin said, gently pulling the little golem back away from the edge of the barge, lest he overbalance and go head-first into the lava. "As I said, Shantaar is the shadow the Holylands cast . . . the dark to its light."

She looked up at the onyx city sitting in a sky veined with red and maroon and purple and black. "It's dark, all right," she agreed.

The barge sailed on, and soon it entered the burning city.

"I didn't get married to anyone last night, did I?" Lambert asked with a tongue as thick and stale as shoe leather. He had passed out at the table where he and Tyler sat, and woke with a flopping, bumping, blinding headache. Lambert tried to raise his head, felt the pain in his skull slosh from one side to the other like liquid in a cup, and put his head back down on the table.

Tyler laughed and banged the tabletop with his palm. Lambert jerked, and a black wrecking ball of pain began demolition inside his skull. His eyes felt like shriveled grapes.

"No, but we can probably find somebody for you, if you want," Tyler joked, and looked around the bar. It was midday, but the Dewlap never closed, and several of the revelers from last night were still here, passed out where they sat. New faces piled in, and pushed the unconscious reptiles out of their seats, claiming the chairs for their own. By that evening, the pattern would reverse itself.

"Please don't," Lambert begged.

Tyler shrugged. "Your loss," he said. "There's a cute little Chameleon over there in the corner, think she's had her eye on you all night. I think she's looking for a change."

Lambert wrapped his arms tightly around his head, still resting on the grimy tabletop. He was grimly convinced it was only the strength of his arms that kept his skull from exploding into a million fragments, like a hollow ceramic statue whacked with a sledgehammer.

"We have a big day today, Mr. Lambert," Tyler continued. He was not banging the tabletop, at least, but neither did he modulate his voice. "Dynasties to overthrow, armies to raise and all that. But first . . . how about breakfast?"

Lambert hurled.

Later that day, when Lambert was reassured it would be about as easy to live with the remnants of his hangover as it would be to kill himself, he went off to procure some female companionship for Tyler. The smell of open sewers followed Lambert through the twisted, narrow streets, and he felt his stomach roll over dangerously. The heat was baking the life out of Lambert and the original Psycho Crew, but Tyler and his new army of reptiles didn't seem to notice.

And that worried Lambert. If Tyler could so easily add soldiers to his army, as he had done in the desert and as he was about to do in Shantaar, what did he care if his original group of fighters died in this godforsaken place? Lambert again told himself Tyler had no intentions of simply sharing immortality with them, any of them, so Lambert was resolved to survive long enough to steal some of the liquid for himself.

Things were racing toward a conclusion, Lambert felt. But if he wanted to be standing on his own two feet when that end came, he knew he'd better do as Tyler ordered and come back with a woman. The time had not yet come for rebellion. As he moved deeper into the maze-like center of the burning city, Lambert found his way to the fleshpot, where everyone's companionship was for sale.

Lambert stopped cold when he saw the woman. She was strikingly beautiful, despite her short, jagged hair and green-tinted skin. He moved closer to her, and she regarded him with a fire in her eyes that had long vanished from the eyes of the other women in this part of the city. Closer now, Lambert could see the woman had numerous bruises that she tried to conceal with green-and-black tiger-striped makeup.

"What do you want?" she asked him, diffidently.

"Eternal life," he answered. "But for now, you'll do."

The thirsty sands drank the blood as soon as it spilled.

Tyler watched with a vague sense of interest as the two brawling lizards fought each other down in the arena. His hooded eyes scanned the amphitheater audience, flitting from one creature to the next. There were quite a few big bruisers watching the scrap, and probably several more in the slave pens down below, who would in turn be let out to duel in the arena, like ancient gladiators. Tyler thought there were more than enough strong backs and tiny brains here to suit his purpose—cannon fodder to take the heat when he led them against the Holylands.

The audience roared with excitement, and Tyler looked to see what had happened. The first lizard had dealt its opponent a gruesome slash across its soft, unprotected stomach. The wounded creature charged on, it taking a while for the message to reach his brain he was in deep trouble. When the news finally broke, he stumbled forward, impaling himself by accident on the victor's sword.

The crowd went crazy and jumped to their feet, stomping their tails excitedly on the hardened magma benches. The victorious lizard stood over his slain opponent, his bloody sword held high, his head thrown back to roar his success to the world. He paced around the arena, arms held over his head in a wide V, accepting their adulation. He had no way of knowing that his foeman, even as he was dying, had buried his own dirk deep in the victor's heart. In a few moments, he would realize that the victory was pyrrhic. But for now, he was enjoying the fame.

Tyler shook his head and said to himself, "I've coughed up scarier stuff than this."

As the guards were dragging the bodies of both dead gladiators to the open pool of lava in the center of the arena, Tyler continued to scan the seats for what he was looking for, and found it. The ruler sat comfortably in his high, isolated terrace box, flanked by heavily-armed guards, but there seemed to be very few threats that this monster could not have taken care of himself. He was huge, and his body's natural plating looked as if it could have deflected the worst an enemy could do. The end of his long, lithe tail ended in a ball of spikes, capable of either crushing a foeman's thick, plated skull, or impaling him.

Down below, two more combatants entered the arena; they were grossly overweight, wearing thonged bikinis that rode them tightly. The creatures slowly, warily circled one another at the very edge of the volcanic pool, each taking the measure of the other. Then they raced forward at one another, faster than it seemed their girth might allow, and collided their huge, round stomachs together. Their short, fat talons locked into the other's arms, and they began to grapple toward the firepits.

Tyler was only dimly aware of this; he was making his way over to the shaded terrace on which the king sat upon his throne. As he neared the box seat, Tyler popped an ampule and drained the contents into his mouth. He pitched aside the empty vial. He could feel the liquid already burning through his veins like a radioactive bullet, fueling his strength, stoking his insanity.

Tyler shot the first guard who blocked his way, and stepped over his still-twitching corpse. He tapped the king on the shoulder and said, deliberately, "Excuse me, but I believe you're in my seat."

The leader turned to Tyler with a look or surprise and outrage and blank confusion. Tyler grabbed the king by his shoulder and jerked him to his feet.

"C'mon, other people need to use the throne!" Tyler shouted. The liquid was giving him a burn he'd never felt before.

The king's second guard moved to grab Tyler, but the king waved him off. His surprise had worn off, and he would handle this bloodbag himself.

The Psycho Crew had positioned themselves around the arena, their weapons ready, should the king's army try to stop the confrontation Tyler had instigated. But the soldiers seemed unconcerned, assuming the king would make short shrift of the meatsack.

The ruler snatched a massive battle-ax from his dead guard, and advanced on Tyler, a menacing smile parting his lips to reveal row upon row of serrated teeth. The audience had turned to watch this battle play itself out, and the wrestlers in the arena began to wind down their own match. The wrestlers looked at one another, nodded a momentary truce, and stood near the lava pit, watching the king fight his challenger.

Tyler feinted a rush at the king, and the lizard swung the heavy ax. Committed to the swing, the ruler could do nothing as Tyler flexed his mighty leg muscles and leapt above the deadly arc described by the blade. Tyler's foot landed on the king's head, and he pushed off from there and landed behind the lizard. Tyler balled his fists together and struck the king aterrible blow to the back of the head, and the lizard king staggered.

Now the crowd was roaring, chanting, urging this combat on to a gory finale.

"You don't seem all that popular," Tyler said, and delivered a roundhouse kick to the king's hard stomach.

The lizard roared and swung the ax and his tail. Tyler ducked the blade, but not the ball of spikes. The sharp horns pierced his side in a dozen places, and the king wrenched his tail free. Tyler glanced down at his wound, decided nothing inside was going to end up on the outside in the next couple of minutes, and threw himself at the ruler.

He brought his booted foot down hard on the ruler's bent knee, shattering the thigh bone and simultaneously using the creature's leg like a living step. Tyler grabbed the ruler by the neck and used his own momentum to bear the creature over and down.

The wrestlers were watching this exchange raptly, and began making friendly bets. The king's subjects were standing in their seats, drumming their tails on the stone benches, rocking the coliseum with their cheers for blood.

"What'd you do to piss 'em off so much?" Tyler asked the ruler, and tried to break the creature's neck with his bare hands. He might have done it, had the king not coiled his tail around Tyler's bull neck and lifted him off. The king whipped Tyler back and forth at the end of his tail, slamming him into the hard, stone walls of the terrace, onto the ground, and off the walls again. The sound of Tyler's breaking bones rang out like gunshots in the now-silent arena.

Tyler's bloody body hung limply at the end of the king's coiled tail, and the audience seemed to hold its breath as one. The king, himself suffering scores of wounds, turned his angry gaze to this seditious pack of rabble, and that look said there would be reprisals.

The king brought Tyler closer to his own face to study his enemy in death; the meatsack's face was swollen and the color of a gangrenous wound. The king's mouth opened, and he drooled in idiot anticipation of this morsel. His tail moved Tyler's head closer to the king's teeth.

Tyler's eyes opened with a snap. "Bite me," he said, and grabbed the lizard's tail in his hands. The meatsack braced himself against the stone seats and pulled with all his might, tearing the powerful appendage from its socket. The king shrieked in mortal agony, and his tail, still coiled around Tyler's throat, whipped and jerked spasmodically. Tyler managed to free himself from its clutches even as the king, focusing on his rage and not his pain, came after the blood-bag once again.

The lizard king brought down his massive ax in an overhand blow. Tyler rolled out of the way, and the ax sliced into the flopping tail. The tail reacted to the pain and snapped at its attacker, catching the leader off guard for a moment. It was all the moment Tyler needed, for he was up in a flash and was piggybacking the king. Tyler wrapped his steely legs around the king's waist and locked his arm around the reptile's throat. He began pulling the ruler's head back with an inexorable pressure, and they could both hear the vertebrae in the lizard's neck begin to groan and creak.

The king flailed, trying to reach around behind his own back to grab Tyler, but his short, stumpy arms were built for power, not reach. Tyler bent the lizard's head back a little farther, and something popped like a champagne cork. The king gasped, staggered around, and tripped over his own dismembered tail. The lizard went down, falling on Tyler. The impact jarred Tyler loose, and the king, wounded unto death but too angry to die before killing his own assassin, raised his ax once more and this time, connected with Tyler.

Tyler gasped and clutched at his chest, blood squirting through his grasping hands. He parted his fingers just enough to see he had suffered a gaping, sucking chest wound, and dropped to a sitting posture, his back braced against the side of a stone bench.

The lizard turned his attention to the now-silent arena, leaning against the shaft of the ax, trying not to show how badly he was injured. He called for his guards, and demanded they lock the exits and set fire to the coliseum. He'd take this traitorous mob with him when he went.

"Oh, *this* doesn't look good," Smegma said to Koontz, one of the other Psycho Crew members.

But the second man sat back comfortably in his seat. "Nah, this is just one of Tyler's . . . whaddyacall it, his . . ."

"Idioms?" Smegma suggested.

Koontz considered, discarded. "Close, but I was thinking more like . . . trademark moves."

The lizard had turned his back on Tyler to shout orders to his soldiers. The guards hesitated to carry them out, reckoning if they could just stall a few more minutes, the leader would die and they would be safe. But he didn't look as if he planned on dying until everyone else was reduced to ash and smoke.

Behind him, Tyler stood up, his chest wound healing as he did. The guard whom the king was excoriating gaped in awe. At first, the leader assumed he had finally gotten through to the dim soldier, but when he heard the crowd gasp, he snapped his head around.

"I don't know how many times I've told people: When you kill someone, make sure they're dead before you turn your back on them!" Tyler laughed, his voice growing stronger by the moment. He was healed, all right.

Tyler smashed the gawping lizard on the end of his snout, driving bone splinters up into his tiny brain. The king dropped his ax and grabbed his gushing nose. Tyler picked up the ax and broke the handle in half; he jammed the broken shaft into the lizard's snapping jaws, wedging his mouth open. He tried to break it with the sheer strength of his jaws, but succeeded only in driving the spiked, broken end deeper into the soft palate of his mouth.

Tyler hefted the thrashing lizard up over his head, standing at the edge of the terraced viewing box. The crowd roared its approval once more, louder than ever. Tyler ignored them and looked questioningly instead at the two wrestlers still standing in the pit. The wrestlers looked furtively at one another, not quite understanding at first, but then enlightenment dawned like a bomb blast. They both held out their stocky arms toward Tyler, thumbs up, and slowly, with great circumstance, rotated their thumbs down.

Tyler nodded. "Thy will be done!" he cried, and threw the still-struggling king into the lava pit in the center of the arena.

The ruler hit the firepit with a horrible but thankfully brief shriek; the magma bubbled up, engulfed the lizard's body, and seared the flesh from his bones. Tyler stood in the king's terraced box, looking out at the cheering coliseum.

"Permit me to introduce myself," he spoke loudly, clearly. "I am your new leader... Lord Tyler!"

The name rolled from tongue to tongue, and the walls of the coliseum were soon rocking with the chant: "Ty-lor! Ty-lor! Ty-lor!"

Smegma and Koontz were standing beside the new ruler of Shantaar, and they ceremoniously placed the rotting skull of the desert warlord back on Tyler's head. Most of the flesh had sloughed off, but bone and horn remained. It was looking more like a crown, at least.

The crowd roared louder still. Tyler glanced back with a sly smile at his royal attendants, and said, "It's good to be the king."

"Listen..." F.A.K.K.² said, holding up her hand. She and her companions were dressed in hooded robes and moved through the shadow-jumbled streets like acolytes on their way to devotions. But F.A.K.K.² had heard something that sounded like...

She paused, straining her ears to catch it.

The sound, echoing and re-echoing off the claustrophobic, tunnel-like streets, came again: "Ty-lor! Ty-lor!"

F.A.K.K.² slammed her fist into the porous wall, as dark as char, and let fly a string of invectives she was, until this moment, unaware she even knew.

"He *is* still alive!" she said. "After all this..."

She stood at arm's length, her palms flat against the wall, cowled head hung low between her arms, chin resting on her chest. *No matter how much I pay, it's never enough,* she thought. But she couldn't stop now. That would make all of her other losses even more pointless, and she refused to let that be the case.

She paced to one end of the alleyway, listened, paced back to the other end, and listened. It was hard to tell exactly where the shouts were coming from, but it was obviously a place large enough to hold several hundred—perhaps several thousand—of Shantaar's citizens.

"Is there a coliseum near here?" she asked Odin.

Ten

Tyler's victory over the lizard king had brought the citizenry to a frenzy. The king had been a tyrant, a despot, a looter of the city's treasury and plunderer of Shantaar's most fetching females, and the oppressed masses were glad to see him gone. Tyler's recently-conscripted Igua-nomads had briefed him on the ruler, and the city's impotent hatred for him. It was a rage Tyler knew he could exploit, because love was never far from hate. They hated the king, and now they loved Tyler for disposing of the monarchy. It was a risky gambit, with the potential of bringing the whole city down on Tyler's head if his sources had been wrong, but it had paid off.

Now, he had not only the royal army to march at his back, he could easily demand that every able-bodied lizard in Shantaar join the attack on the Holylands. It took little to stir these creatures' hot blood—it was as if the lava that coursed through the streets surged through their veins, as well. It would be a simple matter to convince them it was time to march on the Holylands. But for today, for now, he would make no demands, other than that his new subjects should revel in this newfound—if fleeting—golden age.

Still concealed by their cloaks, F.A.K.K.², Odin, and Zeek entered the coliseum without notice. Everyone was too interested in Tyler. He had ordered the death-duels in the fighting pit to continue, much to the grave disappointment of the two wrestlers. They had hoped things would be different under the new administration, but barely ten minutes in, it was the same old thing. But even more insulting, as the two Sumo-like reptiles fought to the death, no one was watching them. All eyes were on Tyler instead.

The two wrestlers had tried to slip away, but Tyler had posted guards on all the arena exits with the order to kill anyone who refused to fight. The creatures quickly found themselves back on the edge of the magma pit, each straining to unbalance the other and toss him into a fiery death.

Zeek pointed toward Tyler and turned to Odin. "Master, he's the one with the key, isn't he?"

The old wizard nodded grimly, watching Tyler from their place directly opposite the royal box. "He is. And I fear he is far too powerful for us to deal with alone."

"I don't care about your key," F.A.K.K.² said. "How do we *kill* him?"

But before Odin could answer, if he even had an answer, F.A.K.K.² noticed a stone gutter above the terraced box, through which a stream of molten lava flowed. Tyler sat just below this trough, and F.A.K.K.² wondered if Tyler would make his way back from the other side so quickly if his body had been completely reduced to ash on this side. Would he resurrect from total immolation? Blackened bone and steam and ash? It was worth a shot.

She bent low and whispered something into Zeek's ear.

His series of eyes grew wide at what she told him, but he nodded his understanding and hurried off through the crowd to do as she had instructed.

"Where did you send Zeek?" Odin asked suspiciously.

F.A.K.K.² stood with her hands on the low, stone balustrade that separated the balcony from the next level of seats. "He went to see a man about some plumbing," she said, watching Zeek's progress as best she could. Occasionally, the top of his cowled head would just be visible through the chanting crowd, and then she would lose him in the mob.

"This is not the time," Odin warned her. "Tyler is too powerful right now for us to stop."

She looked sidelong at the old wizard. "Take a look around you," she said. "He just gets more powerful by the moment. He's like a black hole, drawing all of this–" she indicated the arena full of the converted with an inclination of her head "–to him. If he's too powerful now, what's he going to be like tomorrow? Or the day after?"

"It is not the time," Odin said again, heatedly. "We must find the key. Tyler is only one small part of the threat."

Movement on the parapet above Tyler's box seat caught F.A.K.K.²'s eye. Zeek, looking like a midget ghost in his acolyte's robes, had reached the lava gutter and was already moving into position to break it.

"Too late now," she told the old wizard, and pointed. Odin's face grew as dark as stormclouds when he saw Zeek and realized his intention.

Zeek braced his broad little back against the wall and wedged his feet against the edge of the stone gutter. He began to exert all the pressure his legs could manage, but even with his great strength, the gutter was going to be hard to break. It had to be, to channel such hellish forces.

Things might have turned out quite differently all

around, had Lambert not returned at that moment with the woman Tyler had sent him for. Lambert dragged the green-striped woman along behind him, through the royal chamber entrance behind the terraced box seats. F.A.K.K.² watched without interest as Lambert and Tyler spoke briefly. Tyler rose from his throne and stood before the unfortunate woman, gripping her face between his strong fingers.

Zeek thought he could feel the gutter starting to give, just a little. He repositioned himself to take advantage of this new leverage, and re-doubled his efforts. The gutter *did* move, and that bit of hope gave him renewed strength to continue.

"That woman is going to die along with Tyler," Odin told F.A.K.K.². "Don't you even care about her?"

She scowled. "Whatever it takes," she finally answered. But it *did* bother her. F.A.K.K.² could tell the woman did not want to be there—she spat in Tyler's eye as he moved in for a kiss. Even from here, F.A.K.K.² could see that. Still . . . whatever it took.

But there was something else about the woman's overt defiance, something that made alarm bells jangle inside her head, because the striped woman reminded her of . . . that was impossible, and yet . . .

"Oh, my God!" F.A.K.K.² whispered. "I thought she was dead!"

She had recognized, even through the paint and close-cropped hair, the woman with whom she had shared her life, and the place before that life began.

"Kerrie!" she cried.

And then she noticed Zeek had almost managed to dislodge a section of the trough above Tyler . . . and her sister. It would only be a matter of moments, and all of that scalding lava would come raining down on both of them. Tyler might struggle back into existence, even from wisps of steam, but Kerrie most definitely would not.

F.A.K.K.² gauged the distance between herself and the terraced box. She could never reach Zeek in time to stop him, not on foot. Reflexively, she drew her pistol from her hip holster and aimed it at Zeek. She had to make this one count, because there wouldn't be time for another.

She tickled the trigger, and the bullet struck Zeek on the shoulder, surprising him as a shower of sparks and pebbles flew up in his face. He squeaked his alarm, and scampered back from the edge of the roof, seeking cover.

F.A.K.K.² had already holstered her gun. No one had heard the shot above the din of cheers, and Tyler was too interested in this spitfire with whom Lambert had presented him. F.A.K.K.² leaned against the stone retaining wall, shaking her head.

"What happened to 'whatever it takes'?" Odin asked.

"That's my sister with him," she glowered. "I'm going to have to find another way."

"As I told you, this is not the time," Odin reminded her; there was just the slightest hint of self-righteousness in his voice. "The involvement of your sister stayed your hand until the proper moment."

Tyler held Kerrie firmly by the arm, facing the coliseum. She bowed her head, feeling terribly exposed and shamed. "Time to meet your new subjects, darling," he told her. And, raising his voice to be heard over the cacophony, he shouted to the assemblage, "Bow to your new queen!"

The crowd cheered. Unnoticed, in the fighting pit, both Sumo-lizards tumbled into the well of lava. They vaporized instantly, and it took a while before anyone realized they were gone.

"Blind adulation gets me hot," Tyler said with a leer to

Kerrie. He gripped her even more tightly by the arm, and jerked her along behind him into the passageway behind the box to the royal chambers beyond. At that moment, the weakened stone gutter at last gave way, and magma rained down on the palace guard unfortunate enough to still be standing there. The crowd cheered blindly. This was turning out to be a good day, all around.

Zeek had made his way back to where Odin and F.A.K.K.² stood at the balcony's edge. Zeek's robe had a burned patch on the shoulder where the bullet had struck, and he was still in a state of near-panic. "Soft one," he began, the words tripping over one another; he couldn't apologize quickly enough. "I'm sorry I failed you! Someone shot me and—"

F.A.K.K.²'s grim look told Zeek everything. "He has my sister," she said. "I have to save her first."

"You saw his power," Odin argued. "We can't hope to fight him here. We have to let him reach the Holylands."

But F.A.K.K.² didn't hear. "I failed her once," she muttered, shaking her head. "I won't fail again."

"Just a little more time—" Odin counseled. F.A.K.K.² shook his hand from her arm and ran off into the throng, casting off her cloak as she went. "Julie!" Odin shouted, but she was gone.

"Master, we have to help the soft one!" Zeek implored, his eyes bright with panic. "I know, my little friend," Odin replied, stroking his chin absently. "Let me think . . ."

"We *must*," Zeek insisted. "I'm not made of stone!" Odin looked at the little golem ironically. "Well, you know . . ."

"Yes, of course, but there is much at stake here. We cannot allow emotion to rule our minds."

"But, Master . . ." the stone man said, and it was clear to both of them that was exactly what was going to happen.

*   *   *

Behind the throne, through the corridor and within the palace, Tyler gleefully checked out his new surroundings. A large canopied bed, made from the buffed ribs of some hard-slain, giant desert lizard, dominated the room. On the wall above the bed, the creature's skull, watching the world with empty sockets. Situated at the far end of the room, a fireplace that spewed lava, as did everything else on this planet, it seemed. This was the room's source of heat and whatever light it had. But none of this mattered to Tyler. His attention was turned to the assortment of weapons the king had collected for himself: on walls, on tables, in cabinets, every possible kind of weapon. Axes, broad-axes, maces, spears, spiked shields, bows and arrows, cudgels, swords, dirks, daggers, cestus gloves . . .

Tyler shook his head in admiring wonder, placing his skull-crown down on the table near the bed. Kerrie slumped against the wooden chest at the foot of the bed.

"Okay, I admit, it's a little retro, but I love that lizard's sense of home security!" Tyler exclaimed, picking up the ax and swinging it. He set it back, picked up the bow and arrow and tested the tension. The king was probably the only one—before Tyler came along, anyway—who could have pulled that heavy gauge. He moved from weapon to weapon like a survivalist in a terrorist Santa Claus' workshop.

Kerrie glanced at the horned helmet on the table next to her. She looked to see if Tyler was watching her, but he was more interested in the ordnance than her subordinance at the moment. She lightly touched the tip of the great horns on the skull, and jerked her hand away in pain. Kerrie saw even that light touch had pierced her flesh. She sucked the blood from her fingers, and did her best not to look at the helmet again, lest she give too much away.

"Oh, what a hectic day at the office, but we're alone at

last," Tyler said, swaggering closer to where she sat. He sat beside her, and she inched away. "I like coy," he told her, and removed the distance between them. Fine with Kerrie; every time she moved away, it brought her a little closer to that helmet.

"My little sugar in shoes," Tyler continued, "you have no idea how long I've been looking forward to spending some quality time with you. Just you and me . . . like it used to be before the world got so crazy. Remember those days?"

" 'Those days' being a reference to when you kept me in a steel cage with razored spikes," she reminded him. He either chose to ignore the venom in her words, or failed to notice.

"Yes!" he said, his face lighting. "Yes! Yes! Yes! You *do* remember! So much has happened since you've been gone, I didn't dare to think—"

"Yeah, well, I've been through some changes myself," she answered, risking a quick glance at the helmet. He was too busy with his adolescent attempt at baring his soul to her to attach any significance to that look.

"I feel we've fallen in such a rut lately, don't you?" he continued. He sounded like some bad actor reciting bad dialogue in some bad holo-flick. Kerrie wondered quite seriously if this was how he truly thought romance went. Maybe the holo-flicks were as close to those emotions as Tyler had ever gotten.

"I mean, kill this, conquer that, and really, what's it all for?" Tyler asked, turning his palms upward. "It has to be about something, it has to be for some reason. Honey, I think it's time we started a family."

That one caught her like a sucker-punch, and she found herself laughing. But it wasn't with Tyler. "I cannot believe how sick and twisted you really are!" she said, shaking her head. She sidled a little farther away from him, a little closer to the helmet.

His rough hand stroked her soft shoulder, but it was more like some kid without a clue. Tyler may as well have been kneading dough for all the softness in his touch. He leaned in closer, nuzzling her throat with his beard-stubbled chin. It felt like needles to Kerrie.

"Compliments will get you everywhere," he purred. "After you get to know me a little better, I think you'll find I'm just like everyone else … self-absorbed … sadistic … with an insatiable drive to own it all. In short, a yuppie."

He kissed her jawline, his whiskers bristling on her soft flesh. Tyler lay back on the bed; the mattress was hard, of course. Everything was hard on this world; life, death, everything.

"All I want is the love of a good woman," he summed it up. "And immortality. Actually, immortality, then the love of a good woman. Is that so wrong?" And now his case was before the jury.

"Where do I fit into all this?" she asked. She moved toward him where he lay on the bed, like the tigress she had been painted to resemble.

"By my side, of course," he said, and put his arms behind his head. She leaned down and lightly kissed the corner of his mouth. "For all eternity."

This was where it started to get tricky for her, to continue to pretend desire when all she felt for this terrible creature was hatred. *The worst my tongue can tell, I wish for you,* she thought.

"Well, it'd take quite a man to please me for that long," she purred, wrapping his long hair around her fingers. Kerrie pulled him closer, his face to her chest, and hugged him to her. And with her free hand, she picked up the heavy skull helmet from the table. It was heavier than she'd expected, and she almost dropped it. If she did, she would never get another chance.

"Well, my charm and chiseled good looks have never let me down yet," he told her warm, sweet chest.

"Feeling horny?" she asked with a high, crazy laugh, and pushed him away from her. As she did, she swung the helmet, driving the massive horns through first one side of Tyler's throat, then out the other. Blood fountained in a jittering, jumping explosion, and Tyler stumbled back, his mouth gaping, his eyes wide.

Tyler fumbled in his boot and pulled out one of the ampules of liquid. His blood-slickened fingers made it difficult to hold, and it slipped from his hand and bounced on the bed. Kerrie knew she had to keep him from it, and she lunged to throw herself across the vial. Tyler sensed her intentions and delivered a powerful blow to her chin, snapping her head back and throwing her off the bed.

She hit the floor hard, but she forced herself to keep moving. Kerrie grabbed Tyler's pistol, but couldn't get it unholstered. She cursed and tried to fire it through the holster, but she had been unable to aim, and the bullet *whang*ed off the stone fireplace, missing Tyler completely. Tyler didn't notice; he barely managed to uncork the vial and drink the fluid before his legs went wobbly and he sat down hard, his entire upper body black with his own blood.

Kerrie could only watch with frightened eyes as the hideous wound began to heal. He stared at her with the fires of madness burning in his eyes. "I'd planned on a romantic evening, but if you want it rough, I can do rough!"

He stood and threw aside the empty vial. Kerrie still held the pistol, but she seemed to have forgotten that because she could only watch as he stalked closer. But then, she knew the pistol would do her no good against this creature. She doubted that anything would. Had her thoughts been less muddled, Kerrie might have turned the gun on herself.

"I'm gonna rrrrrrip you in half!" he told her, his hands trembling with barely-contained fury. In a moment, he would lose all control. Kerrie hoped her death would be swift.

But then the window blew in, showering the room with glass. Tyler instinctively threw his hand up to protect his eyes, but Kerrie saw what he did not.

"Julie!" she cried, and she was surprised to feel the burn of tears in her eyes.

F.A.K.K.² had rappelled down the outside palace wall into the royal chambers and now crouched before Tyler. One predator stalking another.

F.A.K.K.² moved between her sister and the world-killer, but she never took her eyes from his. She had learned from what he had told her in the bar; really, Tyler's advice was not so different from something her father had said: *Looking back over your shoulder too much can get you just as dead as not looking at all.*

"You and I have some unfinished business," she told Tyler.

"And you are . . . ?" Tyler asked, genuinely puzzled.

F.A.K.K.² felt the rage boil up in her like the volcanoes that pocked this planet, and she threw herself at Tyler. The force of her momentum rocked the madman back off his feet and they tumbled together toward the blazing fireplace. Kerrie could only watch in petrified horror what was about to happen.

Tyler fell and landed with his head near the gushing lava in the fireplace, and F.A.K.K.² tried to drag his head under the flow of magma. "Physician, heal thyself!" she spat.

"No, no, I'm terrible with names," Tyler went on, insanely. He was worse than F.A.K.K.² had remembered—killing this sick animal would be doing the universe a favor. "But I never forget a body, especially one like yours."

Kerrie shook her paralysis off and moved forward to help her sister drag Tyler's head under the fiery stream. Perhaps, together, they might have destroyed him, but Lambert had heard the ruction from the royal chambers and led a handful of the original Psycho Crew into the room. He understood at once what was happening, and grabbed Kerrie off of Tyler. The other henchmen moved to separate F.A.K.K.² from her intended victim.

"Let me go!" she spat, and flailed with her long nails, raking open the face of the nearest crewman. He cried out and slapped his hand to his cheek; his fingers came away wet with blood.

Behind them, Tyler stood, his face blackened, his hair smoking wisps from the heat. But his eyes burned brighter than ever. "Now I know you!" he said. "Club Dead, right? Honest, babe, I would've called, but I had to blow the joint. Literally."

He looked to Lambert, faithful Lambert, and said, "Why don't you shut the door? No need to wake the neighbors."

Lambert, still gripping Kerrie, dragged her over and kicked the door shut.

F.A.K.K.²'s captors held her tightly, her arms pinned behind her back, unable to move, but still she struggled.

"Sisters," Tyler remarked. "And it's not even my birthday!"

Tyler grabbed F.A.K.K.²'s throat with his powerful fingers and squeezed. She tensed her neck muscles, but it was token resistance. She could feel her breath being choked off as purple splashes strobed wildly before her eyes. A few moments later, she went spiraling down into velvet darkness, and Tyler relaxed his grip. She collapsed at his feet.

Tyler raised his booted foot, about to crush her skull.

The two henchmen who had been holding her turned away from this, and crossed to the closed door.

"Sure you don't want to watch?" Tyler asked, his foot still held above F.A.K.K.²'s unconscious head. "I've always wondered what goes on in a woman's head, and this is our chance to find out."

Things happened at a pretty rapid clip after that. Zeek, rolled up into a tight, hard stone knot, splintered the door with his cannonball-body. He struck the two crewmen nearest the door, then hit the floor and rolled toward Tyler, who still stood with one leg raised like a flamingo. Zeek slammed into Tyler's grounded leg and bowled him over like a skittle. He flew back against the mantel, cracking his skull and landing hard.

Tyler struggled to sit, rising into the path of Zeek's balled fist. The sound of bone breaking was as loud as thunder, and Tyler's jaw canted sickly to the side of his face. He fell back again, grappling with his shattered jaw.

Lambert was getting used to these impossible situations and the constant chaos, and he held fast to Kerrie, despite her increased struggles. Zeek bounded over the thugs as they tried to rise, and scooped the unconscious F.A.K.K.² onto his shoulder. He raced for the window through which the soft one had entered only moments earlier, pausing at the gruesome sound of Tyler wrenching his mangled jaw back into place. With a last, hideous crunch, Tyler re-set his broken mandible and began spewing his insanity.

"How's a man of romance supposed to concentrate under these conditions?" he cried.

Zeek slammed his fist into the wall beside the window, bringing rubble and lathe down atop Tyler and his goons.

"You're a bad, bad man," Zeek told Tyler, and, with the soft one still over his shoulder, leapt from the chambers. Tyler unearthed himself from the fallen stone, frustrated and angry.

"Stop them!" he shouted at his men. He grabbed the jerkin of the first henchman and shook him, but his head lolled stupidly on his neck like a balloon on the end of a stick. "Send out the order to stop them!"

"Uh, I'll see to that, shall I?" Lambert meekly interjected, and hurried from the room to do just that.

F.A.K.K.²'s rappelling rope still hung outside the smashed window, and Zeek gripped it in one hand to slow their fall. The friction of the rope passing though his fist caused him no pain, and the cable was strong enough to bear his and F.A.K.K.²'s combined weights long enough for them to reach the bottom, where Odin waited.

Odin led Zeek, who still bore F.A.K.K.² across his shoulder, through the seas of shadow clotting the winding back alleys and side streets choked with refuse, always bearing nearer to the dock and the Seventh Bridge.

"Did you see it?" Odin asked over his shoulder. "The key? Did Tyler have the key?"

Zeek shook his head. "I didn't see it, Master. But there wasn't much time to look."

"No, of course," Odin agreed, and dismissed the subject.

They reached the dock, where the barges that floated above the lava were moored to stone pilings. Two big lizard guards stood with their broad backs to the approaching fugitives; they were talking about the rumors that the Shantaarians would soon invade the Holylands.

"Can't happen soon enough for me," the slightly-uglier one said. "Finally get to see a little action!" The lizards harbored resentment for the Holylanders because their ancestors had been forced into servitude long ago to build the Chambers of Immortality.

The guard looked down, noticed the bloody tip of a sword protruding several inches from the center of his chest. He was puzzled, and touched the sharp edge gingerly. "How long has that been there?" he asked the other guard, embarrassed and annoyed at the same time. "Why didn't you tell me?"

Odin twisted the sword, and the first guard went down with a soft, rattling, bloody cough, as if he were trying to clear his throat. The second guard spun around to face Odin, who was still trying to wrench his blade from the dead soldier. Odin had misjudged; the remaining guard was the true danger, for he reacted to all threats quickly and harshly. The guard's sword had cleared its scabbard and was already coming down at Odin, and doubtlessly would have cleaved the old wizard in two, had Zeek not seen his Master's peril and acted immediately.

Zeek dumped F.A.K.K.² onto the igneous dockfront, and launched himself forward, tucking and curling into a stone ball as he went. The guard was too solid for Zeek to upset, as he had those back in Tyler's quarters, but Zeek managed to strike the lizard's unprotected wrist, jangling the cluster of nerves there and forcing the sword to drop without a sound into the lava lapping at the pilings.

The little golem nearly went over as well, but caught the mooring cable with his hands at the last moment. Odin had by now freed his sword and driven it up through the reptile's soft throat and into its walnut-sized brain. He tried to curse his killer, but his words made no sense because the sword had impaled his tongue to the roof of his mouth, so he left this life making nonsense sounds and baby talk.

Odin heard the sound of Tyler's Psycho Crew rumbling through the streets, barreling closer to the docks. He scooped up F.A.K.K.² and jumped from the pier into the waiting hover-craft.

Zeek still clung to the mooring cable, looking down at the bubbling magma. The lava swelled, nearly engulfing Zeek. Lava was one of the few things he feared, for he knew it would destroy him quickly and surely, and he froze with indecision.

"Quick!" Odin was shouting from below. "Jump! Zeek, jump!"

The stone man hesitated a moment longer, trying to overcome his preternatural fear of lava by concentrating on what would happen to his Master and the soft one if Tyler's guards caught them . . . and they would, if Zeek waited any longer.

Zeek swung his little body on the cable, and at the apogee of the arc, hesitantly let go. But his hesitation threw off his trajectory, and he fell past the barge. His stone fingers scrambled furiously, just managing to clamp them into the steel side of the skiff. Odin cast off the line and the barge began to move.

"Kerrie . . . ?" F.A.K.K.² mumbled thickly, her senses coming back like the tide, washing in and out. She tried to sit up, but the movement of the skiff unbalanced her, and she flopped over onto the deck. "Where is she?"

Zeek hefted himself over the port side and tumbled clumsily to the deckplates. "I'm sorry, but I could only carry one and I chose you," he said.

Odin knelt beside F.A.K.K.² and brushed her lank, black

hair from her eyes. "I had no idea things had gone this far. I never guessed he would become so powerful, so soon."

"Tyler's not an easy man to kill, Master," Zeek opined.

"Neither am I," F.A.K.K.² declared. Perhaps that was true, but the number and nature of her wounds made it clear she could be hurt, and some wounds ran deeper than these.

"We may have bitten off more than we can chew," Zeek lamented.

"Then we just learn to chew bigger," F.A.K.K.² said, managing to wrestle herself into a seated position. "We have to go back for Kerrie. I can't leave her with that monster!"

"There are too many of them," Zeek said, not unkindly.

"We've got to get you to the Holylands," Odin said. F.A.K.K.² opened her mouth to argue, but Odin pressed on. "What Tyler seeks lies within the walls of the Holylands, but a powerful army will oppose him there. He'll bring your sister, I have no doubt. You will have another chance to rescue her." A look of disbelief crossed her eyes like a cloud across the face of the sun, and Odin added, "Trust me. I've seen his kind before."

"We're about to see it again, and real soon," Zeek cautioned, tugging on Odin's sleeve.

Odin looked to where Zeek was pointing, and saw two of the royal skiffs pulling away from the dock. The skiffs were faster than the barge on which the fugitives were making their escape, and had weapons as well.

On the onyx docks, Tyler stood fuming and cursing, surrounded by the Psycho Crew and city guards. Over the boiling, hissing lava, his words floated, as if buoyed by the rising heat and deadly gasses from the magma; his words and rage were no less fatal than the lava.

"You've let them get away!" he roared, pacing back and forth in impotent anger on the edge of the pier.

His pacings brought him face to face with two of his Psycho Crew who had, until this moment, avoided his towering gaze, but that look fell upon them now, and they knew they could measure the remaining span of their lives in seconds. Tyler grabbed each man by the throat and lifted them high, shaking them like a terrier playing with a rat.

"Failure is not in my vocabulary!" he shrieked, and flung them off the dock into the lapping magma. They opened their mouths to scream, but the lava had dissolved their jaws and tongues, and the rest of them quickly followed.

There was no pity connected to these deaths, for the reptiles on the dock began laughing at the misfortune of their unlucky brothers-at-arms. Or perhaps they were laughing in relief that Tyler had, if only for the moment, spared them.

"There's nothing funny about death," Tyler said sternly, and the creatures stopped laughing at once. His face split into a maniacal grin, and mad laughter bellowed up like the gasses rising from the lava. "Nah, I'm kiddin'—it's a gutbuster!" he said, wheezing breathlessly, doubled at the waist, his hands supporting him against his knees. Spittle dripped from the corners of his mouth and hissed as it pattered down upon the hot dock.

The barge lumbered slowly toward the shimmering curtain of energy through which it had entered Shantaar, but it wasn't going to reach it before the skiffs caught up with them.

. "We're going to have to fight," Odin announced as calmly as a man might declare those gray clouds on the horizon would surely bring rain, and placed his hand on the hilt of his great sword.

F.A.K.K.² was still muzzy-headed, but she stood and unholstered her pistol, and set her steely eyes and jaw. Zeek placed himself before both of them; their attackers would have to break him to gravel before he allowed them to reach his Master and the soft one.

"I'm sorry I involved you both in this," F.A.K.K.² said softly, and the first shot cleared their bow. It was not a cannon, as they had expected, but a grappling line and hook which embedded itself into the steel housing. The guard began cranking the winch, reeling their own smaller skiff closer to the barge. Off starboard, another boom and sussurus of cable unspooling.

The lizards were running across the grappling lines like highwire artists. Odin tried to break the cables, but they were too thick, made for this very purpose. F.A.K.K.² shot the first creature onto the barge through the eye. He screamed and fell back, knocking into the next reptile on the cable, and both fell into the lava.

Odin was parrying with one of the lizards; in swordsmanship, Odin was one of the best on the planet. The problem was, his opponent was stronger, and his sheer brute strength drove Odin back across the deck, closer and closer to the edge. Odin slumped against the railing, his enemy towering above him, sword clutched in both hands over his head.

"Please . . . mercy . . ." Odin said hoarsely.

The creature laughed and brought his sword down, and Odin rolled between the lizard's spread legs before the blade could strike. Too late, the lizard understood he had been tricked by the old man. Odin shoved hard, adding his weight to the reptile's own forward momentum from his downward slash, and he tumbled gracelessly over the low railing, head first for the lava.

He grabbed the railing with his tail, hanging upside down scant inches above the roiling magma. Odin stood beside the tail.

"Please . . . mercy . . ." the creature implored.

Odin chopped through the tail, and the lizard continued his plunge to his death.

"Maybe next life," Odin said. "But for this one, I'll show you the same mercy you would have shown me."

F.A.K.K.² managed to disengage the grappling hook from the metal housing of the barge, and the sudden slackness in the line caused the lizards running along the cable to drop like dominoes into the magma. She swung the weighted end of the grappling line over her head as if it were a lasso, and cast it toward the skiff that had fired it. The skiff was held aloft by the rising gasses from the lava, but it was propelled forward by a fan on its stern. The lizards still aboard the skiff ducked as the metal line sailed over the heads, realizing too late what the woman's intentions were.

The steel line was caught by the fan's whirling blades, and wound tightly around the pivot. The fan whined and screamed like a creature in torment, and the skiff began to rock and buck, up, down, side to side. The lizards tried vainly to cut the cable around the stalled fan, but it was, of course, made for this purpose. The engine began smoking, smoldering, and a geyser of sparks and flame exploded upward through the steel deckplates.

The lizards screamed as the skiff went careening out of control across the fiery bay, and at last overturned, throwing its occupants into the flames and lava.

But the crew of the second skiff had taken advantage of the mayhem to board the barge, and they were herding the fugitives closer and closer to the railing. The barge, no longer immobilized by the opposing pull of two skiffs, drifted nearer to the shimmering wall of eldrich energy.

"What do we do?" F.A.K.K.² asked Odin. "Go down swinging, or jump?"

"The latter would be quicker," Odin agreed, "but while there's life, there's hope."

Zeek shook his head, looking back over the railing at the orange and black and red magma. "I don't like lava. It'll take me longer to dissolve!"

"Tyler wouldn't like that," one of the Psycho Crew advised the trio. "He was very insistent we bring you all back to suffer."

Another Psycho corrected him. "What he said was, 'Bring that witch's head back to me, but make her suffer first.' "

"My mistake," conceded the first, and stepped forward, gripping a thick handful of F.A.K.K.²'s hair and twisting it tightly around his fist. He threw her over the railing, dangling her above the lava by the hair. "Let's look at this as a learning experience," he told the struggling woman. "At last, we answer that age-old question: why do fools fall in lava?"

He laughed, and began lowering her toward the magma.

Eleven

F.A.K.K.² was sure she was dead.

She could feel herself dissolving, but there was no pain. Perhaps the indescribable heat of the lava was too great to feel, or her nerves were burned away, and death would come calling like an old friend instead of a dark intruder in the middle of the night.

But when she opened her eyes, she saw she was not alone, nor was she suspended any longer over the fiery bay. The fugitives were traveling once more through the six fantastical landscapes, falling and flying all at once. Gravity was all nonsense now, and she felt like laughing.

The barge had continued drifting toward the dimensional gate, and the trio had bought a round trip from the guardian of the Red River. Once the barge hit that shimmering curtain, the fugitives were recalled to where they had started.

F.A.K.K.² looked around, wondering what had happened to the Psycho Crew who had entered with them, taking the trip unknowingly. She thought she saw them, obliquely, as if they traveled alongside them, but not in the same dimension, nor across the same Seven Bridges. F.A.K.K.² could just imagine the hideous troll, the gatekeeper, saying indignantly, "No hitch-hikers!" The Psycho Crew were doubtless lost between dimensions, the price stowaways pay.

And then, she, Zeek, and Odin were spat out like seeds from the moss-draped portal of the old witch's body. Chartog cried out in alarm, unprepared for this sudden return, and fell backwards heavily, landing on the bucket beneath the pump spout.

"Odin . . . Zeek?" F.A.K.K.² asked, brushing herself off.

Odin, sprawled on the ground where he'd been cast, pushed himself to his feet, using his staff and Zeek's shoulder for support. Chartog noticed a glint of something silver heliographing sunlight, and stooped to retrieve it. It was a dull silver amulet hanging at the end of a broken chain necklace, and it had been lying where Odin fell.

The guardian of the Red River surreptitiously palmed the piece. There was as much misdirection in real magic as there was in stage magic, and the old witch knew all the moves.

"Hurry! We must go!" Odin said, all but pushing F.A.K.K.² before him with his staff.

Zeek was tossing junk to one side of the buggy's wide bench seat, clearing a spot for his passengers. He had a hunch the guardian had probably taken anything of value from the buggy while they were in Shantaar, but there was no point and less time to argue the matter. Once his Master and the soft one were seated, Zeek picked up the rickshaw's handles and set off across the desert in a gallop.

Chartog watched them go, and opened its hand to inspect what Odin had lost—it was an amulet, but like none Chartog had seen. Engraved in its time-worn face was a sun setting between two pillars. The old witch shuddered without knowing why, and, acting on impulse, cast the necklace into the fiery gorge beyond its hut.

Tyler saw from the pier that his henchmen had failed to stop the escape of that bitch and her companions. For a moment, he had dared hope she had died while dangling over the lava, but he didn't believe it. Hope and belief are not the same dog running in circles trying to grab its own tail—they're separate creatures. Now he sat brooding inconsolably in his quarters.

Tyler was at a loss as to his next move. He held the obelisk in his hands, absently tracing the cuneiforms etched thereon with the ball of his thumb. He could feel the key talking to him, a vibration in the bones and the hollows of his skull, and it was telling him it was time. Time to march on the Holylands, and time to grab his destiny.

"Big guns, big key," Kerrie observed. She was bound hand and foot on the floor next to Tyler's feet. "You sure you don't have some inadequacy issues you haven't worked out yet?"

"Good one," Tyler chortled, but he hadn't really heard what Kerrie said. He was still inside the key, flying over the heat-shattered landscape, watching the world slip away beneath him. Faster now, as if the anticipation was too much, and the land below was just a red blur.

And suddenly, there were the gated walls of the Holylands. And beyond the gates, over the dead and the dying, the Chamber of Immortality, the mountain face around it carved in the likeness of a woman, the portal located between her kneeling legs.

The doors opened like a lover's arms to welcome Tyler, and he smiled beatifically in the glow of the light that washed out to caress him.

"I never dreamed," he murmured. "Never imagined..."

But then he was being pulled backward out of the Chamber and the doors were slamming shut, and he was bulleting ever faster back across the landscape. He returned to his body with a jolt, startled to find himself once more in these dreary surroundings, ashamed that he may have spoken aloud his wonderment of the Holylands before this woman.

The symbolism was obvious.

Inadequate, am I? he thought. Tyler stood, gripping the key tightly in his fist. The light that burned in the obelisk blazed through his hand, showing the bone beneath, illuminating the sharp, hard planes of his face like a demon's mask. His eyes glowed with hellfire, as if it filled him. As if he were hell, given form.

"Mr. Lambert!" Tyler called. "Prepare the men. We march at once on the Holylands!"

The buggy broke its axle not far out of Shantaar, and Zeek wasted almost an hour trying to repair it. Ultimately, he had to admit it was a waste of time, because the tools he needed to mend the axle were missing from their kipsack.

"Chartog," Odin muttered, like slow steam escaping. "That packrat must have rummaged our goods while we were in Shantaar."

F.A.K.K.² didn't bother to look back the way they had come. She knew the hut was too far away to return to for the tools. Instead, she fixed her attention on the jagged spine of mountains sitting on the distant, heat-rippled horizon. "How far?" she asked.

Odin studied the terrain, shrugged. "If we walk all night, we'll be there by morning."

Without another word, F.A.K.K.² began to march for the

mountains. Odin sat down on a low, flat black rock; it looked like the back of some great beast breaking surface in an ocean of red water.

When she realized the old man was not with her, F.A.K.K.² looked back for him.

"Julie," he said, "I must rest. I'm not as young as I once was."

Who is? she thought bitterly, but said nothing. He was helping her, after all, and as hard as it was, she forced herself to return to Odin's side. She sat next to him. Zeek cursed the broken buggy and kicked the wheel. He stormed over to his master and the soft one and joined them on the rock.

F.A.K.K.² smeared the sweat away from her eyes with her forearm. "Is it always this hot here?" she asked, making conversation.

"This is a nice day," Odin said. "It's the humidity that gets you. Well, that, and the constant volcanic activity." It took F.A.K.K.² a moment to realize he was making a joke.

"Good one," she said, glancing sidelong at the old wizard. She caught herself almost laughing. Almost being human again.

"What of your world, soft one?" Zeek asked. "Is it not hot there as well?"

It had been a mistake to laugh. She had let her defenses down, and Zeek's unintentional one-two punch knocked the wind out of her.

"My world?" F.A.K.K.² said, and appeared to be thinking. In fact, she was simply gathering her emotional armor about herself once more. "No," she replied at length. "Eden was beautiful. Eden was ... *Eden.*"

"Eden?" Odin repeated. "Then, your planet's history must tell you of the Arakacians?"

F.A.K.K.² felt she was on safer ground now. She could

discuss her world without emotion, as long as it was the distant past. After all, that history had never happened to her, or involved anyone she had loved. Of course she had heard the stories. Her father had told them to her and Kerrie at bedtime, as if the past was nothing but a fairy tale that may or may not have a happy ending. And, one day, she thought, this present would be someone else's past, another fairy story that may or may not end well. You could never tell how a story would unfold, or if it was ever really over. Endings were sometimes vague, or false. If you waited for happiness as a marker that the story was over, you might have a long wait.

Once upon a time, she thought, *and once again . . .*

"Of course," she said. "When they ruled the galaxies, Eden was occupied by the vile creatures. It was the memory of their obscene horrors that convinced my people to designate ourselves as a F.A.K.K.[2] planet . . . to maintain complete isolation."

Odin planted the end of his staff in the hard soil at his feet, and gripped the staff in his right hand. "I, also, harbor terrible memories of the Arakacians, but none more terrible than those of the human, Rutger, who led their murdering hordes into battle, shoulder to shoulder, with his psychopathic general, Moebius." His face seemed as hard and stern as the far mountains.

"He was a bad, bad man," Zeek added.

"You don't look old enough to have seen him, Zeek," F.A.K.K.[2] said. "You don't even look old enough to shave . . . or sandblast."

Zeek giggled like a schoolboy. "I'm not!" he exclaimed, and laughed again. "But my Master has told me the stories."

The stories, yes. F.A.K.K.[2] wondered why she had never realized the stories were a thread to the past. Every culture on every world had its fairy tales and legends. Perhaps they changed a bit from teller to teller, generation to generation, but they were the voices of the past, trying to speak to those in the present.

"Under their daemonic rule, my people were enslaved and forced to endure centuries of abuse and torture . . ." Odin continued. The voice of the past was strong and unwavering, just cold facts; but the voice of the teller cracked a bit under the weight of emotion. ". . . before finally rising up and destroying them all."

F.A.K.K.² nodded. "It was your people's bravery that helped liberate Eden," she said, and knew it was inevitable that she should help liberate the Holylands, if that was the way the story chose to end itself. The universe had a sense of symmetry, assuming you lived long enough to see the subtle patterns. "But what happened after the final battle?" By that point, her people had been returned to Eden by the Elders, and there their stories diverged.

"Many of the Arakacians were hunted down and killed," he spoke bitterly. "Some disappeared forever. Unfortunately, it is believed that Rutger survived."

He stood, still gripping the staff he had planted in the earth, and looked back over his shoulder at F.A.K.K.². "Julie, this man you call Tyler . . . I fear he is Rutger."

Within the walls of the burning city, blades were sharpened, war wagons loaded, and good-byes made, and then, Tyler's ragtag army was ready to march into battle.

A horn blew, loud, long, and clear, and the lizard warriors licked their hideous lips in anticipation of what lay at the end of the march. Their howls rose to a vast roar, and Tyler stood looking down from his balcony, nodding his approval. Soon, he would join them.

"All this...just to impress one woman?" Lambert chided him. "I'd call that overkill, wouldn't you?"

Tyler's gloved fist snapped out and gripped him by the throat. He jerked him closer, holding him one-handed over the edge of the parapet. Lambert dangled there like a marionette, his legs kicking, trying to find solid footing. His hands gripped Tyler's steely wrist, but he knew if the madman chose to really drop him, Lambert couldn't do anything to stop his fall.

"Sometimes, I wonder why I let an idiot like you still breathe," Tyler said, and shook his head.

"Maybe I remind you... of the man you once were?" Lambert choked.

Tyler glowered a moment, then pulled his first mate back onto the balcony and dropped him to the rough floor. Tyler turned his back to him, and finished putting on his battle-gear. Lastly, he donned a heavy metal forearm shield. Of no small coincidence was the engram Tyler had etched there himself: a symbol of two pillars with a glittering sun made of precious stone rising behind them.

Rising... or setting.

As Odin marshaled his strength for the arduous trek that lay ahead of them, F.A.K.K.² rummaged in her nearly-empty kit-bag and, after a moment or two, found what she had been looking for. She withdrew a sheet of paper, laid it flat on the rock upon which she and the old wizard sat, and folded it into sharp triangles, and folded these into smaller triangles again. Zeek watched her raptly, unconsciously rocking his weight from one leg to the other.

"Hobby of mine," she told him, and gently tossed the little paper airplane into the air. Even in this breathless place, the plane found wind enough to float, climb, glide, and Zeek clapped his hands together as if the soft one had actually invented flight. But at last, the plane got nailed by a downdraft and simply dropped onto its nose at Zeek's feet. He picked it up, carefully, gently, for fear of damaging such a delicate, magical thing, and ceremoniously returned it to F.A.K.K.²'s hands.

"Must be wonderful to be light enough to soar through the air like that," he said, his eyes still on the plane. Its nose had gotten crumpled by its crash, but F.A.K.K.²'s nimble fingers smoothed it out, good as new.

"So long as you don't crash," she said. She handed the plane to Zeek, who reacted as if he'd been given some holy artifact instead of a child's toy. "Here, you try it."

Zeek took the plane between his coarse fingers and tried to lob it into the air, but he tried too hard, and the plane looped-the-loop and pounded into the ground.

Zeek laughed and went to retrieve it. F.A.K.K.² supposed, given the way the universe works, it was just a miracle more things didn't fall out of the sky.

Tyler's army marched across the red face of Uroboris, like soldier ants, leaving nothing of value standing in their wake. What few villages that lay between them and their destination of the Holylands were plundered for their meager foodstocks, and those men foolhardy enough to defend their homes and family were put to the blade. A few villagers, sensing the way the wind blew, threw in with Tyler and his marauders, and helped destroy the very village in which they had lived for so long.

The great, rumbling wheel of destiny continued to roll across the world, bearing ever closer to the Holylands.

They found the wreckage of the *Cortez* just after moonrise.

It lay in a long, narrow valley, hidden from their eyes until the trio crested the rise of the last of the sand dunes. In this silvering moonlight, the low, rippling dunes looked like frozen waves on the face of the ocean. Passage could not have been more troublesome for Zeek had the dunes been actual ocean waves, for his little legs and body density made him sink waist-deep in sand with each step he took. F.A.K.K.² and Odin, on either side of the golem, would pull him free each time, and on and on across the treacherous desert they progressed in this slow manner.

"Tyler's ship," F.A.K.K.² gasped, and stupidly, her mind cross-patched with the handsignals she and Kerrie had worked out for hunting: *The beast is over the rise.* She lay on her belly on the edge of the drop, looking at the ship through her binoculars.

At first glance, she mistook the dark lumps lying all about the wreckage of the main surviving section of the *Cortez* to be twisted, mangled masses of equipment, melted into unrecognizable shapes by the fire that must have followed the crash. And then she saw them for what they truly were.

"Oh, my God," she gasped again. They were the bodies of Tyler's Psycho Crew, locked in a battle to the death and beyond with the invading Igua-nomads. Tyler had left them all where they fell, to serve as carrion to the scavengers of the desert . . . and as a warning.

The glasses brought their horrific bloat and decay right into her face, and she fumbled to remove them. But the sight they had shown remained with her, as if the image had somehow imprinted itself upon her retinas.

"There isn't time," Odin reminded her. "This can't help us."

"I have to check it out," F.A.K.K.² argued, her face buried

between her arms on the sand. She pointed to the two guards positioned outside the fire-blackened hull. "Why would Tyler go to the trouble of posting guards on a wreck if there wasn't something important in there he didn't want anyone else to have?" She raised her head and looked at Odin, who kneeled beside her. "It may hold some secret to killing that pig."

Before Odin could say anything more, she began slithering, lizard-like, down the sandy slope into the shallow valley.

Not that many miles ahead, in the desert, Tyler and his army stopped for the night. His war-tent was the biggest, of course, and took the longest to erect. It was also filled with many of the amenities of his hard-won royal quarters from the palace of Shantaar. The weapons, the massive bed, and, of course, the woman. His woman. It vaguely occurred to Tyler he didn't know her name. But then, it didn't matter. Why bother naming property? It was what you told it to be.

Kerrie was strapped into a yoke-like harness, a heavy wooden pole that sat athwart her shoulders, wrists tied with leather thongs to both ends of the yoke. During the day, she was leashed and made to walk along behind Tyler's throne-chair, which was carried by soldiers. Sometimes she fell, and the wagon would simply drag her across the basalt plains, flensing the skin from her knees and abrading her stomach. Kerrie received no help from the nearby soldiers when this happened; she quickly learned that lesson, and righted herself as soon as possible.

"Note to self," Tyler muttered as he lifted aside the heavy flap of his war-tent, and entered. "The next planet I conquer must have more trees." The orange glow from the campfire beyond the open flap ingratiated itself into the tent, but it did more than that. Its soft light fell on Kerrie's already-beautiful face and smoothed away whatever bruises or scratches or drawn lines she may have worn, transforming her from merely lovely to breathtaking.

"And more accommodating women," he added, staring at her. "Hey. Are you getting sexier, or am I just horny?"

She growled and swung the end of her heavy yoke at Tyler. He easily deflected the clumsy attack, using her own momentum and the weight of the pole to knock her to the ground. Her hands tied, she was unable to break her fall, and the air banged out of her lungs in a rush.

"Don't push your luck," Tyler advised. "Warm or cold, it doesn't matter to me."

The tent flap fell closed, and whatever softness the firelight might have brought was banished, and the room was crowded with shadows once more.

The guards posted on the *Cortez* had been on duty, without relief, since Tyler first assumed the mantle of nomad warlord several days ago, and had grown tired and careless. But then, word was out about the demon from the sky, spreading like wildfire through the region, and not the worst scavenger would dare plunder the wreckage of the *Cortez*. So the guards risked sleep, sitting before the closed hatch leading inside the downed ship.

F.A.K.K.² had managed to get this close without detection, but doubted she could enter the ship without alerting the guards. Kneeling behind them, swaddled in shadow, she kissed one of the guards wetly on the cheek, then dropped back down into darkness.

The object of F.A.K.K.²'s affection blinked awake, touching his fingers to his cheek, which was moist from the kiss. He glanced over at his partner, still dozing next to him, but with an unsettling smile bowing the corners of his mouth. The first guard landed a powerful roundhouse right on the sleeping man's chin, shoving him several levels deeper into unconsciousness.

"How many times do I have to tell you—NO!" the guard cried, smearing at his wet cheek.

"You say no, but you mean yes," F.A.K.K.2 said, rising. The guard spun in the direction of the voice, but not in time to avoid the heavy piece of pipe she brought down hard across his head. His eyes rolled up as if to inspect his skull for signs of interior damage, and he slumped sideways, coming to rest in the other guard's lap.

F.A.K.K.² opened the hatch and cautiously entered the *Cortez.* There was a dead crew member just inside, his body quilled with arrows from the nomads' raid. He had gotten as far as the ship's hatch, but it wasn't the arrows that had killed him. Clearly, Tyler had shot him dead as a coward for leaving the battlefield.

This man's death was no more horrific or tragic than the rest, and F.A.K.K.² stepped over him and continued down the corridor.

The ship was resting at an angle, so the climb up the slanted passageway became more arduous the farther in she progressed. But F.A.K.K.² thought that if she was going to find any answers, it would be on the bridge. Germain St. Germain had told her he was an officer aboard the *Cortez,* and presumably kept a workstation on the helm.

There were a few emergency lights glowing mutely in the wreckage, making her progress somewhat easier, but then, that beggared the question, why maintain power at all for the ship? It wasn't as if it was ever going to fly again.

Cables as thick as a man's leg dangled like vines from the ruptured ceiling panels, and small electrical fires still burned in places; presumably, they would burn so long, extinguish themselves, then break out again at some other point.

The command deck was on an upper level, she realized, and was wondering how she would be able to reach it when she spotted the grate hanging askew on the wall. F.A.K.K.² wrenched it free from its last retaining bolt and pulled herself up to peer inside the opening she had exposed. It was a service shaft, allowing the technos to repair the machinery and circuits within the walls without having to remove the steel plating of the bulkheads. Dull red emergency lights studded the serviceway, and she could see the shaft branched off at the end of the main access. F.A.K.K.² chewed her lower lip thoughtfully, and, deciding, pulled herself up and in.

The damage to the ship was almost as bad in the gangway as it was in the main corridors, with spills of cable and twisted steel, but unless she wanted to retrace her steps (and she doubted she could turn around in this narrow warren of conduits and cables) and try to find another way up to the bridge, she would just have to continue, and hope the way ahead wasn't completely choked shut by debris.

Here's a thought, her mind suddenly popped up like a sniper in the jungle. *What if some of those desert scavengers are in this passageway with you? What if they've made their home in these walls? Are you sure this is such a good idea?*

No. No, she wasn't sure of anything anymore, but it was the only idea she had, and there was nothing to do but see it through.

F.A.K.K.² arrived at the junction of tunnels, and paused a moment to try to recall the ship's layout from what she had seen in the corridors. Deciding, she angled to the right, and was rewarded for the correct choice by a vertical shaft at the end of this passageway. She knelt at the bottom of this shaft, gazing up. There were lights set into the walls, and ladder rungs to facilitate the climb.

And what if there's another of those furry things, like a whirlwind with fangs and claws, waiting for you at one of the intersecting horizontal passages? What if it just comes flying out of the tunnel and clamps its teeth into your throat? What then?

"I give up," she murmured irritably to herself. "What then?"

That seemed to quiet her claustrophobic thoughts, if only for the moment, and the moment was all she needed to finish her climb to the helm. She peered through the mesh grate, determined she was indeed on the bridge, and kicked the covering free from its retaining bolts. She dropped down into the command center, which was canted at an uphill slant.

The Captain's chair—and quite a big section of the deck plating to which it had been mounted—was missing, and nowhere to be found in the debris scattered about the helm. Tyler had obviously removed it for whatever reason only his madman's mind could comprehend, but the rest of the workstations seemed to be intact. F.A.K.K.² tried to imagine where the officers would have sat: first mate, navigations, communications...

She located the workstation that seemed most likely to have been St. Germain's (the glossy photos of women taped to the computer bank were pretty much the giveaway), and sat in his chair. The spilled blood had long dried and flaked away. She hoped he kept his personal log up to date, and managed to key up the video diary.

The emergency lights on the bridge actually dimmed from the extra juice it took to power up the computers, and for a moment, F.A.K.K.² thought the whole electrical system would fail, leaving her sitting in tomb-like darkness. But the last of the reserve power kicked in, and the gray computer screen filled with a sputtering, snowy image of St. Germain. He was clean-cut when this first entry was made, not as wild-eyed and close to madness as the man she had encountered. For a moment, F.A.K.K.² wondered if she had found the wrong workstation, after all.

The voice from the computer was filtered and staticky, as if she were communicating with St. Germain's spirit through some kind of electronic seance, and not the video diary. "Metal Mammoth Mining, Personal log employee ID: 47, 16 point 9," the log reported dutifully.

The image sputtered and fritzed. It couldn't last long, she knew, and F.A.K.K.² picked up the keypad, hit the function key, and voiced her command. "Computer, search: Tyler."

St. Germain's image wavered; whatever walls or curtains separated this life from the next were clearly not easy to penetrate. At last, the tragic, doomed face before F.A.K.K.² spoke, but furtively now, and there was just the first trace of fear in his dark eyes.

"Tyler, Science Officer . . . took over . . . ip. Son-of-a-BZZZTTT! . . . kind of power tri . . . BZZZT! . . . key to unloc . . . immortality . . ." The sound fell out completely at that point, and F.A.K.K.² worried it was gone for good, but it came back a moment later: ". . . total psychopath!"

She shook her head. Nothing here; nothing she didn't already know. She picked up the keypad once more.

"Computer, search: F.A.K.K.²," she ordered.

The screen grayed down, nearing the end of its battery power, but suddenly filled with brightness, almost too bright, washing out the images, but in a moment, F.A.K.K.² would be grateful for that.

"... entered Quadrant Six," St. Germain reported. His eyes were constantly darting back and forth, as if he feared detection at any moment. Even with the poor contrast on the screen, F.A.K.K.² could tell how haggard he looked, like some wild-eyed desert prophet who one day wandered into town with a message to deliver. "Colony outplanet ... Just massacred an entire commune ..."

She hadn't expected this, but the image shifted to the Eden colony, in the immediate aftermath of Tyler's attack. Her mind had been right about dangerous creatures laying in wait for her aboard the ship and striking at her out of nowhere; it was just mistaken as to the nature of those monsters. They weren't some exotic species at all, but familiar, everyday faces and places. There was no way to protect herself from the whirlwind of fang and claw that ripped at her heart. She would simply have to hope it got tired of hurting her and went away after a while.

On screen, the washed-out images showed Tyler's black-clad Psycho Crew dragging the lifeless bodies of the Eden Colonists into several piles, those piles being loaded onto the black fighters that would ferry them back to the orbiting *Cortez*.

"... charged to do his dirty work ..." St. Germain's voice sputtered. It occurred to F.A.K.K.² that he must have risked carrying a hidden vid-cam down to Eden with him to document these atrocities. Perhaps, even then, St. Germain had hopes this nightmare would end and Tyler would be brought to justice before some Grand Tribunal. Or maybe he was just covering his own ass.

The screen began to smoke, and grew brighter still. A high, shrill whine rattled through the video speakers, and the image blanked out altogether, leaving only a black screen.

"No!" F.A.K.K.² shouted, banging her fists down on the keyboard. "Not yet! How do I kill him? Tell me how to kill Tyler!"

She lifted the keypad over her head and smashed it down, again and again, into the blank, idiot monitor. The glass imploded, but she didn't stop until the whole console had been left as badly ruined as her life.

They're here, her mind finally ventured at the wind-down of her rant. *You saw them loading the bodies, so they must be here. Maybe, if you find out why, that will tell you how to destroy Tyler.*

After knocking the guards unconscious for the second time, Zeek finally had to admit to his master he was concerned about the missing member of their little trio. "The soft one has been inside the ship for too long," he stated.

Odin nodded. "Wait for me here, Zeek," he said, and entered the open hatchway.

F.A.K.K.² had retraced her steps through the access shafts, stopping at every grated service entry panel she passed long enough to peer into the rooms beyond, hoping to find her people, simultaneously praying she would not.

Prayers were apparently not recognized here in hell, because the next room she peered into both rewarded her search and at once dashed any hopes she may have harbored of finding anyone else from Eden alive.

She could see only a few figures in this dim light, and couldn't make much sense of the little she saw. She rocked back on her haunches, braced her arms on either side of the shaft, and kicked the grating loose with one mighty thrust. She dropped down and started across the room, but froze in horror when she realized what her eyes were trying to tell her.

The bodies of the Edenites were entombed in giant glass jars, bobbing in the mystic green liquid filling their containers. The bodies were all desiccated and mummified, as if they were ancient corpses recently discovered by an archeological dig instead of her fellow colonists. Their eyes were open, blank, and dead as marbles.

Her own eyes and brain revealed only pieces of the picture a little at a time, as if protecting her sanity as best they could, but now F.A.K.K.² saw there were rubber tubes inserted into the sternum and skull of each corpse, recirculating their bodily fluids. But the law of diminishing returns was taking its toll, leaving the corpses shriveled and withered. She hesitantly, reluctantly, followed the tube from the corpses to its culmination as a tiny drip spout on the outside of the jars. Beneath each spigot stood a small army of glass ampules, each waiting its turn to be filled by whatever was being distilled from the dead.

She moved from canister to canister, barely recognizing the faces of most of the dead, so badly desiccated were they. They floated like question marks, punctuating questions she could not hear, nor could she answer. She didn't know. She didn't understand.

And now she noticed that Tyler, or one of his mad dog henchmen, had painted as a joke on the side of the jars: LITE. DRAFT. DARK. IMPORTED. ALE.

"Oh, you sick, miserable, mother-grabbing—" she began, but lost her voice when she stepped into a stagnant puddle of the hideous liquid pooling on the floor. One of the pickling jars had shattered in the rough crash, and spilled its contents on the deck. She looked down, saw the body that had been disinterred from its liquid grave, and felt a violent chill. She knew that jerkin. She just hoped she was wrong.

She knelt next to the corpse, tenderly touching its shoulder; the body was almost weightless, and her hand sank into its tar-like flesh. The body rolled over onto its back with a fluid *THWACK!*

F.A.K.K.[2] felt despair welling up within her from some deep, dark place whose existence she hadn't even suspected, and then it was rising somehow. A weight that great should not be able to wing so blithely up, but here it was, bursting from her lips in a scream and rising up through the octaves with crazy ease.

And then the scream seemed to shatter like crystal under its own weight, and that part of it was done. Afterwards, there was only one thing she could say, just one word, but she said it over and over again, until the word no longer contained any sense, until her throat felt raw and bloody, until she was quite sure she would go mad, take her mind off the hook and simply refuse to answer any incoming calls:

"Father," she sobbed. "Father . . ."

A firm hand fell across her shoulder, and a voice said, "Julie . . ."

Tyler had excused himself from Kerrie's presence long enough to tend to some piffling matter Lambert had insisted upon bringing to Tyler's attention. Alone now, Kerrie tried to break the yoke that hobbled her by falling against the hard ground inside the tent, but the impact that juddered through the wood and her body quickly discouraged that. She would more likely break herself before the petrified wood to which she was bound.

She lay where she fell, the weight of the yoke pressing her down, making it impossible to sit up.

"Julie," she whispered. "Where are you?"

F.A.K.K.²'s pistol was in her hand, the barrel pointed at the underside of the man's jaw before she recognized him as Odin. She heaved a sigh of relief, but there was a bit of regret as well, because for one wild moment there, she wanted this man to be one of Tyler's guards, so she could shoot him dead. It would never even the score, but it was a start.

"I came looking," Odin explained, kneeling next to her. "I heard your screams and followed them here..."

He looked at the seemingly-endless rows of giant sterilization containers, and the rubber tubing, and the spigots from which dripped their distilled life-essence, and he understood at once what Tyler had done.

"Where the key goes, horror follows," he told F.A.K.K.².

"What does a key have to do with this madness?" she demanded.

"Not just a key, Julie, but the key Tyler now possesses ... the key to the Chamber of Immortality."

She regarded him with skepticism. "Immortality?"

"The Arakacians, centuries ago, discovered a tear in the fabric of the universe through which flowed a liquid capable of bestowing life eternal upon whomever drank it," Odin answered. "My ancestors built a chamber to contain these unnatural forces."

Realization dawned like a sunrise. "The Holylands," she said.

"The chamber could only be opened with the key of which I speak," he continued. "To prevent the Arakacians from seizing the key, the chamber was locked, the key cast out ... deep into space. Without their life-giving waters, the Arakacians became mortal, and were defeated. But Rutger somehow found the key, and the nightmare is beginning again."

F.A.K.K.[2] rose, walking slowly between the containers, studying the faces of the dead. A few of them rode the currents within the jars, nodding their heads as if in agreement to something only they could hear ... or perhaps sensing her thoughts, and approving.

"Why does Tyler need the chambers at all?" she asked, placing her palm against the cool, curved glass of the nearest container. The head of the dead woman within was haloed by her own hair, floating on the green liquid. "He's already invincible."

"Not quite," Odin corrected, coming around to where she stood. She pressed her forehead against the glass. Her people were forever beyond her reach. If she needed a reminder, this would serve. "The key contains two secrets. It contains a map that is designed to lead its carrier to the waters. This key also led him to Eden."

F.A.K.K.[2] raised her head from the glass, studied Odin's reflection in the surface. It looked as if he were floating in the jar as well. "Why us?" she asked. "What do we have to do with the waters, except for the shared history your people and mine have? If it isn't obvious ..." she said, indicating the slain colonists with a vague wave of her hand, "we aren't immortal."

Odin gripped his ash staff and studied the faces of the dead. He saw his own face reflected over that of the man in the jar before him, and looked away. "The liquid spilled on certain worlds before the breach was sealed," Odin told her.

"Yours was one of those worlds. But only trace amounts survived, absorbed by your people through the food chain. Not enough to keep them immortal, but enough for Tyler to distill into some manner of elixir."

"The ampules he keeps popping," F.A.K.K.² realized. "He has to keep drinking them to sustain his immortality."

She looked again at the ampules waiting beneath the spigots, the faithful waiting for the benediction. "He's been distilling it from their bodies," she said, and her throat felt as small and tight as a pinhole in fabric. "It's given him enough strength to get this far... maybe enough to reach the Holylands."

Odin nodded grimly. She guessed there was more he wasn't telling her, and he admitted to the key's second secret: "The key causes insanity to anyone who touches it."

She laughed without much mirth. "He was crazy to start with."

"But now he's dangerous," Odin reminded her. "Like a wounded animal, driven mad with pain."

The beast is over the rise, she thought. "I'll do anything I can to stop Tyler... or Rutger... or whoever he is," she assured Odin.

"I know you will, Julie," he replied. "Good or evil, if one being becomes immortal, life as we know it will end."

F.A.K.K.² looked at the countless jars, and the people who floated within like dead fish on a black sea. It wouldn't be such a bad thing if this life, as she knew it, were to end, and a sane, rational one were to take its place, but she understood what the old wizard meant.

F.A.K.K.² found she was able to hack into the Captain's computer on the bridge from the massive electronic brains within the lab. She thumbed the function key, and entered her commands. On the dull screen before her, faded and difficult to read, appeared the words 15 minutes to self-destruct.

"Self-destruct sequence has been activated," the SYSOP warned. The drained emergency reserves of power made the artificial voice slur drunkenly, but this was not some intoxicated rant. This was for real. Alarms and sirens began to sound half-heartedly, as if they were reluctant to commit. F.A.K.K.² had already ushered Odin from the labs; she wanted to make her last good-byes to her father alone.

She knelt beside his withered corpse, but the words wouldn't come. Not because there weren't any, but because there were too many. In the end, all she could say was she loved him.

In the end, maybe that's all there ever is to say.

F.A.K.K.² glanced at the hateful distilling apparatus and stopped cold. She looked again to make certain she had seen things correctly, and, accepting that she had, rushed from the labs, slid down the smooth, sloped metal deck corridor, to find Zeek and Odin waiting for her by the escape capsule launching bay.

"Soft one?" Zeek began, unsure what was going on. "What are you—?"

"Trying to set the night on fire," she answered, and shoved him in.

Ironically, that was Tyler's intention as well, but in a radically different sense.

He had returned to the tent to find Kerrie still struggling under the weight of her yoke, and jerked her to her feet. "Enough of this sensitive male crap," he said. "Let's party."

He pulled her closer to him, and leaned in to kiss her

mouth. He held the yoke fast, so she couldn't avert her face, and she felt his tongue flicking lightly across her lips.

But then a massive blast shook the landscape and the intense light from the fireball that ensued lit the interior of the tent without shadows. Tyler shoved Kerrie roughly away from him, and she fell backwards across his bed. He cursed and ran from the tent, into the incredible confusionof the campground.

"Do you people understand blue-balls on this world?!" he shouted at the nearest reptile. Tyler stopped when he saw what everyone was staring at: a rising column of fire veined with black smoke in the distance, over the rise.

"The *Cortez*!" Lambert voiced Tyler's fear first. "The *Cortez*!"

"My ampules!" Tyler roared, fisting his hands and throwing his head back in a blind rage.

Lambert knew what was coming, and knew enough to make himself scarce. Unfortunately, the reptile standing at Tyler's right hand didn't know the extent of his new leader's madness, and he paid the price. Tyler swore and threw the lizard down, ripping the broad-ax from the soldier's scabbard. Tyler raised the ax over his head like a woodsman about to split logs, and the reptile understood what a mistake he'd made in standing in that spot.

It was the biggest mistake of his life, but, on the plus side, it was also the last mistake the reptile would ever make.

His face and chest stippled with the lizard's blood, Tyler stood, panting from exertion, and turned toward the rising finger of flame. "You miserable witch!" he shrieked. "You did this! I'm going to make you immortal just so I can kill you every hour of every day for all eternity!"

He wheeled on his army, who stood watching the fiery

spike on the horizon. "Pull up camp!" Tyler roared. "We move on the Holylands—NOW!"

Within the small, cramped escape module, the trio could hear the *Cortez*'s SYSOP continue its emotionless countdown. The craft's engine whined, as if it were about to launch the escape capsule away from the doomed ship, but powered down with a spray of sparks from beneath the console. The lights within the module darkened, then emergency lights slowly came up.

"Perhaps we should walk," Odin suggested, trying the hatch. "It's, uhm, rather a nice night, after all . . ."

F.A.K.K.² shook her head.

"The hatch won't open once the module's engaged," she told him. "We're stuck. But the module obviously isn't going anywhere. Not in one piece, anyway," she added, sotto voce. *We've done Tyler's work for him,* she thought.

"How long?" Zeek asked.

"Four minutes to self-destruct," the SYSOP answered with infuriating calm. "All personnel are advised to leave the ship now. Three minutes, fifty-five seconds . . ."

Twelve

F.A.K.K.² thought Zeek could probably force the hatch open, but even if he could do it in time, they could never get far enough away from the blast-site before the ship went up. Even had they left on foot as soon as F.A.K.K.² armed the self-destruction sequence, they couldn't have traveled far enough or found sturdy enough shelter to protect them from the blast. There would be massive amounts of energy released in the explosion when the *Cortez*'s hyperdrive crystals blew. It would be equivalent to a couple of nuclear missiles detonating.

"Three minutes, fifteen seconds to self-destruct," the ship's computer stated flatly.

F.A.K.K.² again set the launch sequence for the escape module, and again the engines whined as they cycled up to ignition. As before, a spray of sparks erupted from beneath the console, and the power damped down, leaving the interior in semi-darkness and stand-by mode.

"Can't you make it fly, soft one?" Zeek asked, hopefully.

"Nathan could, but—" she began. *But Nathan's not here,*

and you are. So the question is, what are you going to do about it?

She unbolted the access panel under the console, and saw at once what the problem was: To prevent his men from jumping ship when he commandeered the *Cortez*, Tyler had systematically gone through each of the escape pods and cut the power line from the craft's brain to its engines. Thus, the power couldn't complete the circuit, and the system reset itself, awaiting input. Crazy as he was, even Tyler didn't want to completely destroy the escape pods, just in case he himself needed to jettison to safety.

Unfortunately, there wasn't time to splice the clipped wires back together. F.A.K.K.² became aware of Zeek's presence at her side, peering under the console. She turned to him.

"Zeek, I have a little job for you . . ."

The module boomed out of the top side of the *Cortez* like the bullet it resembled, its trajectory skittish, but nonetheless determined. The craft arced up into the jeweled night, like a falling star ascending to the heavens for one more chance.

Zeek held the clipped wires together between his stone fists, using his hands to contain a scary load of energy. Zeek said it didn't hurt, but F.A.K.K.² suspected that was just brave talk. He looked scared, she thought, but not for himself. He was frightened of failing his master and the soft one.

Moments later, the *Cortez* vanished in a blinding white light, and a giant tree of fire with spreading leaves of black smoke grew up from where the evil ship once stood. It was not the burial F.A.K.K.² might have hoped for her people, but at least it gave them back the dignity Tyler had stolen.

She stopped herself from looking back through the little portal.

"I remember, Dad," Julie whispered, and smiled.

The blastwaves caught up with the escape craft and it jerked and juddered like a toboggan overshooting the snow and skidding on dry pavement. The ship's gyros tried to compensate, but it was an escape pod, after all, not a fighter, and there was not much to do but hang on.

The glow from the swirling firestorm painted the desert and the night sky the color of blood.

"You missed a spot," Tyler said, watching the crimson sky from the rise as his men struck camp. "But I'll touch it up for you."

The army was ready to march, and the light from the burning ship lit their way.

The escape craft's trajectory brought it down just a couple kliks away from the gates of the Holylands. Inside the module, altimeters sensed the shell's descent, and instant-hardening crash foam was deployed, to absorb the shock of the landing impact.

Within moments, the foam dissolved, and F.A.K.K.² released the hatch locks. The door opened and she stepped out, followed by Odin and Zeek.

"Good job, Zeek," F.A.K.K.² acknowledged. "We would've been sunk without you."

Odin inclined his head in the direction of the fiery maelstrom, or, more accurately, the cloud of dust rising on the table-top horizon. "Rutger's army," he said. "They're marching on the Holylands, even now."

"How long, Master?" Zeek asked.

Odin studied the cloud. It seemed to be larger and much nearer already. "Daybreak," he supposed. "Perhaps sooner."

"Guess we'd better get moving, then," F.A.K.K.² said, and set off for the mountains.

Zeek hurried to catch up and, after a beat, Odin followed.

The guard on the gate was able to see the approaching trio well before they reached the Holylands, thanks to the light from the burning Cortez. He had alerted the Three Elders of Odin's imminent return, and they anxiously waited for what news he carried back to them.

Odin was not alone, the Elders saw, and were instantly wary of this strange woman.

Archers stood poised along the ramparts, minutely adjusting the trajectory of their nocked arrows to track the trio's approach, should they need to let the deadly cargo fly. F.A.K.K.² looked up at them without raising her head.

"Let me guess," she said to Odin. "You don't get many salesmen around here."

"They suspect all strangers," Odin said simply, and raised his staff as a signal to let the guard know the old wizard was not in danger, and all was well. Somewhere within the great, walled city, a horn blew, and the massive gates, crisscrossed with thick beams and studded with rust-colored spikes (as she got a little closer, F.A.K.K.² saw that it wasn't rust that discolored the spikes, but dried blood), swung outward, allowing them entry to the large, vaulted foyer.

"Seems like I'm the one outnumbered here," F.A.K.K.² reminded Odin hotly. "If anyone should be suspicious . . ."

She became instantly aware of the archers inside the foyer as well, watching their approach from the niches within the stone wall, and fell silent.

At the end of the long, broad stone foyer, a heavy steel portcullis trundled up into place, allowing the trio entry to the Holylands.

The steel gate slammed back down as soon as they had cleared the threshold, and despite herself, F.A.K.K.² could not help but gasp in awe at the walled city unfolding before her.

Odin had spoken rightly when he called Shantaar the shadow of the Holylands' light, for the buildings here were made of translucent, alabaster stone, and great, cobbled streets lined with obsidian statuary spread out in neatly ordered grids, unlike the rumble-tumble rat's warren streets of Shantaar. The buildings were like ancient ziggurats, their peaks planed off. Great, gleaming white obelisks jutted up as straight as soldiers on parade at the four corners of the buildings, and minarets sat atop towers like a king's crown. In the distance (not rippled or hazed by heat, F.A.K.K.² realized, and with that realization, she felt a chill. She suspected heat did not pound like a hammer on an anvil here within these walls) was a domed, windowless building, surrounded by more of the great stone spires.

Trees and close-cropped shrubbery bordered the long, shallow reflecting pools of clear water that shimmered in the pearly, pre-dawn light, and F.A.K.K.² reacted with a start when she recognized the soft trilling and cooing of birds. She had not noticed the absence of birds until now, had forgotten the simple beauty in their song. She stood facing the mountains at the base of which the Holylands nuzzled like a puppy at its mother's breast, and a cool, soft breeze gently lifted her dark bangs from her high, clear forehead. The breeze was not hot and gritty, as blew in the desert when there was breeze at all—this was like the breath of life into drowned lungs.

No wonder the Shantaarians want to conquer the Holy-lands, she thought. Nipping at the heels of that, she imagined Tyler and his bloodthirsty minions storming into this gated oasis, and her memory dredged up a ludicrous cross-reference of when she and Kerrie's adolescent rough-housing would result in the breakage of some little toy or whatnot, and her mother would admonish them, saying, *"You see? This is why we can never have anything nice."*

The absurdity of that comment, juxtaposed with their immediate dire situation, made F.A.K.K.[2] break into laughter. The Elders regarded her as if the sun had baked her brain to the size and general usefulness of a date. She laughed harder and waved them off.

"Nothing," she said, her face red with breathlessness. "Just remembering something—" And she was off again, sailing away on seizures of laughter.

"The key," the main Elder said in a voice that cut across F.A.K.K.[2]'s laughter. "Is it here?"

"I fear so," Odin replied, studying his companion. She had gotten it under control finally, and stood relaxed and alert. "The key has returned to Uroboris, but worse . . . it's in the hands of Rutger!"

"Rutger!" the Elders gasped as one, sounding like some odd three-headed creature. They murmured amongst themselves, regarding F.A.K.K.[2] with darting, wary eyes.

"Hey, we only went out a few times," she said flippantly, hoping to lighten the mood but falling considerably short of the desired results. "It was an abusive relationship, so I ended it . . . by trying to kill him."

She wanted to tweak their noses, but wasn't sure why. Perhaps because she had learned from her father the difference between authority and authoritarian, or perhaps it was because they had paradise here in their grasp, and as far as they were concerned, no one was worthy of admittance. They had used the slow-witted Shantaarians long ago to build this place and their Chamber, and then cast them out, once the lizards' usefulness was at an end.

"As we speak, Rutger's murderous hordes descend upon our holy city," Odin said. "The day we've dreaded for so long is finally here."

The main Elder could hold his sharp tongue no longer, and he addressed Odin as if F.A.K.K.² were not there, or as if she were some odd pet he had picked up along his travels. "Who is this malodorous stranger?" he asked primly.

"She is a great warrior goddess, come from the stars to help us," Odin answered.

F.A.K.K.² hadn't felt this awkward since her first date, nor this scrutinized. "Hardly that," she said, trying to fall in line with the sense of prevailing decorum. "But give me a weapon and I'll do what I can."

"As you wish," the main Elder replied, sniffing the air and crinkling his nose as he did. "But first, please accept our—ahem—hospitality." He clapped his hands twice, the fingers of one hand tapping the palm of the other. One of the guards stepped forward two measured paces. "Take our guest to the baths . . . quickly," the Elder said, disdainfully.

As F.A.K.K.² followed the guard, she raised her arm and sniffed. Impulsively, she put her hand under her raised armpit and made a rude noise, making the Elder, his back to her, shiver with disgust.

The planed and orderly lines of the outside architecture continued inside the quarters to which F.A.K.K.² was taken; everything was spacious and open and tiered, while the ceilings and corridors, like the doors and windows, were slightly arched. Early morning sunlight spilled like liquid through the roundel skylights, printing ovoid spots on the floor and wall.

F.A.K.K.²'s bathing pool was an ornately detailed miniature version of the reflecting pools outside, and cascading spouts of water bubbled playfully up from the surface of the baths.

She laid the back of her head against the low tiled banking of the pool, and allowed her body to float on the effervescent waters. Our lives are lived in anticipation of the days of heaven, she thought, and smiled languidly. A few moments later, she was asleep, but the smile remained.

Not far from the walled city, Tyler's army paused to study the lay of the land. They would pitch tents, bring up siege dragons, set rank. Tyler had no pretenses that this would be easy. He would lose many of the lizard warriors with every attacking wave the Holylanders repelled, but what did he care? He'd shatter the whole planet if that's what it took to walk through those gates.

He felt a pustule open on his face, and wiped the goo away from his cheek with the back of his hand. He glanced down and saw he had wiped away a gobbet of his flesh, as well. His heart broke into a wild gallop: his old wounds were re-opening.

"So soon?" he asked softly, like a frightened child in the dark. "I thought I had more time..."

Without a constant supply of the liquid to repair his countless wounds, Tyler knew he was a dead man. The attack had to be soon, and it had to be successful. He could not afford to wait it out.

Tyler opened his hand and looked at the last ampule of forever fluid. That was it. With the *Cortez* destroyed, the only other source of the waters was within the Chamber of

Immortality. Tyler closed his hand into a tight ball encircling the last popper. He could withstand the pain his re-emerging wounds caused him for as long as it took to take the city, and kill that meddlesome witch. His hatred and this last vial would just have to get him through the rest.

The key hummed in his belt like a struck tuning fork, urging him on. Tyler wanted time to think, to plan his attack, to approach this with all the cool logic and mathematical precision he used to enjoy.

The key's vibrations grew more intense, and rattled those thoughts and memories right out of Tyler's aching skull.

He raised his hand and, on his order, the troops began to march again.

The alarm went through the mountain city just after sunrise, and F.A.K.K.² ran from her quarters, pulling on her battle armor as she went. She clambered up the steps to the ramparts above the great gate, and watched as Tyler's warriors assembled for a massive assault.

The earth shook as huge, multi-horned, multi-tusked Tricer-iguanas pulled the weapons-heavy war-wagons into the camp that was being hastily erected just past the reach of the best archer's arrow. These heavily-armored beasts would soon be called upon to give their life in a charge on the thick gates. F.A.K.K.² could see these creatures were faster than would seem likely, given their great bulk, for one of the beast-riders cracked his whip and the dragon he rode charged forward on thick, powerful legs with the swaying gait of a crocodile. It swung its tail as it ran, and F.A.K.K.² could see the tail ended in a deadly clump of sharpened bony knobs.

The rider of this juggernaut looked up to the ramparts, his keen eyes instantly spotting F.A.K.K.² standing amidst the rows of archers, and he pointed at her, an evil smile splitting his reptilian features. He said something only the warriors near him could hear, and they all laughed. Horrible war horns blared all the time Tyler's men were setting camp, and F.A.K.K.² could see strong and brave men trembling with fear beside her.

Thick clouds of dust hung in the torpid air, and F.A.K.K.² watched a phantom shadow move without care or hurry through the occluding grit. She knew that arrogant swagger, knew well the name of the monster to whom it belonged.

"Tyler," she spat.

The archer next to her shifted uncomfortably, but held his arrow nocked against the bow-string.

The red dust-cloud parted—although it seemed from the ramparts as if the madman had simply materialized out of the dust, like some blood-drinking creature of elder legend—and Tyler stood looking at the gated city, hands clasped together behind his back as if in contemplation. At last he seemed to sense he was being watched, casually looked up at the battlements and cocked his head to one side. He looked like a little boy who had some bit of mischief he wanted to keep concealed, but this was more than a spider down the back of some unsuspecting girl's dress.

"You," he said at length, pointing with one hand at F.A.K.K.². His other hand he kept hidden behind his back. Even above the creak and crack and groan of the beasts hauling the war wagons into the encampment, his voice carried high and clear. "You have been a *very* naughty girl."

He waggled an admonishing finger at her, and F.A.K.K.² thought again of her mother, saying *"This is why we can't have anything nice."* But this time, it didn't seem as funny. No, not nearly.

"You know ol' Tyler needs his medicine," he said, "and you went and blew it up. So, here's the deal—"

"No deals!" F.A.K.K.² shouted down. She had a very unsettling feeling she knew already what his offer was going to be.

But Tyler pressed on as if he hadn't heard. "You open the gates, and let me and my men march in and take what we're going to take anyway—"

"No deals!" she said again, louder this time. "We have a stalemate. We can last in here for a long time, but how long can you last without your elixir?"

Tyler chuckled, clasped his hands together once more behind his back. "Well, see, that's what I thought too, at first," he said, and now F.A.K.K.² could see he held one end of a long, braided leather leash. He began reeling it in, fist over fist. A smaller shape, still occluded by the chalky dirt hanging in the air, was at the end of that leash, and F.A.K.K.² felt the air leave her lungs and the steel leave her heart.

"Until I realized I still had one bottle of elixir left," Tyler said, jerking hard on the shortened leash.

Kerrie, the other end noosed about her neck, her hands tied behind her back, stumbled gracelessly into view through the dust cloud. Tyler held her in front of him like a shield, and nuzzled his teeth into her neck.

"So, what do you say? Open the gates and let me through . . . or do I break the top off this longneck and drink her dry?"

F.A.K.K.² bit down on her lower lip, and raised the bow and arrow, sighting Tyler's head, behind and just above Kerrie's shoulder, and pulled the bow taut.

"That's an impossible shot," the archer beside her said disparagingly. "You can't—"

"How 'bout you keep an eye out for me?" F.A.K.K.² said, and released the arrow.

The shaft struck Tyler dead in the left eye, and he screamed and staggered backwards, releasing Kerrie. She tried to run for the gates, but Tyler, despite the pain, stomped his foot down on the trailing end of the leash. When the leash snapped taut, Kerrie was jerked off her feet.

She fell hard on the ground, and Lambert cautiously moved forward, all the while keeping an eye on the archers on the battlements. He dragged her back, trying to use her as a shield just in case there was one more impossible shot left in F.A.K.K.²'s bow-arm.

Tyler wrenched the bloody shaft out of his eye, and the eye out of the socket with a wet, sucking sound. He gasped in pain, but refused to show it. He clapped a hand over the puckered socket, and tossed the gore-tipped shaft aside. The deflated eye still clung to it like a rotted vegetable on a shish kebab skewer. Humorous fluid dripped down his cheek like tears, and he turned and strode off the battlefield and into his tent.

"No mercy!" he shouted to his men. "We're going to kill them all! No survivors!"

"Just take your eye and go home, you big baby." F.A.K.K.² muttered sarcastically, watching Tyler's retreating back. He was already too far for her to hit, but that was all right. That one shot had told her a lot. She had hurt him worse than he let on.

Around and below her in the compound, the men began to chant her name, loosely at first, but before long they were all chanting as if with one throat, one voice.

"Looks like we've found our warlord," Odin commented.

Thirteen

The day passed in dribs and drabs, with Tyler sequestered in his tent and refusing to speak to his men. He was trying to cobble together a makeshift distillation device using the crude equipment at hand, but the scientist he once was seemed to be the first fatality of this war. He couldn't concentrate with the urgent screaming of the obelisk in his head crowding out his thoughts; the key kept slamming images of the Chamber of Immortality into his brain, insisting he attack now.

Tyler's wounds were beginning to reassert themselves more now, and his eye had barely regenerated; vision in that eye was as opaque as watching the world through a shower curtain. The pain was worsening, and Tyler struggled against the impulse to chug his last ampule. He would need it for the battle ahead.

In a rage, he destroyed what little of the distillation device he had been able to reconstruct. It was not much more than a barrel with a few tubes.

And still the key urged him to attack now. He clutched

the sides of his head, trying to keep out the voices, but they were coming from somewhere deep within his forebrain. Tyler gripped a flagon of wine and drained it in just a few big gulps. If he couldn't drown out the voices, perhaps he could simply drown them. He cursed the drink that gave him hope, then poured himself another.

Tyler's soldiers had had pretty much the same idea, but for different reasons. They were not accustomed to waiting, nor were they given to introspection. They were men of action, and, failing that, they were hard-drinking thugs. As the day wound down and the preparations for war were completed, the lizards and remaining members of the Psycho Crew opened the kegs and casks of the foul Shantaarian brew and proceeded to get sloppy drunk.

With Tyler removed from the picture, if only for the moment, there were those original members of his shock squad who had time to wonder just what they were doing, attacking such a well-defended city. It could only end badly for them. Tyler would gladly sacrifice them all, as long as it meant he was still on his feet at the end and able to walk into the sacred chambers. The smart thing to do, they realized, would be to hide out somewhere and come back when it was all over.

"I have a plan, Mr. B.," Bald Rick said.

"Is it a cunning plan?" Mr. B. Adder asked.

"Very cunning," his little companion assured him.

"As cunning as a fox that's just been appointed Head of Cunning at Oxford University?" Mr. B. further inquired.

The little man nodded. "Unfortunately," he admitted, "the success of my cunning plan requires that we be somewhere other than here. Perhaps as far removed from here as Shantaar."

Mr. B. could find no flaw in this cunning plan, and so,

under cover of darkness, after the bloody red wound of a sun had set and before the Gemini moons had risen, the two men slipped out of camp and back across the desert, where they quickly fell prey to the night hunters.

F.A.K.K.² had not been idle during Tyler's uncharacteristic delay in attacking the Holylands. Earlier, she had asked Zeek if there was any more of the same lightweight material at hand that Odin's buggy had been made of. Zeek smiled and led her to the old wizard's labs, where rods of the hollow steel lay stacked in piles like cordwood. She selected the pieces she thought she would need, and quickly sketched a blueprint to show Zeek.

"Do you think you could bend these rods for me?" F.A.K.K.² asked the little stone man. Zeek studied the sketch, sized up the rods, and got to work.

Tyler had more or less passed out from the combination of pain and alcohol. Without the poppers to continually re-generate his system, the alcohol hit him nearly as hard as any other man. He was almost grateful for that. He wouldn't be when he woke up in his own sick, but for now, the voices in his head were still, and the pain was just background noise.

Kerrie sat on the floor of Tyler's tent. Her hands were still lashed together behind her back, but Lambert hadn't bothered to tie her ankles when he brought her here earlier. She had been able to secretly palm a sharp stone when she fell, and smuggle it back to the tent, where she'd spent the last few hours surreptitiously sawing at the thick leather thongs around her wrists.

Once Kerrie was certain Tyler had passed out, she was able to quickly finish the job on her bindings, rubbing pins and needles of returning awareness back into her hands. She stood looking at her captor, passed out on the bed, left arm thrown up across his eyes as if he were some swooning heroine in a holo-vid melodrama, and thought for a moment of finding a dagger and plunging it through his heart.

But what if it doesn't kill him? she thought.

She studied his slack-jawed face. More of the gangrenous, suppurating wounds were flowering there like a bad case of acne. He wasn't as powerful as he once was ... but she had the sense there was still a lot of damage he could inflict if her first blow didn't do the job.

Kerrie moved closer still, and as she did, the obelisk Tyler wore at his waist began to glow brighter, filling the tent with its sickly green light. This close, she could just make out some eerie, otherworldly chanting, and she thought the key might be trying to warn Tyler he was in danger. He stirred restlessly in his sleep, as if on the verge of waking.

She stepped away from him, and the glow faded instantly. Tyler grunted once or twice more, then his breathing resumed an even rhythm suggesting deep sleep.

Kerrie recalled the layout of the tents and the war camp from Lambert escorting her here, and she knew Tyler's was the last tent—its back faced only the flat, endless desert. She laid down on the pumice, and slipped quietly out beneath the heavy folds of canvas. The tent fell back into place behind her.

She was looking at the makeshift pens in which the Tricer-iguanas were kept. They were docile at the moment, but Kerrie knew if these siege-dragons decided they didn't want to be penned, there was little anyone could do to persuade them otherwise. They regarded her with huge, black eyes full of muddy intelligence. She moved slowly away from them. Their night vision was no better than hers, nor were their olfactory senses heightened to any advantageous degree. They were not trackers, not hunters, just simple, mindless juggernauts bred for bashing down gates and losing their life in the process.

Kerrie hugged the shadows filling the narrow spaces between the tents, wishing she had at least stolen a dagger for protection, then realized a dagger wouldn't do much good against most of Tyler's lizard warriors. Still, she didn't like being unarmed as she was. Drawing nearer the main bonfire, she could hear the drunken grunts and roars of the lizards; a few sounded as if they were trying to sing, or perhaps they weren't able to hold their liquor. It was hard to tell.

Still, it was going to be difficult, if not impossible, to cross the encampment unseen; she would almost surely be re-captured before she could reach the gates. Re-captured ... or worse. Tyler was starting to consider other uses for Kerrie besides the usual man/woman relationship ... unless most men tried to find a way to distill their women into a life-giving elixir. If that was typical of most couples, she was glad to be unattached.

Kerrie had reached the last of the tents and stood swaddled in the jagged shadows, weighing her chances; most of the lizards had been drinking all day and were passed out, but a few remained upright, if not sober. She thought maybe if she could sneak a burning log from the fire without being seen, set a couple of tents on fire ...

Or maybe she should release the Tricer-iguanas from their pen. Anything to keep the soldiers occupied while she made her mad dash across the open sands to the gated city.

As she was deciding, she heard the sound of leathery wings from somewhere high above and drawing closer.

Kerrie looked up, at first not able to detect the source of the sound. But then she noticed a green glow, like two malevolent eyes. With those eyes as a focal point, she could then make out the giant spread of wings; whatever it was, the creature was enormous. The wing-span must have been nearly twenty feet across.

The lizards were oblivious to the thing's swooping descent. Perhaps it would go after one of them and leave her alone, and she could escape in the confusion.

Sure.

The creature dropped closer still; it didn't seem to take its eyes off of Kerrie. She wished again she had taken the time to find a weapon, because whatever it was, it had selected her for its main course. It was angling closer.

There was nothing to do for it now but go down swinging. Kerrie bolted for the bonfire, seized the end of a flaming faggot, and swung the firebrand at the descending bat-thing. The lizards watched it all in drunken fascination; it didn't occur to them to wonder why Ty-lor's woman was wandering around loose. Some laughed, most slept through it. Kerrie held the burning wood like a baseball bat, waving it over her head, trying to frighten the creature off, away from her and into the throng of lizards.

But it dipped a bit closer, and now she could hear it calling her name. "Kerrie!" it said. "Stop it! It's Julie!"

She lowered the flaming club, looking up at the bat. As it descended into the glow of the fire, she could see it was Julie, harnessed into a makeshift hang-glider. The eyeshine Kerrie had seen was the electric glow from Julie's night goggles.

"Julie!" she cried.

"Get ready!" F.A.K.K.² shouted, and swooped in low, skimming through the leaping flames of the campfire. Kerrie pitched aside the firebrand, and the tent near where she stood began to smolder as vines of flame climbed up its side, spreading like ivy.

A couple of the soldiers reacted to the intruder, and unsheathed their swords. It was fortunate the lizards were slow-witted, but even so, they weren't autistic. This was going to be close.

Kerrie stood with her arms upraised, and F.A.K.K.² held her left arm down for her sister to clamp onto. Kerrie grabbed F.A.K.K.² by the forearm and swung her legs up to lock the backs of her knees around the hang-glider's passenger frame. She struggled to heft herself up to a seated position, at least enough so that Julie could let her go and use both hands on the glider. The right wing was burning, describing a flaming tail like a comet. F.A.K.K.² banked the glider, trying to compensate for Kerrie's weight throwing them off course.

F.A.K.K.² was just able to nose the glider up, passing low over the tops of the tents, ruffling their canvas in the glider's backwash of current. Burning tatters of canvas dropped from the glider's wing, setting the dry material of the tents ablaze.

The lizards were shouting now, running between the tents in close pursuit.

"So, what's new?" F.A.K.K.² asked Kerrie, trying to keep the tone jovial, although she supposed her sister already knew they were in deep trouble unless they could get this thing banked and headed back for the city.

"I met the most interesting guy," Kerrie said, adding her own weight to F.A.K.K.²'s attempt to steer the runaway glider, and her own lightness to the mood.

"Really? Me, too!" Slowly, slowly, the glider began to wheel on invisible tides of air, swinging out wide over the tops of the tents, and more of the lizards charged out after them. The glider was just out of reach of the reptiles' hands and swords, but pretty soon, someone would almost certainly think to get a bow and arrow. "Maybe we could double some time?"

And now the glider was doubling back, over the camp once more, back toward the gated city. The fire was leaping across the first wing, intent on spreading to the other. Kerrie noticed it, but said nothing. Julie knew the score as well as she did. If her sister wanted to kid, well, that was her right as the oldest. Those five minutes made a big difference.

"His name's Tyler," Kerrie said, and now she had to shield her face from the embers that rained down on her from the wing.

"What? But, that's *my* guy's name!" F.A.K.K.[2] said in mock surprise. She had pulled her gun and was shooting at the Psycho Crewmen directly before and below them who had drawn their pistols. The soldiers were easier targets than she and Kerrie in their erratic flying wing.

They soared past the edge of the encampment, and now they were over the flat, sandy plain that rolled up to the city's walls. Behind them, they could hear gunfire, and bullets whizzed past them like angry insects. The fire from their wing printed the glider's shadow on the ground.

Tyler had finally awakened, the shouts of the men making his head throb like a rotten tooth. He staggered bleary-eyed from his quarters, and grabbed the first man he saw. "What's happening?" he demanded. "What's going on?"

"The girl," Georgeoff said, pointing toward the flaming contrails of the glider.

Tyler looked up, past the men, past the tents, and saw what Georgeoff was trying to say. Tyler screamed in rage, lifted the man off the ground and shook him. "Why didn't anyone tell me?" he yelled into Georgeoff's face, baptizing him with spittle.

"You said you didn't want to be ... disturbed ..." the soldier replied. He knew it was the wrong answer. Tyler charged through the tangle of tents, Georgeoff still hoisted high, and threw him like a shot-put over the rails of the Tricer-iguanas' corral. Georgeoff hit the ground with a thud, somewhere in that tangle of legs and tails, and his screams didn't last for more than a few seconds.

Tyler stalked away from the pen, through the warren of tents, some now reduced to smoldering rags and ruin, and into the main encampment. He watched the glider in the distance, burning a hole through the night, then pulling the darkness closed behind it.

"Of course, you realize, this means war," Tyler said.

Fourteen

"They're coming!" the sentry shouted from his watchtower. "Make ready for war!"

The cry was picked up and carried from sentry to sentry, and the battle horn blew its only song: after countless centuries, the Holylands were under attack once more.

Archers and pikemen quickly lined the battlements; the second line of defense, inside the gates, took their posts as well. F.A.K.K.² ran from station to station, making certain everyone was in position for the coming onslaught. That done, she quickly climbed the steps to the ramparts and stood in the front lines, watching as Tyler's warriors whipped the great Tricer-iguanas onward.

"Get the lava ready," she ordered. Steam boiled up from sluicegates above the door as the flow of magma was diverted to defensive purposes.

The first Tricer-iguana charged up the long, low flight of steps to the massive gates. The sluicegates were cranked open, and a gout of lava cascaded from above, covering the beast. Its rider was instantly incinerated, but the beast, maddened with pain, charged on, slamming its multi-horned head into the gate. The great bolt inside the fortress cracked and bowed from the enormous impact, but held. Panels of wood jittered free from the door, and daylight could be seen through the splits.

The gate was damaged, but it had held. This time.

The sky darkened with a flight of spears and arrows from the battlements; below, the nearest of Tyler's warriors managed to deflect the deadly rain with their shields, and on they charged, swinging their gruesome horned weapons. The soldiers were prepared for death from above, but were taken off guard when neat rows of hidden slits opened in the gate, and a volley of arrows spat out at them.

The creatures stumbled forward a few paces, and fell, the wave of soldiers behind them trampling their still-twitching bodies into the pumice. The second horde was cut down by the crossfire of arrows from above and straight ahead, striking their soft, unprotected throats and bellies. But the shadow army was too large, and their own natural armor allowed them to take several hits without fatalities. The first warriors to the walled city were the geckos, able to climb the smooth walls with their suction-tipped hands and feet. They moved fast, zigzagging from side to side as the arrows were fired at them. In a moment, they would crest the battlements.

"Get ready for hand-to-hand combat!" F.A.K.K.² cried, unholstering her own pistol. In her other hand, she held a gleaming broadsword.

The first lizard over the top leaped past the heads of the archers and landed on the narrow stone passageway, facing F.A.K.K.². It let fly a horrible, trilling shriek and charged at her, its mouth wide, saliva flying backwards like drops of rain. F.A.K.K.² brought her pistol up and fired directly into the creature's open jaws, through the roof of its mouth, and into its walnut-sized brain.

"Go brighten up hell, choirboy," she said. The lizard's momentum propelled its dead body forward, but F.A.K.K.² sidestepped and it struck the edge of the parapet, tumbling end over end to the jagged rocks below.

But now more of the geckos were clambering up the wall and over the ramparts, their swords rising and falling like deadly metronomes. The lizards' superior height and weight made it nearly impossible for the Holyland soldiers to long deflect the sword blows, but they took with them as many of the shadow warriors as they could.

The second Tricer-iguana thundered toward the splintered gates, clawing its way up the steps, over the smoking remains of the first siege-dragon, and through the stream of lava. The monster bellowed its pain, and plowed on, blasting its battering-ram of a head into the already-weakened gates. The wood groaned, and the dragon reared back for one last charge. Holylanders threw themselves against the buckling gates, trying to use their own strength of arms to keep them closed until the beast succumbed to the stream of lava. The huge bolt barring the doors broke in two, and the gates swung open.

The Tricer-iguana, mortally wounded, huge fissures opening in its plating from the pouring lava, nevertheless had enough strength left to roll over the soldiers trying to bring it down.

The juggernaut rumbled down the length of the cobble-stoned foyer, taking arrow after arrow from the archers secreted in the wall aureoles. It shrieked mournfully, whipping its spiked tail back and forth like a scorpion, pulping its attackers against the walls or cobblestones.

The heavy portcullis gate was raised to allow the Holylanders into the foyer to barricade the outer doors; now, as the Tricer-iguana pounded through the entryway, the gateman dropped the grating.

The spiked ends of the barred gate plunged through the back of the dying dragon's neck, pinning it to the ground. It shrieked miserably, and dropped flat on its belly. Its whipping tail lashed out blindly, killing the shadow warriors as impartially as the Holylanders. The Tricer-iguana's panicked efforts to free itself only made the portcullis' iron teeth bite deeper still into the monster's neck. The dragon bleated sadly, not understanding any of this, and a death spasm rippled through its horribly wounded body.

Still, that was a small victory; if the shadow warriors were allowed to enter the vaulted foyer, the iron portcullis would not hold them out for long. Ballistas threw flaming debris and stones down from the embattled parapets, dropping across the open gateway, impeding the lizards' progress long enough for the archers and pikemen to gather behind the portcullis.

Tyler stood back from the swarming soldiers, looking up at the parapets, finding F.A.K.K.² and smiling at her. "Don't you kids make me come up there!" he shouted. "Give me what I want, and I'll leave you alone."

F.A.K.K.² cut the rope holding the ballista's flaming payload, and a bale of burning goatsgrass was catapulted over the ramparts and crashed down next to Tyler. He cursed and leapt aside as the flaming debris landed.

"Have you taken a good look at yourself lately?" F.A.K.K.² yelled back. "I don't think the blemish stick is helping!"

Tyler's hand unconsciously went to his face, and came away slimed with purge fluid and pus. The witch was right.

He wasn't looking so good, and the pain was worsening with every runaway beat of his heart.

But he'd outlive that witch.

Tyler summoned his own catapults forward, and ordered them filled with payloads of multi-bladed spears. The soldiers released the safety cords holding the pitching arms down, and the spears climbed their deadly arcs, raining down on the Holylanders lining the ramparts. A dozen men were impaled by the spears. F.A.K.K.²'s shoulder pauldron turned the tip of the spear away, but she could still feel the warm, slow seep of blood down her arm.

More of the shadow warriors charged forward, erecting their clumsy assault ladders at the base of the walls surrounding the city. They began scaling the ladders, but the Holyland Acolytes diverted the flow of lava from the sluicegates above the main gateway, and back into stone troughs along the ramparts. The flaming liquid rained down from a hundred different slots in the gutters, drooling onto the troops and trapping them on their makeshift ladders. Most of the warriors chose to leap to their horrible fates on the sharp rocks below. Those less fortunate ignited into shrieking fireballs, who then fell to their deaths on the razored stones.

Her wounded arm was starting to bleed more heavily now, but F.A.K.K.² ignored it. She strode along the besieged ramparts, overseeing the defenses. A few small rivulets of lava continued dribbling out of the many spouts and corbels fronting the battlements.

The geckos had done a massive amount of damage to the first line of defense on the ramparts before finally being routed themselves. Many of the archers were badly wounded, and many more dead. But the wounded men held their posts, and vowed to their new warlord they would be faithful to their duty even unto death, and beyond.

F.A.K.K.² hoped she could simply delay Tyler entering the city long enough for his countless wounds to reappear and claim his life, but she wasn't sure how long that would take. Already in the first few minutes of the siege, both sides had suffered a heavy number of casualties.

The problem was, the shadow warriors could usually kill or cripple at least two or three of the Holylanders before being brought down themselves, and F.A.K.K.² didn't need a degree in quantum physics to do the math: the numbers were not good. Not for the Holylanders, anyway.

At the base of the escarpment, Tyler's troops brought up a weapon of Tyler's devising; a crossbow gattling gun. Perhaps his genius as a scientist had deserted him, but his cunning in the ways of death and destruction had gotten a good foothold, inspiring his twisted ingenuity to even greater heights.

Tyler's archers aimed the massive gattling guns at the escarpment, and released the safety cord. The arrows had heads of steel fashioned from the hull of the *Cortez*, and were more than a match for the stone walls of the fortress. The tips punched through the rock, and the grappling lines the arrows trailed behind them unspooled, dangling down for the next shock troops to try their luck at breaching the wall.

The foot soldiers advanced with a roar, grabbed the cables and began climbing the wall. But their weight on the wall triggered concealed booby traps, and spiked poles exploded out of the face of false stones, and drove through the lizards. Their bodies hung on the wall, twitching and jerking, until, one by one, they stilled.

From a distance, Tyler watched everything with contempt and scorn. "This is just typical," he said to Lambert.

"Perhaps if you led them," Lambert suggested.

Tyler glared sidelong at his second in command. "Soon," he answered. "I will control the Holylands by sundown, no matter what."

He watched the bloody sun sail over the pillared gates, and something in that tableau struck a chord of memory. Tyler removed the obelisk from his sash and studied the pictograms engraved on its smooth face; the sun between two pillars. He smiled. If he believed in signs in lieu of science, Tyler would have to say this was a good one.

"Very soon, I think," he added.

And still the shadow warriors attacked, as relentless as the tide on the beach, as numberless as the grains of sand. More of the soldiers made it up the wall, and at the top they met the Holylanders in brutal hand-to-hand combat. F.A.K.K.² rushed to the aid of a soldier, slicing the lizard's soft throat open. It clapped its hand to its neck, trying to staunch the spray of blood, and fell off the battlement.

But even as she exposed herself to attack by coming to the aid of another, Zeek was covering her back. One of the lizards, still on the other side of the parapet, reached over the wall for her, but Zeek saw him, and slammed his thick stone head with all his might into the reptile's skull. Bone and brain crunched, and the lizard dropped where he was, half over the ramparts.

F.A.K.K.² brought her sword down, driving the blade halfway through the attacking shadow warrior's chest, but she couldn't wrest the sword free in time to defend herself from an oncoming lizard. Zeek leapt up, and brought his balled fists down on top of the second soldier's head. Blood and brain jetted from the lizard's earholes.

"Good work, Zeek," F.A.K.K.² said, at last working her blade out of the corpse.

"Just watching your back, soft one," he replied.

"You just be sure that's all you're watching!"

She looked out across the desert and felt her heart sink when she saw Tyler's vast army. As many of the shadow warriors as the Holylanders had slain in combat, still the army seemed to stretch from here to the horizon, filling her vision east and west. There were so many of them, so tightly packed together that they seemed to be one black, shapeless beast, with countless heads and limbs.

F.A.K.K.² leaned wearily against the ramparts. It wasn't going to be enough. They couldn't hope to stop Tyler's army forever.

"No," she said to herself, her face stern, her lips a thin, drawn line. "Not forever. Just long enough."

"What is?" the archer next to her asked, favoring her with a coy smile. She saw in that smile Nathan, like a ghost that haunted her heart.

Sometimes, you couldn't help but look back. The problem was, you couldn't always choose when you did it. They called it the past for a reason, but it never really seemed to be.

Tyler leaned heavily against the helm of his sword, its tip buried in the hard ground. It was about all that was holding him up at the moment. That, and his hate for that long-legged witch.

The obelisk was shrieking at him, urging him to throw aside caution and charge the gates himself, and he knew he wouldn't be able to resist the commands much longer. He coughed, and spit out something wet and red that looked like it might have been a piece of lung. He was going to have to do it, after all. Tyler wrenched his sword free of the earth, and, steeling himself, he ran for the sundered gates.

Next to him, Lambert watched in surprise. Then, not wanting to be left behind, he too began to ran. Remarkably, none of the arrows or spears that flew down at them even came close.

Maybe, Lambert thought, just maybe they would make it.

Inside the small gatehouse, from which point the portcullis could be raised or lowered, a single guard stood his vigil. He watched through the small niche in the stone wall before him as the shadow warriors repeatedly flung themselves at the massive iron bars of the gate. Inside the compound grounds, Holyland archers and pikemen repelled every assault with arrow and spear. Outside the gate, inside the vaulted cobblestone foyer, the bodies of the dead piled up like a twitching green mountain.

The gatekeeper did not notice the shadow that fell across him through the doorway, did not hear the soft whicker of the sword that slashed his throat. He heard only dimly the rattaplan of his blood striking the walls. The same hand that slew the guard pressed the perfectly balanced counter-weight, and the heavy stone descended into the well beneath the gatehouse. At the same time, the portcullis started rising. The spikes wrenched themselves free of the Tricer-iguana still pinned beneath them, and the gate rode smoothly up into its recessed housing.

The lizards began swarming under the space between the spikes and the floor even before it had risen more than a foot or two. The guards within the compound, overwhelmingly outnumbered, nonetheless stood their ground, locking the shadow warriors in man-to-monster combat.

And then, the portcullis slammed into place above, and the rest of Tyler's army, seeing what had happened, surged forward, up the stairs, through the gates, and into the compound as one.

"What's happening?" F.A.K.K.² cried, not yet believing they had been betrayed. "Who opened the gates?"

The lizards tried to swarm up the circular stone staircase leading to the parapet. Zeek and F.A.K.K.² pushed the last of the stones and flaming debris down the steps, blocking the advance of the soldiers. Their progress slowed, F.A.K.K.² and Zeek were able to cut them down in single file order. But that wouldn't make any difference now. She knew they had to get down to the compound, where the lizards were flowing in like foul water filling a jar.

"Fall back!" Odin cried from the compound. "Defend the Chamber at all costs!"

"Zeek," F.A.K.K.² said, gripping the little golem by either shoulder. "Whatever happens . . . I'm counting on you to protect my sister."

Zeek didn't have time to answer, but he didn't need to. She knew he would do as she asked. She jumped from the parapet, to the top of a wagonload of spiky grass lashed in bales, to be set ablaze and thrown by catapults, and then she was in the compound and running with her soldiers, to defend against the final push at the Chamber.

Still the last few Holylanders at the gate fought on, despite hopeless odds. Tyler and Lambert strode regally up the wide, low stone staircase to the massive gates, laid open to them. Even from here, Tyler could see the mountains beyond the city, the place the Acolytes called Tall Mesa, its peaks lost in the clouds. But in those mountains, he knew, waited the Chamber of Immortality. The end of the quest.

"There it is," he said to Lambert. Despite the pain, and his re-opening wounds, Tyler was his imperious self once again. "The Chamber of Immortality! Even a trembling worm like you will have the pleasure of serving me forever!"

Before Lambert could reply, an arrow seemed to appear as if by magic in his chest. It had pierced a lung, and he was drowning in blood. He choked, dropped to one knee, flailing weakly at Tyler for help. And then, he noticed the last ampule Tyler wore at his belt, and Lambert reached out and plucked it loose for himself, the last apple on the tree in fall. Tyler became aware of what was happening, and he gripped Lambert's wrist, trying to wrest the vial away from the dying man's pursed lips.

Lambert's fingers snapped open, and the ampule tumbled end over end away from both men. They watched in helpless horror as everything happened in slow motion: the vial hit the cobblestones, bounced once, twice, and broke apart on the hard pumice. They watched the thirsty soil greedily drink the last of the elixir. In a moment, the ground was dry once more.

"Nooooo!" Tyler wailed, his head back. His voice echoed and re-echoed off the walls of the compound. "You clumsy idiot! That was the last one!"

"Please, oh please—" Lambert managed to gargle through his blood-filled throat.

Tyler swung his battle-ax, and Lambert closed his eyes, awaiting the terrible, burning impact. But it never came. He cautiously opened first one eye, then the other, and examined his chest. His jerkin was slightly torn, and a thin rill of blood dribbled down like an idiot drooling saliva, but he didn't seem to be too badly injured. Maybe Tyler turned his blow at the last instant, because he realized he needed Lambert.

As he was thinking that, what there was of him above the slanted wound began to slide sideways and slapped to the ground. The body below the wound tottered backward and fell.

Tyler had already turned from Lambert and dropped to his knees beside the slightly discolored patch of ground where the liquid had spilled. He scooped up trembling hands full of the sodden earth and stuffed it in his mouth, trying to suck the elixir from it, but he coughed and choked, blowing the dusty wads from his mouth. Mud striped his chin and chest. Tyler raised his head and looked once more at the mountains. A moment later, he was on his feet and running.

F.A.K.K.² hit the ground next to the scrub-grass-laden wagon just a moment after Tyler took off running, punching and hacking his way through the soldiers, killing his own men as well as the Holylanders who blocked his path to the Chamber.

She saw Lambert's dismembered body, and retrieved the ax Tyler had used to dispatch his second in command. There was a sense of rightness here, using Tyler's own blade to kill him. F.A.K.K.² pounded after him, and found herself in the tangled mass of soldiers.

"Julie . . ."

She barely heard the old wizard call to her. Tyler had just passed through here a moment earlier, and had slashed Odin across the belly with his sword. Odin was lying on the ground, his hand outraised to F.A.K.K.². She hesitated, looking after Tyler, already near the final long set of stairs leading to the Chamber, then at Odin. She hissed at her own indecision, and helped the old wizard to his feet, her arm around his waist, steadying him with her other hand.

"He cannot be allowed . . . to use the key!" Odin wheezed. His face was ashen, partly from shock and partly from bloodloss. His white robes were almost completely scarlet from the waist down. "Go," he said. "I'll follow as best I can."

F.A.K.K.² said nothing, but was running after Tyler up the gradual incline of steps.

Zeek managed to make his way down to the compound in the same way F.A.K.K.² had, and tried to battle his way through the swarming shadow warriors to the side of his Master and the soft one, but the road ahead seemed ridiculously filled with lizards. As he paused to look in the direction of Tall Mesa, one of the lizard warriors struck Zeek a horrific blow from behind with a spiked cudgel. Zeek gripped his head and toppled over, dazed by the force of the blow.

"I'm gonna make gravel out of you!" the lizard growled, and raised his deadly mallet. But before he could bring it down, a sword-tip exploded through his neck like some gruesome jack-in-the-box. The mallet slipped from his nerveless fingers and clattered to the ground. The soldier crumpled across Zeek, and the little stone man could see his savior, standing revealed now.

"That's for saving my sister's life," Kerrie said, freeing her sword.

Zeek wrestled himself free of the pinning weight, and moved closer to Kerrie. He gently took her small, blood-spattered hand in his, bowed his head, and softly kissed her fingers.

"And that's for saving mine," he said.

F.A.K.K.² looked at the destruction that lay all around her—the bodies, the buildings in flame, the ruin—and then saw Tyler, standing at the altar before a pair of locked gates shaped to look like a woman. It made sense, she supposed:

women were the life-givers, after all, and men the destroyers, the shadow cast by her light.

You're the reason we can't have anything nice, she thought, and hefted the great ax in her hands. She began stalking up the steps, her eyes hooded and filled with images of Tyler's death.

His real one. His last one.

"I want you to remember one word when I send you to hell," she said. She could see Tyler's shoulders tense at the sound of her voice. "F.A.K.K.²."

"Spell it?" he asked sarcastically. He turned to face her, and she reeled from the amount of decay in his face. She could see patinas of blood welling up within his jumpsuit as well, and she wasn't sure his injuries were all from this battle.

And then he simply turned his back on her once more, dismissing her threat entirely. He was studying the cuneiforms on the altar, looking for the proper slot in which to insert the key.

F.A.K.K.² voiced a throaty scream of rage and hatred and dashed the last few yards between Tyler and herself. As she ran, she raised the ax high above her head, but Tyler had goaded her into yet another mistake. Instead of defending himself, he stepped into her attack, too close to F.A.K.K.² to allow her to bring the ax down. Her murderous blow checked, Tyler was able to grab the shaft just below the blade with his right hand, and slam his left fist into the handle. The handle splintered in half, and now Tyler held the heavy blade.

Tyler hooked his foot into the backs of F.A.K.K.²'s ankles and swept her off her feet. She fell to her left, the impact jolting the broken ax handle out of her hands. It bounced once, rolled toward the edge of the top step, wobbled indecisively, then went over.

Tyler charged at her, wielding the broken top half of the ax. He stood over her, and smiled demonically. "Time to split," he said, and drew the ax back for the final blow. But he stood astride her, his crotch unprotected, and F.A.K.K.² shot out her foot like a piston, catching him square. He shrieked and doubled over in agony, dropping the ax head as he clutched his throbbing crotch.

She bolted past him up the stairs, and turned to strike a defensive pose. Tyler, tears of blood in his eyes, roared his anger; he was beyond words now, and only stupid animal sounds could express the depths of his hatred. He stormed up the steps, locking his arms around her and bearing her farther up the risers.

He was still impossibly strong, and had her locked in a bear hug. She could feel her ribs grinding together, and it was just a question of which would happen first: if her ribs would pierce her lungs, or if her spine would break in half. She put everything she had into a powerful roundhouse right, connecting full with Tyler's face. A great, bloody wad of gangrenous flesh squished off the bone and splatted on the steps. He cried out in pain, and let her go to clasp a trembling hand to his wound.

"Let's just call it a draw, okay?" Tyler said thickly, struggling to speak through the pulpy flesh filling his mouth. He spat it out, and thought maybe some of that was his jaw. "You know, agree to disagree..."

Even as he said that, he boiled up the steps once more like black lightning, but F.A.K.K.² had anticipated this, and delivered a whirling back-kick to his ribs, and another to his stomach. He gasped and fell forward, but F.A.K.K.²

brought her foot up one more time before Tyler could complete the fall, and she drop-kicked him on the chin. His head snapped back so hard she could hear vertebra popping, and he somersaulted helplessly down the steps, landing in a graceless, bloody heap at the bottom. F.A.K.K.² took a small running start and leapt from the top step, arcing through the air and landing with both knees on Tyler's stomach.

The air exploded from his lungs, and his hideous, rotting face twisted in agony. Her rage finally set free, F.A.K.K.² fell atop Tyler and gripped her hands tightly about his throat, and squeezed with all her might, adding her weight to the task as well. His face began to darken, shading from blue to red as quickly as one of the chameleons in Shantaar. Tyler clawed helplessly at her hands, but she locked on tighter. She would not be denied this time.

His eyes orbited like crazy moons, and his face was so red it was nearly black. F.A.K.K.² could feel the decaying flesh beneath her nails splitting, fissuring open, and purge fluid washed over her hands in a hot, sickly wave. She was just surprised it wasn't acid.

Tyler put everything he had into a last, desperate blow, balling his right fist and slamming it into F.A.K.K.²'s left temple. She grunted and rolled off of him, dazed and semiconscious. Tyler coughed air into his laboring lungs, and sat up, rubbing his swollen throat. With effort, he stood, and landed a solid kick on her head.

Tyler smeared blood and goo away from his mouth, which was not much more than a ragged tear at this point, and stumbled toward the steps. His decomposition was rapidly accelerating, due to the exertion of the fight, and only sheer willpower held his tattered flesh, hanging like pennants, together at this point. That, and the glue of madness.

At the top of the stairs, Tyler approached the altar

slowly, and anyone watching would think he approached it almost reverentially. They would be mistaken, for the climb up the steps had left him drained, and he felt the decay taking another big bite out of his flesh. Still, he fumbled the obelisk from his belt, and moved to the head of the altar. He listened to the key, telling him which slot was the proper one, and Tyler raised the key with both hands above his head. The voices and chanting grew unbearably loud, and Tyler slammed the key into the groove.

"Open 'em, babe," he commanded the giant stone goddess who guarded the gates.

Below, far, far below, somewhere in the mountains, or somewhere deeper than that, the rumbling roar as if of something indescribably huge and powerful waking from a long sleep began. The entire mountain range started trembling spastically, and gigantic boulders were torn free from the ancient roots and cast down the sheer face.

And then, above, a swirling vortex of clouds suddenly opened, and lightning laddered its way down from the heights. More bolts of jagged lightning scribbled across the sky, like badly drawn cartoon stickmen, chased by thunder; nature's rhyme. Behind him, the stone formation comprising the gates opened to him, revealing the entrance to the Chamber. Crazy zigzags of white light washed out, growing in size and intensity as the gates continued to trundle open.

"Bring it on," Tyler whispered. "I ain't got all day."

Far below, in the compound, the warring Shantaarians and the Holylanders all stopped their battle in mid-blow, and turned to stare at the column of white light (except it wasn't really white; it was more like an absence of color, as if something there had been erased, leaving only the blank page beneath it) that shot from the cloudy top of the moun-

tains and disappeared into the heavens. Kerrie thought perhaps they were looking at one of the strings of creation that
binds all things together. And she had a feeling Tyler was
about to snip that thread.

If she knew anything about the universe, she knew it
was cheaply made, and clipping one string could cause the
whole thing to come unwound.

Both armies fell to their knees and bowed their heads,
and if they were sore afraid, they should be forgiven.

Tyler moved mesmerically toward the tendrils of light that
coiled sinuously about him, like an eager lover's exploring
fingers, and he could feel his strength returning already.
Soon, he would bathe in the Waters of Immortality, and
then—

"Hey, yam-head!" F.A.K.K.[2] cried from the stairs behind
him.

He spun reflexively at the sound of the threat, and
turned right into the path of the hurtling ax handle. The
jagged end of the broken shaft plunged into his right eye,
driving him back a couple of paces, nearer the threshold ...

And then his anger overtook him, and he charged forward to meet F.A.K.K.[2]'s mad charge up the steps. She held
the broken ax blade, ready to cut Tyler's head from his
shoulders, but he obviously wasn't quite through using it,
for he lashed out with a furious roundhouse kick. The blow
sent her reeling backward, against the low stone balustrade
banking either side of the steps. Tyler retrieved the fallen
ax head and moved in to finish the job. But as he did, Odin,
still bleeding badly from his earlier wound at Tyler's hand,
tried to moved past them both to the Chamber.

"That's not a public pool, bub," Tyler growled, and buried the head of the ax deep in Odin's chest. The old wizard

grunted, as if he had merely had the wind knocked out of him instead of being clove nearly in two, and sat down hard on the steps. Tyler jerked the ax free from the Holylander's narrow chest, and brought it up for the final blow. Odin feebly raised his arm as if to deflect the ax-fall.

F.A.K.K.² had spent these brief moments regaining her senses, and, with a tremendous kick, broke the putrefying bones in Tyler's forearm. She ripped the ax from his grasp, taking a few fingers with it, and struck him with the flat of the blade. He fell to his knees, more pus gushing from his kneecaps on impact with the stones, and wobbled over onto his back.

Hideous, black liquid began pouring from the rips and sleeves and collar in Tyler's black flightsuit, as if all that held him together in the shape of a man was his clothes. His flesh rippled, as if a swarm of insects burrowed just beneath the surface, then burst into huge boils and sores. They could hear the sound of broken bones, healed by the elixir, coming apart, and the wet, sloppy sound of flesh sloughing off the bone and muscle. He stared up at her, but it was impossible to read much in his face. In his eyes, though, the hellfire seemed to burn brighter still, as if it were consuming him from within even as the decay devoured him from without.

"Please, I don't want you to see me like this," he sneered. "I want you to remember me just as I was, when I killed your dungheap of a world."

"Don't worry," F.A.K.K.² assured him, and hefted the blood-smeared ax blade. "I'm not gonna turn my back on you 'til I'm sure you're dead!"

"Mortality sucks!" he gurgled, and screamed as the weapon began its descent. The scream was cut off neatly by the falling blade. The silence that followed was deafening.

"Sometimes, you don't see how it's possible," Julie murmured softly, "but there *are* some things worse than death." Slowly, she turned away from Tyler's lifeless body.

At last, after far too long, the people of Eden had been avenged.

Now that it was over, Julie wanted to feel something—anything—to take the place of the anger that had blazed in her heart, but there was nothing there. Not relief, not peace, not even a sense of balance and justice. There was just a gap in her soul where the anger had been excised, and she couldn't guess what would fill that void. In time, she supposed she would find a puzzle-piece that, if not quite the same size and shape of the void, would at least go some distance toward completing her once more.

A low, pained hiss from behind her snapped her from her musings. She turned to see Odin frantically searching in his blood-sodden robes for something.

One battle, Julie knew, was at last over.

Now, the real war would begin.

Fifteen

"You did it, Julie," Odin said, and as he spoke, a murky ribbon of blood oozed from the corner of his mouth. "You destroyed Rutger ... without my help. Heh. I underestimated you. You're much more clever than I thought. But we must ... close the gates." He tried to stand, couldn't, sank back down on the steps. "Help me up, please? Help me to the gates."

As Odin spoke, clutching his arms across his grievous chest and stomach wounds, Julie tried to casually step between the old wizard and the yawning Chamber door, but she did not move to help him. She could actually feel the light—*hear* it calling to them. It didn't care who answered the call. It was dialing blind, and sooner or later, someone would respond.

"Thank the powers that you had the strength necessary for the both of us," Odin continued, trying to push himself to his feet. A tacky puddle of blood stained the steps where he sat. "The universe is forever in your debt ... for killing Rutger." He forced himself up, steadying his shaky legs against the low banister. Odin moved one step higher, and then another. Julie matched his progress, still keeping herself positioned between him and the Chamber.

"It's hard to kill someone who never existed in the first place," she said. "Even harder than it was to kill Tyler."

Odin left a trail of bloody footprints and palmprints on the steps and balustrade as he went, forcing himself on toward his goal. "I'm not sure I understand," he admitted. But the cornered look in his eyes said he did.

"Well, this has puzzled me all along," Julie said, and climbed another step higher above Odin. "How did the Arakacians manage to open and close the Chamber *without* touching the key?" Closer to the gateway, she could feel the light plucking at her hair and ruffling her clothes, as if it were an impatient child seeking attention.

Odin shook his head mournfully, and pushed himself up another step. "One by one, my people were forced to operate the key, and one by one, they died, insane . . . in terrible agony."

"But who enforced this, Odin?"

At the foot of the steps, Zeek arrived with Kerrie. His little body had suffered many chips and cracks and splinters from the battle, but he was otherwise whole and well. Kerrie had acquitted herself quite nicely against the invaders, but now she silently motioned Zeek into hiding. They slipped behind the balustrade, just near enough to hear the old wizard's words.

"Rutger, of course," Odin replied. His words were slow, like the last insects of summer. But there was something different—something guarded—about his tone of voice. It was more than the wounds that made his speech halting and unsure. "Their lives meant nothing to that cunning monster."

"It's odd that someone as cunning as Rutger would simply forget the power the obelisk contained," Julie wondered aloud.

"What do you mean?" There was a hint of menace in his voice, like the low growl of a cornered animal about to turn on its tormentors.

"Tyler wasn't Rutger," she said, shaking her head. "Rutger would never have touched the key, knowing what it would do to him. There never *was* a Rutger."

Odin stumbled slightly on the steps. From the pained expression etched on his face, he looked as though his life was draining from him, faster now, like sand falling into the receiving globe of an hourglass. He searched his sodden robes with quick, desperate movements, making odd, glottal noises as his panic increased.

Julie removed the ampule she had stashed in her ammo belt, and held it up for Odin to see. "Looking for this . . . *Moebius?*"

"Damn you!" he cursed through clenched and bloodied teeth.

At the base of the steps, Zeek started at the revelation. He had suffered many injuries during the battle, but none worse than this. His Master was the vile Moebius all along? Surely the soft one was wrong . . . and yet, he knew in his stone heart she was not.

Kerrie understood the look of grief on his face, and took his hand in hers. It was scant comfort, but better than none. You grab what comfort you may in this world, and return it when you can.

"I was blind with grief on the *Cortez*," Julie continued, and she thumbed the top off of the ampule. "But not stupid. I couldn't help notice one of the vials in the lab had disappeared, when only you and I had been in there."

"How very *observant* of you, Julie," Odin spat venomously.

She shook her head. "I'm a cop's daughter—I don't miss anything. When I helped you back on your feet in the battle, I took this from your robe." She tipped the vial just slightly, allowing a bit of the elixir to spill out. She uprighted the ampule once more, stopping the flow. Odin was panting like a dog on a hot day, barely able to contain his outrage at this callous treatment of the elixir. *His* elixir. "You opened the outer gates, didn't you? To let Tyler—and the key—make their way to the Chamber. That was your plan all along, wasn't it?"

He found strength somewhere within him, and strode menacingly closer to her. Julie took a step back to match each of his advances. "For decades—centuries—I've survived on this hellhole," he said. His words were not cautious now, but spilled out like blood. "My charade fooled the oh-so-pious Holylanders ... even that little stone fool! What makes you think a pathetic mortal can stop me now?" he asked, and hooked his hands into murderous claws.

Julie upended the vial, and the last of the elixir poured out onto the stone steps.

"Because you're one, too," she said. "Any other questions?"

The flesh of Odin's face seamed and ripped, splitting down the middle with a sound like burlap tearing. Hideous black, gelatinous body fluids oozed out of him to waterfall down the terraced steps. From within the sagging sack of torn flesh, something monstrously evil was squirming to free itself. Odin was little more than a chrysalis—a walking, talking cocoon that harbored the true lifeform inside it.

With a final purling of faux flesh and robes, the true form of Moebius, the last of the Arakacians, stood revealed before Julie. He was spider-like, hairy body slick with the black fluids that had spilled forth. Hinged legs unfolded, telescoping him up and up, towering above Julie, and she took an involuntary step back. She saw herself reflected again and again in his compound eyes, like countless cameos bearing the likeness of a loved one. When his mouth opened, spike-like mandibles issued forth from both sides of the sickening gash of a mouth. Corrosive acids dripped from slavering jaws, and Julie stepped aside just as the spittle fell onto the steps. A terrible stench arose from the spot where the acid struck, creating a frothing foam of green bubbles and acrid smoke.

Julie rolled out of the way and grabbed the ax with which she had dispatched Tyler, and swung it at Moebius. He was fantastically strong, and fast, and he reared up on his hind legs, towering over her, and made as if to fall across her. If she allowed herself to be pinned, it would all be over for her. She drove the ax up, and the blade sunk into the bulbous black body like a nail in rotten fruit. Moebius squealed his pain and anger, and threw her aside with his skittering legs.

Momentarily stunned, she thought he was going to renew the attack. Instead, he clattered past her, taloned legs making disturbing chittering sounds on the stone steps. He was making for the open Chamber doors.

"No!" she cried, flinging the ax after him. It struck, burying itself in one of his legs, but Moebius had crossed the threshold and was descending into the Waters of Immortality.

Julie rallied the last of her strength and pulled herself up the remaining steps, staggering to the altar. The key was still in the lock, still holding open the doors. Green lightning flared from the obelisk as she drew closer, warning her away. She didn't need the warning, but there was nothing she could do about it.

Steeling herself, she reached for the key.

And Zeek's strong hand closed around her wrist.

"No, soft one," he said. "Now, *I* must fulfill *my* destiny."

Julie didn't argue—what was there to say, anyway? *"Thanks, but if it's all the same to you, usually after I avenge my extinct homeworld, I like to commit suicide as an encore?"* Zeek was right; perhaps the universe had created him, through Moebius, just for this purpose. The universal plan didn't always make sense, but at least it could think fast on its feet or bluff its way through almost any situation. She moved back, and Zeek stepped up on the altar.

Snake-like bolts of lightning writhed in the skies above Tall Mesa, ripping up dirt and flagging stones with every deadly flick of their tongue. From below, in the Chamber, there came the echo of Moebius' evil laugh.

"You're a bad, bad man!" Zeek shouted after his former master, and walked closer to the obelisk. He grasped the key in both hands and jerked it out of the cavity. Instantly, the light cascading from the Chamber vanished, a beam of bright light appearing in the now-vacant key socket.

The gates of the Chamber began to grind shut, and Moebius, still rejuvenating himself in the sacred waters, stared uncomprehendingly at the sight. Impossible! And yet . . .

The light radiating from the keyhole in the altar tumbled around Zeek, lifting him up like a ball riding a column of air. He wrapped his arms around the key, holding it against his chest, rising faster by the moment.

"Zeek!" Julie shouted, extending her hand to him. She jumped atop the altar, but the light was carrying him farther and faster now. In moments he was out of her reach.

"Goodbye, soft one!" he cried back. "I'll never forget you!"

Moebius had climbed out of the Waters of Immortality and was running up the steps leading down into the Chamber. The doors continued to close with all the inevitability of fate. Julie heard Moebius commanding the doors to stop, saw the race could still go either way. She leapt down from the altar, unholstered her pistol, and squeezed off six shots through the gap between the doors and into Moebius' healed chest. The bullets slammed into him like steel-jacketed fists, the impact driving him back.

The bullets wouldn't harm him, but they had delayed him from reaching the gates—long enough that the gap narrowed further still. . . .

There was a loud rumble and the mountaintop shook once more. Zeek was suddenly propelled skyward like soap through a wet fist, and he rocketed away faster and faster.

Julie turned back to the gates in time to see the look of horror on Moebius' face as he realized he was not going to make it. Realized that immortality did him no good if it meant he'd spend eternity sealed in a mountain tomb on a godforsaken planet.

Realized he'd been thwarted by a "pathetic mortal."

He bellowed a seemingly endless cry of denial, as if he could negate this perceived injustice by sheer force of will. He could not, and the gates banged shut in his face. The final image Julie had of the last member of the Arakacian race was the look of fear and anger that blazed in his eyes.

And she had put it there.

Epilogue

Julie looked at the closed gates, and then turned her eyes skyward. She fancied she could just make out Zeek's body glowing white-hot as it exited the atmosphere and began its long, endless journey. He had wanted to fly, she thought, and had finally been granted his wish.

"But eternity's such a long time to spend alone," she said to herself. She wasn't sure, though, if she was talking about Zeek, or immortal Moebius, trapped forever behind the impenetrable gates.

"Julie!"

She turned at the sound of the voice and watched Kerrie run up the stairs to join her. Julie met her halfway, and they both fell laughing and weeping into one another's arms.

Not all endings, Julie realized, are sad, nor are all tears bitter. Not for those who don't only look to the future, but joyfully embrace the sweet memories of the past.

It was only that which made the trip bearable.

*   *   *

And so, as before, the key to the Chamber of Immortality was once again cast into the silent gulfs of space . . .

Zeek told himself this story now and then to keep the memory of those he loved alive and near. In this way, we do live forever. Not by magic waters, but by the simple, yet unstoppable power of memory.

He held the key against his body and curled into a ball around it, guarding it against evil for all eternity. Zeek closed his eyes, and went to sleep. He was never alone, not really, and although he might change the story a bit from time to time, it always ended as happily as it could.

That's all we can hope from any story.

An Open Letter to Our Valued Readers

What do Raymond Chandler, Arthur C. Clarke, Isaac Asimov, Irving Wallace, Ben Bova, Stuart Kaminsky and over a dozen other authors have in common? They are all part of an exciting new line of **ibooks** distributed by Simon and Schuster.

ibooks represent the best of the future and the best of the past...a voyage into the future of books that unites traditional printed books with the excitement of the web.

Please join us in developing the first new publishing imprint of the 21st century.

We're planning terrific offers for ibooks readers...virtual reading groups where you can chat on-line about ibooks authors...message boards where you can communicate with fellow readers...downloadable free chapters of ibooks for your reading pleasure...free readers services such as a directory of where to find electronic books on the web... special discounts on books and other items of interest to readers...

The evolution of the book is www.ibooksinc.com.